D0579380

W^{TO}RITE
A
WRONG

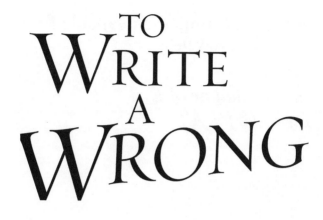

Center Point
Large Print

Also by Robin Caroll and available from
Center Point Large Print:

In the Shadow of Evil
Injustice for All

**This Large Print Book carries the
Seal of Approval of N.A.V.H.**

TO WRITE A WRONG

A JUSTICE SEEKERS NOVEL

ROBIN CAROLL

CENTER POINT LARGE PRINT
THORNDIKE, MAINE

This Center Point Large Print edition is published
in the year 2013 by arrangement with
B & H Publishing Group.

The text of this Large Print edition is unabridged.
In other aspects, this book may
vary from the original edition.
Printed in the United States of America
on permanent paper.
Set in 16-point Times New Roman type.

ISBN: 978-1-61173-603-8

Library of Congress Cataloging-in-Publication Data

Caroll, Robin.
To write a wrong : a Justice Seekers novel / Robin Caroll. —
Center Point Large Print edition.
pages cm
ISBN 978-1-61173-603-8 (library binding : alk. paper)
1. Large type books. I. Title.
PS3603.A7673T69 2013
813'.6—dc23

2012038574

For Benton Alexander Miller Forgy
and Zayden Brody Forgy . . .
because Gran loves you so much.

ACKNOWLEDGMENTS

I cannot ask for a better publishing team than the ones with whom I work at B&H. They are so talented and work extremely hard behind the scenes to bring the novels to life. My heartfelt thanks to the whole Pure Enjoyment team, but especially to those I've been honored to work with closely on this novel: Julie Gwinn, Robin Patterson, Kim Stanford, Greg Pope, Haverly Penington, and Diana Lawrence. The vision of these amazing people push the Pure Enjoyment fiction line to the forefront in the industry. For everyone at B&H, thank you for being part of my publishing "family." I truly appreciate each and every one of you for extending your talent and skill on my behalf.

I can't thank my editor, Julee Schwarzburg, enough for taking the stories in my head and helping to refine them until they shine on the page. You are such an amazing editor, Julee, and I thank you from the bottom of my heart, for not only being an awesome editor, but a true friend. I stand in awe of you.

This book dealt with minute details of our legal system, probation and parole system, medical details, and our prison system. Huge thanks to the following people for sharing their knowledge with me: Rick Acker, Dr. Skipper Bertrand, Dr. Richard Mabry, Cara Putman, and Dr. Ronda Wells. Any mistakes in the representation of legal issues are mine, where I twisted in the best interest of my story.

Thanks to Joyce S. Bridges and Robert F. Hancock (Director of Collections at the Museum of the Confederacy), who answered my tedious questions regarding the War between the States artifacts and values with an enormous amount of patience and kindness. The "adjustments" I made were deliberate for fictional purposes.

While writing this book, I ran into a rough patch that included not being able to locate my favorite "writing food." Wonderful readers that follow me on Facebook and Twitter heard of my plight. Special thanks to Susan and Tom Snodgrass for sending me a box of Tom's Hot Fries so I could finish the book.

Special thanks to the CARA PUTMAN, for helping in plotting and reading this book through before I turned it in. You are amazing and I love you for all your assistance!

As always, there are many in the writing community who help me in so many ways, I can't even begin to list them. My heartfelt thanks to: Colleen Coble, Pam Hillman, Ronie Kendig, Tosca Lee, Dineen Miller, Cara Putman, and Cheryl Wyatt.

My most sincere thanks to my awesome agent,

Steve Laube (HP), who keeps me focused and on task, as well as remaining steady and calm when I need it. THANK YOU.

My extended family members are my biggest fans and greatest cheerleaders. Thank you for ALWAYS being in my corner: Mom and Papa, BB and Robert, Bek and Krys, Bubba and Lisa, Brandon, Rachel, Scott Yarbrough, and Aunt Millicent.

My deep gratitude for the feedback of first reader Lisa Burroughs who read this book for me before deadline, even while on vacation. Whatever would I do without your questions and comments?

I couldn't do what I do without my girls—Emily Carol, Remington Case, and Isabella Co-Ceaux. I love each of you so much! Thank y'all so much for eating cereal for supper and letting me lock myself in my room when I needed to write. And my precious grandsons, Benton and Zayden, you are joys in my life.

There aren't enough words to express the love and gratitude for my husband, Case. Thank you for putting up with my moods, crazy ideas, endless "what-if?" questions, erratic cooking ideas, and deadline insanity. I could not do this without you and I love you with all my heart.

Finally, all glory to my Lord and Savior, Jesus Christ. *I can do all things through Him who gives me strength.*

"Then I said to you, 'Do not be terrified; do not be afraid of them. The Lord your God, who is going before you, will fight for you, as he did for you in Egypt, before your very eyes.'"

DEUTERONOMY 1:29–30

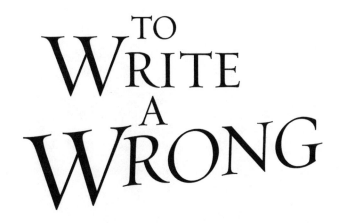

TO WRITE A WRONG

PROLOGUE

A moonbeam stole in and sliced against the polished blade, casting an unanticipated glint across the room. A red indicator blazed on top of the security camera, even though it was no longer connected to the recording system. He knew because he'd cut the wires and disabled the system.

X, or was it Y?—it was impossible to tell with all four of them wearing the same mask—let out a hiss. "Stop playing around and put the sword in the bag." X, definitely.

"Sabre, not sword," he whispered to himself as he slipped the beautiful Civil War artifact into the velvet bag. He was Z, the last one selected for this special mission. The afterthought, but they'd needed a security systems person familiar with this particular setup. He'd never done anything like this before, probably wouldn't again, but his son's increasing medical bills had shoved him into desperation.

Y turned back to the task at hand, reaching for the book resting inside the opened glass case.

"No!" X shook his head. "We're not supposed to take that."

"But it looks like it's worth a lot of money." Y ran a gloved finger along the case. "Why can't we take everything?"

X covered the short span of space between the men and grabbed Y's black collar. "Because. We stick to the plan, we don't get caught."

They'd been over the details, ad nauseam. At least it seemed that way to him. They memorized the list of what to take . . . because W already had buyers lined up. They'd gone over again and again how to get in and out—everything was planned down to the last facet. He didn't even know the other three men's names. Oh, he knew Y's name —Charlie was the one who'd contacted him for this job. Quick and easy, and a good, guaranteed payoff. So he went along with the plan, even the parts he thought silly, like addressing the others by initials only.

So far, everything had worked like a charm. He'd deactivated the security system easily. The extra security had been disposed of before they'd arrived on-site. Everything would go as it should, as long as they stuck to the plan.

"I've got it! We're done." W stepped onto the third floor, his commanding voice barely muffled by the mask. "Time to go."

While he wasn't supposed to know, he was pretty sure W was the private investigator who ran those discount coupons in the monthly sale circular.

"We still have a couple more things on our list," X answered.

"No time. Move." W silently led the way down

14

the stairs to the first floor and out the back door.

The four men, all dressed in black, stole across the plush lawn, dodging the security lights. They slipped into the open side door of the black van, pulling in the four laden velvet bags. W shoved in the key and revved the engine. X reached for the side door's handle.

"Hey!" A uniformed muscled mass of a man sprinted over the grass, drawing his weapon. "Stop!"

W punched the gas.

But Y didn't hesitate. He pulled out a handgun, leveled it at the security officer, and pulled the trigger.

The man fell facedown onto the grass.

W slammed on the brakes. "You shot him? Are you crazy? You weren't even supposed to have a gun!" Hysteria plowed from behind the mastermind's mask. The man who seemed in control since the planning of this job.

Z's chest tightened. A perfectly planned robbery had just escalated to armed robbery, assault, and possibly murder.

They were doomed.

He was doomed.

CHAPTER ONE

"Follow justice and justice alone,
so that you may live and possess
the land the LORD your God is giving you."
DEUTERONOMY 16:20

Was she insane?

Lightning pulsed past the ominous clouds polluting the sky with their foreboding. She shouldn't be here—every ounce of her screamed this was a bad idea. What had she been thinking?

That was the problem—Riley hadn't been thinking lately. Her love life had come to a screeching halt. She'd messed up so badly at work that her boss awarded her a mandatory leave of absence until she redeemed herself, though how she could do that while on leave was a mystery. Now, the hearing. She should go home, bury her head under the covers, and just cry until she couldn't cry any more.

Yet, she wouldn't let herself leave.

Riley pressed her balled hands into her abdomen and leaned back against the door of her car. Her shoulders and neck were so tight and tense, the ache felt as if it'd taken up permanent residence. She'd lost almost ten pounds in the last two weeks, just from the stress of today. There were a million reasons for separate appearances before the board. Why hadn't she heeded any of them?

Because her heart wouldn't let her.

"Ms. Baxter?"

At the attorney's deep baritone, Riley pushed off the dented, scratched compact and pivoted. She smoothed her pants with damp palms.

The cheap pinstriped suit jacket hung off Corey Patterson as he rushed across the parking lot. "I didn't think you'd make it." His blond hair glistened as lightning streaked across the sky again.

He'd sure tried enough times to discourage her. His arguments had almost worked. Just this morning, she'd debated using the weather as a possible excuse to back out. After all, as she heard on the news, April ushered in full tornado season in south Louisiana.

If the weather wasn't bad enough, the barbed wire atop the fence as she entered the property almost did her in. Everyone would understand if she changed her mind. But if she didn't show, she'd never be able to live with herself.

There was no other option. She had to look *him* in the eye, see if the crazed haze still glowered in those irises. Needed to see *him* in person, not on some impersonal terminal via videoconferencing, to know if he still wore the illness in the lines of his face. She had to hear *his* voice to determine if the venom still bittered his words.

"I said I'd be here." She eyed the crowded parking lot as she fell into step beside the aging prosecutor. So many people lining up to board the white visiting buses . . . mainly women and children. Some infants. It broke Riley's heart. Why didn't people think about the consequences on their families before they did something stupid? Such a waste.

The next clap of thunder didn't cover Mr. Patterson's heavy sigh. "You really shouldn't have come. This won't be good for you." Those big, blue eyes of his stared into hers. He squeezed her upper arm.

She denied the urge to sigh herself, already mentally past the argument. They dodged the first raindrops as they made their way along the sidewalk, past the fence with rolls of barbed wire. Riley shivered, then followed Mr. Patterson through the green-trimmed door. The tips of her heels *rat-a-tat-tatted* on the polished brown tile.

"Wait here for a moment." The attorney's damp soles squeaked as he headed down the hall.

She leaned against the white cinder-block wall. Icy cold crept into her spine, chilling her from the inside out. Women and children moved like cattle to sign in for visitation. Her mouth went dry. What would it be like to have to visit someone you loved like this? Maybe *that* was the story she needed to get back in her editor's good graces.

Jeremy was beyond furious with her. He'd

accused her of letting her bias against criminals get in the way of good journalism. His yelled reprimand that she find emotion for the reader and ignore her own still rang in her ears. What better way to steal the hearts of readers than to expose the angles of pain worn raggedly on some of these women's faces?

It would also prove she was capable of writing a story 100 percent unbiased against someone close to criminal involvement. Given the reason she was here and the emotional mess her life had become, that would be no easy feat.

"They're ready." Mr. Patterson appeared at her side, barely touching her elbow. "Do you remember what I told you? The procedure?" He led her down one hallway into another.

They all looked the same to Riley, but it hardly mattered. Nothing about the location mattered. Her stomach threatened to reverse the cappuccino she'd drunk on the drive here. She licked her lips with a dry tongue. "Yes. I remember."

He paused outside a closed gray door. "You can still back out, you know. You can just walk out, get back into your car, and drive off." He cleared his throat. "We could meet for dinner later and I could fill you in."

Her heart pounded. A bead of sweat dotted her upper lip. Temptation swirled like a tornado inside her chest, and for a moment, just a split second, she considered the option.

But then she squared her shoulders. She never backed out. From anything. That wasn't who Riley Baxter was. Especially when this was so important.

And so personal.

"I'm fine." If only her knees would get that message and stop quivering. Good thing she'd worn slacks so nobody could see her shaking. The beads of sweat felt like lead on her upper lip.

"Okay." The disappointment draped off his shoulders as badly as the ill-fitting suit jacket. He opened the door and motioned for her to precede him into the room.

It was smaller than she'd expected. A computer monitor sat on one table, showing three people—two men and one woman—sitting behind a conference table. Directly across from the monitor were two empty wooden chairs. Adjacent to the monitor a video camera rested atop a tripod, pointing at the empty chairs.

A lady wearing a washed-one-too-many-times dress sat behind a desk, an armed guard hovering behind her. Her attention never lifted from the open file in front of her.

Mr. Patterson waved Riley toward a row of chairs along the wall. A lady she'd never seen before sat in one of the chairs. Quite pretty with long, dark hair. Spanish and exotic looking. Beside her sat Alicia Lancaster.

Riley knew who she was only too well: Simon's

older sister. The one who had cried on the witness stand. Who testified at his sentencing hearing that her brother's drinking was an illness brought about by genetics, so he shouldn't be incarcerated, but rather, hospitalized. Who told a story of a boy abused by an alcoholic father who had merely followed in his father's footsteps.

Riley swallowed hard, curling her sweaty palms into a ball. She hadn't known Alicia would be here, but she should've considered the likelihood. As much as Riley wanted Simon to stay behind bars, Alicia wanted him free.

Chest tightening, Riley concentrated on breathing normally. Inhale through the nose, slow exhale through the mouth.

Mr. Patterson gestured for her to sit. He wanted her to sit next to Alicia? The bile rose in Riley's throat. No alternatives miraculously appeared with a second glance. She eased to the edge of a chair and slid as far from the woman as possible. Mr. Patterson studied her as if to satisfy himself she wouldn't bolt, then lowered himself onto the chair beside her. Its leg scraped against the waxed floor, the grating bounced off the cement walls until Riley's teeth sat on edge.

The rattle of keys clanked down an adjacent hall, the unnerving jangle drawing closer to the room. Nearer. Nearer. The door on the opposite side of the room opened. An armed guard entered. Another. A prison official wearing a worn suit.

And then Simon Lancaster shuffled into his parole hearing at the Louisiana State Penitentiary at Angola.

Alicia gasped, and Riley had to press her lips together not to do the same. She didn't know what she'd expected, but this wasn't it. His cheekbones stuck out more prominently than Riley remembered, making him appear gaunt. He wore his hair combed back from his pallid face. He walked with the gait of a man ten years his senior.

The guards ushered Simon to the empty chair and assisted him in sitting. The prison official sat beside him and opened a file, skimming the contents.

Simon smiled over at Alicia and the other lady before letting his gaze trip to Riley. He met her stare, hesitation in his eyes, as if trying to place her. After all, it'd been eight years since he'd seen her. Then, she'd been twenty-five, still so naïve. Oh, how she'd changed since then.

The prison official looked into the camera, rattled off his name, and introduced Simon Lancaster to his parole board. He read directly from the chart how Mr. Lancaster had been a model citizen while incarcerated at Angola, how his work ethic in the silk-screen department was to be commended, and how he'd been active in his religious activities, proving his moral rehabilitation.

Riley thought she might be sick.

One of the men on the monitor cleared his throat and leaned forward. "What do you have to say for yourself, Mr. Lancaster?"

Simon straightened in the chair, stole a quick look at his sister, then stared into the camera on the tripod. "I believe I've changed in here. I take part in AA, I'm now a Christian, and I can be a worthy member of society now."

Worthy member of society? Right. He'd run straight to the nearest bar as soon as he broke free of the prison walls. Riley bit her tongue while clenching her fists. Her nails dug into her palms but she ignored the pain.

The woman on the parole board spoke. "I understand you have family members to speak on your behalf?"

The prison official waved to his sister and the lady. Both rose and crossed the room. Alicia stood beside Simon, tears glistening in her eyes. "I'm Alicia Lancaster. Simon's my baby brother." She wrung her hands in front of her. "You need to let Simon out. He's served his time and needs to come home."

"So if Mr. Lancaster is let out on parole, you'll provide him a place to live?" the woman on the parole board asked.

"Yes, ma'am. He'll be living with me and his fiancée here." Alicia motioned to the pretty lady beside her.

"His fiancée? We don't have any notation of

his engagement," the woman said over the monitor.

What a crock! Riley sat on the edge of the hard chair.

"*Sí*, I marry Simon. As soon as he out."

The pretty lady's broken English confirmed Riley's suspicions—this woman no more loved Simon Lancaster than Riley did, and *that* was as likely as hades freezing over.

"I see." By the parole woman's tone, it was clear she wasn't fooled by this . . . fiancée.

Riley let out the breath she'd held.

"And he has a job waiting on him," Alicia interrupted.

"What type of job?" one of the men asked.

"Working in the shop where I'm the cashier." Alicia nodded. "Boudreaux's Paint and Body. My boss said he'd hire Simon as soon as he was released."

"Doing what?"

"Just being a hand in the shop. Cleaning up spills. Putting tools back in their places." Alicia shrugged. "Doing whatever is needed."

"I see," the second man on the parole board said.

A place to live. A job. People who cared about him. Riley clutched her hands together. Surely they wouldn't consider letting him out? They couldn't.

"Anything else you'd like to add, Mr. Lancaster?" the first man asked.

"Yes." Simon turned and met Riley's stare. "I'm sorry my drinking killed those people. I wish with everything in me that it hadn't happened. But it did. All I can do now is say I'm sorry."

With her stomach reversing the coffee she'd inhaled this morning, Riley shot to her feet and rushed from the room. She couldn't breathe. Couldn't take it anymore. Fresh air . . . she needed fresh air.

And to get away from the scumbag who'd murdered her parents.

Tears burned Jasmine's eyes. She couldn't let them spill out. Not with her mom watching. Mom had been through enough already today. The idiots at the prison . . . She and Mom and Mikey shouldn't be punished because the guards thought Dad did something wrong. Since when was food considered contraband?

Would have been nice had someone told them not to come. They'd already wasted an hour or so driving to the prison, using up gas they didn't have the money for. The storm had made the trip long and tedious. They'd all been tense when they arrived. Now, to be told they couldn't see Dad . . . well, it was just plain wrong.

Her little brother, Mikey, continued his wailing out the front door of the prison and into the parking lot. At only six, he didn't understand why he couldn't see Daddy after Mom had told him they would. He'd been so excited to tell Daddy about his Easter-egg hunt at kindergarten that he'd even let Mom put him in that ridiculously ugly shirt that made him look like a girl.

Jasmine turned and kicked the leg of the bench outside of Angola's front entrance. Her toes crunched against the concrete, but she didn't care. She didn't even pay attention as people came in and out of the prison. She ignored the water puddles, the remnants of the storm from earlier. The rain had disappeared, but the dark skies remained. She'd had enough of Angola already, but if Dad's appeals kept being denied, she would have to deal with it for many more decades. He'd already been in for almost a year now.

"Mikey, honey, I know you want to see Daddy, but we can't today. Just get into your car seat, sweetie. I'll get you McDonald's on the way home if you be a good boy." Mom tried yet again to ease him into the booster seat.

"Buy McDonald's with what, Mom? We put the last twenty we had into the gas tank." The tears slipped down Jasmine's cheeks in spite of her determination not to cry. "And for what? We can't even see Dad." She swiped the back of her hand against her face.

Mom struggled with getting Mike to sit in his seat. "We'll figure it out, Jasmine. Just help me get Mikey settled."

"It's not fair. Dad shouldn't even be here in the

first place because he's innocent, much less not be allowed to see his wife and children because he had a certain kind of food hidden in his locker. It's food, not a weapon or cell phone or anything." Jasmine stomped against the asphalt. "Since when is it a crime to hoard food?"

She stopped fighting the tears. "He's already lost so much weight. I don't understand why we can't see him." She bent her head into the crook of her elbow and sobbed. She didn't want to put any additional stress on her mom, but she couldn't take it anymore.

Plain and simple, they were broke. Dad had been the moneymaker of the family. Mom had gotten a job at the local grocery store chain right after Dad was sentenced, but it wasn't enough. It was never enough. Not enough for gas. Not enough for groceries. Forget about new clothes. They'd lost the house months ago and now rented a mobile home in a trashy trailer park. Just two days ago, she'd heard Mom on the phone to the electric company, begging for an extension and not to cut their power off. If things didn't change soon, they'd be homeless.

"Jasmine, honey, just get in the car. We'll talk about this at home." Mom buckled Mike's seat belt. "Hands on noses, Mikey." When he complied and had his hands safe from getting squished, she slammed the back door and stared over the hood of the Honda. "I know you're disappointed, but there's nothing we can do here. We're both upset right now."

"Upset? Mom, I'm mad as hell. Dad's innocent and we're all paying for something he didn't do."

"Watch your mouth, young lady."

Jasmine waited for Mom to come around and unlock the passenger door. Even the automatic lock and unlock button were broken on the old car. Everything was unfair. Dad hadn't been involved in the stupid robbery. It was all a setup. Why hadn't the jury been able to see that?

"I won't have you talking like a heathen." Mom jammed the key into the door. "No matter how upset and disappointed you are."

A heathen? Really? Where was Mom and Dad's all-powerful God in this? Why had He let an innocent man go to prison? Why was He letting the whole family suffer like this?

"Excuse me."

Jasmine turned as her mother did. The woman standing mere feet from them had a familiar pain in her eye.

"I couldn't help but overhear your conversation." She took a step closer, her brown hair bouncing against the top of her shoulders.

"I'm sorry if we disturbed you." Mom opened the car door. She pushed Jasmine's shoulder, trying to shove her inside.

"No, please." The woman joined them. "I'm sorry, I'm messing this up. Let me start over. My

28

name is Riley Baxter." Her piercing blue gaze darted between Jasmine and her mother. "Did I hear correctly, that your husband isn't allowed visitors today because he hid food?"

"Yes. How stupid is that?" Jasmine blurted out before her mother could respond.

Mom shot her a glare, then focused on Ms. Baxter. "Why are you asking? No offense, but it's really nobody's business."

Talk about rude, and Mom was forever on Jasmine's case about her sharp tongue.

"I'm a journalist and am interested in writing a story from the point of view of an inmate's family."

Mom frowned. "We're not interested." She pushed Jasmine's shoulder again. "Get in the car, sweetie."

"I want to tell readers how hard it is on a family." Ms. Baxter laid her hand on the car door. "How the family is punished just as much as the inmate. Sometimes more."

"Yeah." Jasmine shrugged off Mom's touch. "At least Dad's guaranteed three meals a day and a bed."

"I'm sorry, Ms.—Baxter, did you say?—but we aren't interested." Mom all but shoved Jasmine into the front seat, then slammed the door shut behind her.

Ms. Baxter followed Mom around the front of the car. Jasmine couldn't hear their conversation, but she recognized Mom's body language. What-

29

ever the lady reporter said, it was working. Mom's resistance was crumbling like a package of crackers in the bottom of her purse.

"I wanna see Daddy," Mikey whined from the backseat. "I want McDonald's. Mom promised."

Jasmine ground her teeth. Her brother didn't understand. Couldn't. Even Jasmine didn't understand all the stupid rules of prison. "In a minute, Mikey." She leaned over and opened Mom's door.

"I promise I wouldn't print anything I didn't get directly from you or your family."

Mom hesitated, glancing into the car at Jasmine and Mikey. She ran her tongue over her bottom lip.

The lady laid a hand on Mom's arm. "It could help prevent other women and children from going through this. People who read my magazine are potential jury members. Maybe this could even help your husband, if the right people read the article. I'd send those people a copy of the article."

Jasmine couldn't keep her mouth shut. "Come on, Mom. If it could help Dad . . ." She leaned over the front seat, practically lying prone.

Mom frowned at her but turned to Ms. Baxter. "Fine. You can call. I'm listed in the Baton Rouge book."

Ms. Baxter passed something to Mom. "Here, take this. For hearing me out."

Mom opened her hand. "We don't need your

money. We aren't a charity case." She tried to give it back.

Well . . . Jasmine would argue that point at the moment.

"I delayed you. I heard you promise your son a treat, and I've kept you from that. It's the least I can do."

Mom hesitated, then shoved the money into the side pocket of her purse. "Thank you."

Ms. Baxter nodded. "I'll call you."

Mom slipped behind the wheel and pulled the door closed before starting the Honda. Jasmine smiled through the windshield at the lady. Ms. Baxter gave a finger wave.

Maybe this trip hadn't been such a waste of gas.

CHAPTER TWO

"And the heavens proclaim his righteousness, for he is a God of justice."
PSALM 50:6

"I can't wait to see Bella again. It's been months!" Ardy Simpson shook the kitchen rug with more oomph than most fifty-five-year-olds should. Her honey-colored hair was pulled back in its customary bun, with some escaped strands curling around her neck.

"Remington, Mom. Her name is Remington, not

Bella." Hayden sighed. "And it's only been about five weeks since she visited."

His mother stepped back into the kitchen, letting the screen door bang shut, and laid the rug on the floor in front of the sink. "Whatever. She'll always be Bella to me."

Him too, although he'd worked hard to remember to call her Remington every time they spoke on the phone. She'd come to Hopewell as Bella, but now they knew she was really Remington Wyatt. And he couldn't lie—the five weeks felt like months to him as well. He missed her something fierce. He wanted her to stay Bella Miller, not Remington Wyatt. Wanted her to remain in Hopewell, Louisiana, not Little Rock, Arkansas. Wanted her to keep being a freelance photographer instead of a forensic psychologist working with the FBI. He wanted her to stay his best friend.

And while he really wanted all those things, he wanted her to be happy more.

Chubbers—Remington's black lab they'd been dog sitting since she'd left to move into her godfather's old estate, half Hayden's although he'd signed over his part to Remington—paced the kitchen. It was as if he, too, knew she was on her way and couldn't wait to see her again. This time, however, she'd take him back to Little Rock with her.

"What time do you think she'll be here?" His

mother's petite frame was a blur as she bustled about. She stood barely five feet, a good foot shorter than Hayden.

"She and *Rafe* should get here any time now."

Rafe Baxter . . . FBI agent, rabid SEC—Southeast Conference—football fan, all-around nice guy, and now Bell—Remington's new boyfriend. Hayden liked him.

"He's nice enough. Don't know if he's good enough for our Bella, though."

"Mom . . ." Hayden grabbed a grape from the bowl on the counter and popped it into his mouth to sweeten the bitterness that rose in him toward his mother at her ownership of Bella. But, of course, they'd been cohorts in secret keeping. He swallowed the grape and pushed aside the mistrust. "Rafe's great, and you think so too. You liked him well enough before."

"We'll see." She flitted about the kitchen, stirring the pot on the stove and straightening the canisters on the counter.

If he didn't know better, Hayden would think she was nervous. He sniffed the air. "Dinner sure smells good."

"We're having gumbo and cornbread. Bella loves my gumbo, you know."

"Bell—er, Remington loves your cooking period, Mom."

She smiled back at him. "Emily will be joining us tonight as well, and gumbo is her favorite."

He fought against the groan.

"She's doing great, Hayden. Really." Mom wiped her already-dry hands on the kitchen towel. "It's like having the old Emily again." The chipper tone sounded too forced.

Translation: There was no telling what mood she'd be in tonight. Could be that Emily would be happy and upbeat, a joy to be around. Or she could be angry and rude. Even better, she could be depressed and sullen.

"Mom, have you—?"

A horn blasted outside.

"Bella's here!" She dropped the towel onto the counter and rushed toward the front door, patting her bun as she walked barefoot on the hardwoods. Chubbers met her step for step, nose at the door.

"*They*'re here," Hayden said, but was only speaking to himself as his mother had left him in her wake.

Remington bounded from the car and ran up the stairs, straight into his mother's open arms. "Oh, Ardy, it's so good to see you!"

Rafe lifted two suitcases from the trunk, then dogged Remington's path at a much more sedate pace.

Hayden held out his hand to him. "How was the trip?"

"Long drive, but the scenery was beautiful." Rafe gripped his palm.

Remington knelt, hugging Chubbers. The dog's

34

entire hindquarters swayed as he wagged his tail. Then she stood and flung her arms around Hayden, drawing him against her. "And you." She buried her face in his neck. "I've missed you so much." Her breath was a whisper against his skin. He squeezed her tightly before releasing her. "Let me look at you." He held her at arm's length. She'd let her once caramel-colored hair return to its natural blonde. The effect was staggering when combined with the glow of her face. "You look good, kid. Really good. Arkansas must be treating you right." And she did look great, as if her worries had dissipated with the south Louisiana humidity.

She smiled and held out her hand to Rafe. "You remember Hayden's mom, Ardy, don't you?"

Rafe smiled and gave a quick nod. "Nice to see you again, Mrs. Simpson. Thank you for having us."

Mom pulled him into a hug. "It's Ardy, and I'm thrilled to have y'all." She turned to Hayden. "Well, don't just stand there. Help him get their suitcases in. Rafe's in the guest room, I have the bed made up in the den for his sister when she arrives, and Bella's in Emily's old room."

"It's Remington, Mom." Hayden opened the door and waved Rafe inside.

"It's okay." Remington stepped alongside him, Chubbers heeling automatically. "She can call me Bella." She linked her arm through his and joined him down the hall, whispering, "Emily's *old* room? What's going on?"

While he loved his little sister immensely, Emily worked the range of his emotions. She made bad choices and blamed them on her illness, then expected everyone to overlook her behavior. That would be fine for most, but he was the police commissioner. Some of her bad choices were also against the law, and he'd had to treat her like any other twenty-two-year-old who'd broken the law. Didn't exactly win him any points with his sister . . . or his mother. "She checked herself out of the hospital and moved out of the house into an apartment with a friend. One she met in the hospital."

"Ah, I see." She squeezed his arm, then slipped out of his touch into the bedroom. "Want me to talk to her tonight?"

"I can't ask you to do that." He tossed her duffel on the foot of the bed. Emily was, well . . . Emily. Difficult.

Remington chuckled. "Of course you can. We're family, remember?" She plopped onto the bed, bouncing the duffel.

He shrugged, the pain of her betrayal still too recent for him to shrug it off.

She bounced on the bed like he and Emily had done many, many years ago. "So, tell me all the Hopewell news. Aside from Emily, what else is happening?"

He couldn't help but laugh. "You know how it is, nothing new."

"Aw, c'mon, Hay, tell me something. I'm dying here."

"You want gossip?" He struggled to put on his sternest expression and crossed his arms over his chest. "You know better than that, missy."

She stood and hugged him again, giggling. "Oh, Hay, I've really missed you."

His throat clogged as he returned the embrace. Even now, he loved her so much, which made his issues even more grappling. "Miss you too, kid."

"Hayden! Bella!" His mother's holler made them both laugh.

"Ah, the voice of authority beckons." She grabbed his hand and led him down the hall. Chubbers followed on their heels.

Mom flitted about the stove while Rafe sat at the kitchen bar. Remington dropped onto the stool next to him. "It smells heavenly." She leaned, resting her head on Rafe's shoulder. "Ardy's the best cook this side of Baton Rouge."

"I can't wait to taste it." He leaned forward and flashed his smile at Mom. "Remington raves about your cooking. I think she dreams about it."

Remington threw a mock punch on his arm. "I do not." She chuckled and sniffed. "Well, maybe."

Hayden grabbed the stool on the other side of Remington. "Admit it, food is your weakness."

"You know me too well."

Seeing her so blissful with Rafe truly made Hayden happy, but it also made him all too aware that he had a void in his own life.

"So, Rafe, tell us about your sister." Mom pointed a wooden spoon at him. "She's the reporter, right?"

"Yes, ma'am. She works for *Life in the South* magazine."

"I read that every week. Even have a subscription." Mom stared at Hayden. "You know, the weekly magazine that always has good articles on politics and stuff?"

He nodded, clueless. His idea of reading material was the Bible, mens' studies, books relating to work, and fishing magazines. It was just easier to agree with Mom. If he didn't, she'd pull out copies for him to read this instant.

"That's the one," Rafe continued. "She mainly does the fluff pieces."

"Rafe." Remington tossed him that stern look of hers before smiling at his mother. "She's done a few serious pieces, which didn't make it into print. Then her editor assigned her to a big story and he thought she blew it." She hopped off the stool and went around to the stove, lifted the lid, and sniffed. "Riley's really working hard to find her footing."

Rafe shook his head. "She used to work at the *Memphis Daily News* and had regular assignments."

"The obits and wedding features aren't exactly Pulitzer-prize considerations." Remington grabbed a spoon from the drawer and stole a quick taste of the gumbo. "She wants to be a great investigative reporter. The Diane Sawyer–type."

"So far, she's not doing so hot." Rafe switched his focus. "More of an answer than you wanted to hear, I'm sure, Mrs. Simpson."

"Please, it's Ardy, and I'm sure she'll be fine. It takes a while to get your footing in any profession." She smiled at Remington. "How is it?"

"Divine!"

Mom turned back to Rafe. "My daughter, Emily . . . she's still trying to figure out what she wants to do with her life."

"For the past six months, she's been trying to destroy it." Hayden spoke before he could stop the words.

"She has an illness, Hayden." Mom glared.

Remington pointed the spoon at him. "Bipolar disorder *is* an illness." She set the spoon in the sink and leaned against the counter, attention solely on Mom. "How's Emily doing these days? Hayden told me she's moved out."

He tuned out Mom's response. In her eyes, Emily would always be *misunderstood,* no matter what she did.

And he'd always be the serious, stern one. He couldn't win for losing.

Maybe she shouldn't have pushed, but she'd seen the anger and pain in the line of the teenager's unmarred face—and recognized the emotions from having seen them too many times in her own mirror. No one should have such worry-creases, as her sister, Maddie, called them.

Riley had more than enough of her share. It broke her heart to acknowledge them on the pretty young girl with tawny hair and bright green eyes.

Not to mention that the girl's obvious anger and pain jerked Riley out of her own misery. Wasn't that something her pastor preached: The best way to stop worrying about your problems is to pray and help someone else's with theirs? It'd certainly worked in this instance.

"Riley! Riley!" Mr. Patterson rushed across the parking lot, dodging puddles left and right. "Are you okay?"

He'd made no qualms that he'd like her to go out with him, but she couldn't get past the used-car-salesman feel she got from him. Riley shook off her animosity. It wasn't the attorney's fault Simon Lancaster killed her parents and now had the opportunity for parole. "I'm fine."

"Are you sure?" He peered down at her, worry and concern weighted in his every pore. "I told you this would be difficult. This is the main reason most of the hearings are done via videoconferencing and why victims and their families speak separately from the incarcerated and those speaking on their behalf."

"I'm fine, Mr. Patterson. Really." She rubbed the back of her neck, willing the tension to return to wherever it came from. "So, what was the outcome?"

"As I informed you earlier, they heard from Mr. Lancaster and his sister and his . . . uh, his fiancée. They'll hear from you and your family before they make their decision. It will take weeks for their determination to be finalized."

"Does he stand a chance of getting released?" Just because his sister showed up and cried and produced some woman who agreed to say she'd marry Simon? Had the justice system gone that far downhill?

The attorney shrugged. "There's no way to know for certain, of course. You and your brother are set to speak at the hearing on Monday morning. I'm sure what you have to say will weigh heavily on the board's decision."

Just the thought that he could get out . . . Riley's stomach knotted and burned. She shoved the strap of her purse higher on her shoulder. "I think I'll head out now. Thank you again for coming with me today."

"No problem." He eyed her. "Are you sure you're okay? Would you like me to call your brother?"

"No. No, thank you. I'm on my way to meet him." Just what she didn't need right now—a lecture from Rafe on how she shouldn't have come today. How she was just borrowing trouble.

But he'd gotten to talk to Mom before she died. He'd had the chance to say good-bye. She hadn't.

"I'll be just fine after a hot shower, something to eat, and a good night's sleep." She forced the smile she didn't feel. "I'll see you Monday."

"Ten o'clock, sharp." He nodded.

She pulled up the address in the GPS, then gave a little wave as she pulled out of the parking lot and passed Mr. Patterson standing outside his car. Great. She could just hear his recounting of today to Rafe.

Riley pressed harder on the accelerator as she headed to the interstate toward Hopewell. She'd agreed to stay with Rafe's new girlfriend, Remington, in the Podunk town. She'd miss the beautiful Hyatt hotel in Baton Rouge that she'd checked out of this morning, but she didn't have a choice. Remington and Rafe were probably already in Hopewell. She'd endure the small-town boredom tonight, then tomorrow she'd call on Mrs. Wilson, the lady she'd met today.

Following the instructions of the female robotized GPS voice, she took the ramp onto the interstate and built up speed.

Riley smiled as she recalled the fire and spunk

in the teenager Jasmine. So outspoken and furious . . . so much like Riley had once been. In the meantime, she'd pull up everything she could on Mr. Wilson's case. Jasmine had been adamant her father was innocent. If there was any question of his guilt, this would be a story Jeremy would kill for.

Her editor had told her he'd give her one last chance. If she couldn't pull off her next story, she'd lose her job. She had to come up with something that readers would call the magazine for more of. That kind of response would guarantee she'd keep her job—even get some of the plum assignments.

"Exit ramp right."

Riley slowed and eased off the interstate. She needed her job. Especially after breaking up with Damon. She hated to admit it, but once again, her brother was right about a guy. First Garrison, now Damon. Jerks. And Rafe had called it early on, which annoyed her something awful.

"Turn left, then turn right."

Just because Rafe was all lovey-dovey with his new girlfriend, he thought he knew everything about relationships. *"Damon's trouble."* Well, he was, but that was beside the point. She missed Damon, even though he was a cheat. And a liar. On the day Jeremy had threatened to fire her, she'd gone home, eaten a pint of Ben & Jerry's, and cried herself to sleep. Alone.

"Turn right."

It wasn't that she wasn't happy for Rafe, she was, and she liked Remington. It was just . . . well . . . she didn't like being alone. Loneliness did *not* become her.

"Turn left."

Riley slammed on her brakes. Turn left? There was nothing to turn onto, left or right. She hunched over the steering wheel, grabbed the GPS from its base, and studied the digital screen. A road? Where? She pressed the button to roll down her window for a better look.

That was a road? That barely-wider-than-a-dirt-path? Seriously?

Yep, the GPS had it highlighted.

She turned slowly into the break in the woods. The dirt under her tires had turned to mud with the morning's storm. She pushed the accelerator . . . the back end of the car fishtailed. Riley gripped the steering wheel harder and slowed.

Creeping, she maneuvered around curves and sharp turns. Over rocks that were on their way to becoming boulders. Almost getting lost in potholes big enough for small children to go missing in.

Finally, the car cleared the woods and nosed into a clearing. Then another curve and a beautiful house nestled against a row of trees emerged.

Riley eased alongside Rafe's car. She killed the engine and took a moment to catch her breath.

The front door opened and her brother stepped onto the porch, followed by Remington, an older lady, and . . . a man.

A very handsome man. Standing about six feet tall, his muscular build was defined through the cut of his shirt, the line of his jeans. His dark hair was short and neat, nice. He had the broadest shoulders Riley had seen in some time.

Riley's pulse spiked. Well, now *this* visit could be interesting after all.

CHAPTER THREE

"So justice is far from us, and righteousness
does not reach us. We look for light,
but all is darkness; for brightness,
but we walk in deep shadows."
ISAIAH 59:9

Four years.

That's how long it'd been since he'd taken the steps to come into his own. To take the necessary path to become the man he was born to be. He glanced out his office window, studying the leaves drifting down in the spring breeze. He could now take the time to appreciate the beauty in things. Like nature. And the art hanging on his office walls.

Four years.

Of course, it took patience and time to plan such a detailed and brilliant scheme as his. The research had nearly made him quit, but he'd prevailed. Of course, there were many hours he'd had nothing but time to carefully plan. Once he had a plan, he'd worked every angle, every scenario. He knew each phase would take months to prepare. Acquiring the right people. The right place. The right time. No, these things couldn't be rushed. He'd taken his time.

Four years.

His time, attention, and effort had paid off. Why bother being *elected* into state government when you could control all the ones already there? Much more fun, and a lot more productive. The best thing was that his hands were clean. No one could link anything back to him.

He could move on to the next phase of his plan.

Personal vengeance.

His phone buzzed and he barely glanced at the caller ID. Didn't matter who called, he didn't have anything to say to anybody right now, so why bother talking? He'd call the people he needed to when he wanted something done.

The next move was almost upon him.

He wouldn't rush this. Each piece of the plan had to be perfectly planned to be perfectly executed.

He'd already waited four years, what were a few mere months?

This was Rafe's little sister? The one who wanted to be an investigative journalist?

Hayden tried to imagine her questioning any type of hardened criminal as Rafe rushed down the stairs to greet her. She was a tiny little thing, even shorter than Emily, as she stood on tiptoe to hug her brother, and couldn't weigh more than a buck twenty soaking wet. The afternoon sun caught the highs and lows of her sandy-brown hair bouncing on top of her shoulders.

But something about her twisted Hayden's gut into a massive knot. Like something deep inside him flipped on when he saw her.

"Have you taken leave of your manners? Go help with her things." His mother's words put his feet in motion down the stairs.

Rafe passed Hayden a bag, then reached for another plus a computer bag. "Hayden, this is my sister, Riley. Ri, this is Hayden Simpson, Remington's best friend."

"Nice to meet you." How had his tongue tied so quickly?

She smiled, revealing a row of perfectly straight, perfectly white teeth. Absolutely stunning. "You too."

Within moments, everyone had been introduced and sat comfortably in the living room. Mom sat closest to Riley on one end of the sectional, while Rafe and Remington snuggled on the other with

Chubbers at their feet and Hayden sat opposite his mom and Riley.

His mom leaned closer to Riley, patting her hand. "I love *Life in the South*. I've subscribed for years."

"Thank you. I enjoy working for them." The tip of her tongue ran over her bottom lip.

Why would that statement make her nervous? Maybe he'd misread her body language. Yet Hayden detected the slight quiver of her voice as well. He glanced at Rafe, who gave a split-second frown.

"Rafe said you came early because you were working on a story. Can you tell us about what?" Mom smiled and leaned even closer, fully engaging Riley. "I find reporting all terribly exciting."

Although she kept smiling, Riley hesitated a fraction of a second before replying. "I'm doing a human interest–type story." The smile faltered just a bit. "About families."

"Interesting." His mom leaned back against the couch, propping her feet up on the worn coffee table. "In Baton Rouge?"

"Yes, ma'am, they're from Baton Rouge." Riley swallowed. "The mother and children are still there."

Rafe's eyes narrowed. "What kind of family dynamics are you talking about here?"

The tension stole into the room like a gator

slipping into the murky darkness of the bayou.

She cleared her throat. Hayden almost offered her a glass of water like he would a witness. "A family split apart. Whose love is evident by their dedication to see each other, despite hardships and circumstances keeping them apart."

Her brother's brow rose slightly. "Anybody we know?"

She shook her head. "I don't think so. I just met them today." She swallowed again and smiled at Mom, effectively avoiding eye contact with Rafe. "I have to call them tomorrow to set up the first interview."

"First interview?" His mother asked. "Will it be a series?"

"I hope so." Riley answered Mom, but her eyes locked on her brother.

"What are their extenuating circumstances?" Rafe asked.

Riley swallowed yet again. "The husband, a father of two, is in prison."

Mom glanced at Rafe, took in the red darkening his cheeks, and stood. "Goodness, Emily should be here. Let me give her cell a ring and see if she's on her way." She headed into the kitchen, leaving them alone with the heavy silence.

Hayden could only wish he had a legitimate reason to excuse himself without being obvious.

"You went today, didn't you?" Rafe's voice, while low, thundered.

Riley squared her shoulders and jutted out her chin. "It's not really any of your business if I went."

Rafe shot to his feet, hands curled into fists at his side. "I told you not to."

Hayden tensed, sitting on the edge of his chair. What were they talking about? It was none of his business, but the urge to shelter this young woman he'd just met nearly overwhelmed him.

"I don't care. I'm an adult and can do as I please."

It was like hearing Emily's voice coming out of Riley's mouth. Hayden's chest tightened. For Rafe or for Riley, he didn't know which at this point.

"Why, Ri?" Rafe dropped to the seat beside his sister. "Why would you do this to yourself?"

"Do you know he has someone who claims to be his fiancée? Some woman actually sat there and said she was going to marry him when he was released." Tears shimmered in her eyes.

"What?" Rafe's stiffness disappeared.

Hayden clenched and unclenched his hands. Every gesture, every movement, every indication of Riley screamed of her pain and outrage. He wanted to shield her from this agony. His gaze snagged Remington's, and she gave a slight shake of her head.

"Yeah. Some woman came with Alicia—she could barely speak English—and she told them she was going to marry him." She blinked back tears. "Everyone could tell it was a lie . . . a farce . . . something to help get him out, but Mr. Patterson thinks it could sway the board members."

"No." Rafe shook his head.

Riley nodded, taking her brother's hand. "So we have to really be good in our statements on Monday. Otherwise, there's a good chance he'll get out on parole."

Hayden tensed his muscles. Now it all made sense.

Mom swept back into the room before Rafe could respond. "Emily won't be joining us this evening after all."

Hayden stood and studied her expression. "Everything okay?"

Mom forced a smile. "She didn't answer her cell, but her roommate said they had already made plans for this evening. She must have gotten the days wrong."

No, it meant she blew them off. Not that Hayden minded, one family drama was enough, but it hurt Mom. Despite his angst over her secret keeping, he hated Mom to be hurt. He pulled her into a hug. "That means more gumbo for me." He locked stares with Remington.

She stood as well. "No, it means more for me. I get Emily's share." Remington maneuvered around the coffee table and threw a mock punch at his shoulder. "You get Ardy's cooking all the time. I don't."

Mom's tautness across the shoulders eased.

"So?" He smiled at Remington.

"So I get the extra portions, not you." She turned and held out her hand to Rafe. "Come on, you two. You do not want to miss Ardy's gumbo."

Rafe and his sister both stood but still remained quiet.

Happy again, his mother rushed into the kitchen to serve up gumbo into bowls.

"Thanks," he whispered to Remington.

"No problem," she whispered back before pulling Rafe and Riley toward the table. "It'll be okay, guys."

After witnessing the strain on both the Baxters' faces, Hayden prayed she was right.

His cell phone rang just as he sat down. He snatched his cell from his belt. "Hayden Simpson."

"Hayden, we have an issue."

Even before Officer Bob Travis could give details, Hayden knew it was about Emily. "What?"

"She's okay. It's your sister." Heavy breathing echoed over the connection. "She's been in an, uh, accident. Of sorts."

Hayden cut his gaze to his mother, who thankfully was still occupied with serving up bowls of gumbo. "Details?"

"It appears she stood in front of a car and refused to move."

Of all the stupid—"And?"

"Well, the driver got out and they had . . . um, words."

He closed his eyes, too easy for him to imagine what had gone on from there. Emily's irrationality. Her accusations. Her misplaced anger. "I'll be there as soon as I can." He pushed back his chair and stood.

"Hayden, there's more."

Great. "Yeah?"

"Yeah. The person she got into it with is Caleb Montgomery."

Just when he thought it couldn't get any worse. His sister had to pick the one person in Hopewell who wanted Hayden removed from his position to get into a public argument with.

"He's saying she not only verbally assaulted him, but physically too, and he wants to press charges."

And the blows just kept on coming. "On my way."

His mother stood at his side. "Hayden?"

He leaned over and kissed her forehead. "Duty beckons, Mom. I'll be back as soon as I can." If he didn't get charged with strangling his little sister.

"I hope it's nothing serious." She set down the ladle.

"No, nothing too serious. Just something that needs my attention."

Remington made eye contact across the table.

Her expression let him know she had an idea what the call was about. Shouldn't be too hard, really, since it seemed it was always about Emily these days.

"Ah." Mom beamed toward Riley. "My son's the police commissioner. Sometimes, they just need his approval on some things."

He gave a casual shrug as he pushed his chair under the table. "Please excuse me," he directed to Riley, then included everyone in his forced smile. "I hope I won't be gone long."

But when it involved Emily, it usually took forever to unravel her tangle of lies.

Hayden ran through a million mental scenarios on his drive into the station, but it was no use. Until he got the details, trying to guess what happened was useless.

Three miles later, and Hayden pulled into the police station's lot. He parked, then hustled in the back door. If he could be briefed before seeing Emily or Caleb . . .

"Hayden." Bob Travis stood waiting in the hall. "Sorry to interrupt your long weekend off."

"No problem." And it wasn't Bob's problem. It was his. Emily had been his problem ever since their father died. Well, her father, but that was beside the point. "Fill me in."

"Mr. Montgomery says he had stopped by the grocery store to pick up milk on his way home from work. When he exited the store, he claims

54

he saw Emily at his car. He states he approached her to deter her from vandalizing his personal property, as she has a record of such. At that time, he alleges Emily verbally assaulted him. He said when he tried to move past her to get into his vehicle, she hit him. He wants to press charges against her." Bob's face was already red as he shrugged. "And he says she owes him a gallon of milk since his is still in his car sitting out in front of the station."

Why couldn't anything with Emily be cut and dried? "What does Emily say in her defense?"

"She says she went to the grocery store on her way to visit a friend. She claims when she tried to pull into a parking space on the front row, she couldn't because a car had taken two spaces. She says she parked farther down, and when she walked by the car taking two spaces, she was writing a note to leave for the driver, asking him to be a little more careful in parking so someone else could park in the front row too."

Hayden understood—it irritated him when people were selfish and parked over the lines.

"Emily said that's what she was doing when Mr. Montgomery came out of the store, just leaving a note. She says he approached her and began yelling at her to get away from his car." Bob rubbed his brow. "Best I can make of it, they had words, ending with him saying something along the lines that just because her brother is the police commissioner, doesn't mean she can do whatever she wants and that he wouldn't rest until she and her illegitimate brother were nothing in this town." Bob ducked his head. "And that, according to her, is when she slapped his face."

For once, Hayden's chest swelled with pride. Not that he could tell Emily, at least not here or in front of anyone, but bailing her out of trouble this time would be his pleasure.

He only regretted he hadn't been able to see Caleb's face when she smacked him.

CHAPTER FOUR

"But let justice roll on like a river,
righteousness like a never-failing stream!"
AMOS 5:24

"Thank you so much for allowing me into your home, Mrs. Wilson." Riley had her notebook and recorder in her arms as she sat on the couch where directed. She could imagine the setup was the same as if her hero, Diane Sawyer, were conducting the interview. "Especially on a Saturday."

"It's Peggy, and you're welcome. I didn't have much of a choice." The woman sat on the chair across the living room. Weariness, not makeup, creased in the crow's feet of her eyes.

"Oh?" Riley settled into her seat, arranging her recorder on the coffee table. She tried not to take in the worn carpet, the cheap paneling that peeled, or the pockmarks in the linoleum. Breathing space was a commodity in the mobile home. While awful, it would tug at readers' hearts.

"Jasmine is determined that we talk to you. I'll be honest . . . I don't think this is the best of ideas, but she is convinced you can help her daddy." Peggy's back was straight, her shoulders squared. "I told her you weren't interested in that kind of story, but she's insistent. I had to send her to the library or she'd have been sitting right here with us." She smiled. "If you take the time to get to know her a little, you'll understand she can be quite persuasive."

One of the traits Riley had recognized in the teen. She, too, had been called persuasive more than a time or two in her youth. Well, even more recently than that. Either way, she was drawn to Jasmine and would do what she could. "She's quite something."

"She is that." Peggy relaxed, leaning back in the chair. "So, what do you want to know?"

"Why don't you tell me a little about your family. How you and your husband met, how long you've been married . . . things like that."

"Why, Armand was my high-school sweetheart. We met our freshman year at Central High. He was an amazing young man and just swept me off my feet the first time he spoke to me during orientation."

Riley struggled not to allow herself to get too excited. High-school sweethearts—this was perfect story material, even if it came straight out of a fairy tale.

"We went on our first date that weekend and were inseparable after that." Peggy's eyes glazed over. "We got married the summer after we graduated. Armand looked so handsome. I felt like the luckiest woman alive."

Riley's throat grew tight. What would it be like to love someone like that and have them love you back in the same way?

"Two years later, Jasmine was born. My, but Armand cried like a baby the first time he held her. And then we had trouble getting pregnant again." Tears filled the woman's eyes. "You see, both Armand and I wanted a big family with at least four or five children. But the good Lord had other plans. I didn't even know it until we couldn't get pregnant for a couple of years and I went to the doctor, but I have endometriosis. Doctor said I shouldn't have even been able to get pregnant with Jasmine, and chances of ever getting pregnant again were slim to none."

This story just kept getting better and better—not for Peggy, of course, but for Riley's proposed series. She could already see it: high-school sweethearts, battles with infertility, then the incarceration and poverty for the left-behind wife and children. Yet a twinge of guilt shoved against Riley. To what length would she go in exploiting this woman's pain for her own personal gain? She chewed her bottom lip. She'd have to think about that. Later.

"But again, God had His plans, and nine years later we had Mikey." Peggy shook her head, not even bothering to try to hide the tears in her eyes. "Armand cried even harder the first time he held his son. And also because the doctor had to do an emergency hysterectomy right then or I could have died right there in delivery."

Mouth dry, Riley scribbled notes as fast as she could, thankful the recorder would pick up the tremble in Mrs. Wilson's voice.

"God was good and laid His healing hand on me. I was fine, and we had a healthy daughter and son. Armand said all the time that he was truly a blessed man. I loved him for that and for giving up his dream to have a big family."

A knot formed in Riley's stomach. She'd never dated someone who was selfless to the point of giving up his dream for love. What did that feel like?

"Our marriage is a good one, Ms. Baxter. Even now, with him in prison almost a year now. I love Armand with all my heart. And I'm faithful."

"Please, call me Riley." Her hand shook as she made a notation. She had to push away emotions.

As Jeremy reminded her relentlessly, professional journalists kept an emotional distance from their story subjects. She gripped the pen tighter. "So, tell me why your husband's in prison."

Despite her determination to squelch her feelings, Riley just couldn't imagine a man so in love with his family deliberately doing anything that could cause him to lose them.

"Armand wanted to be on the police force but couldn't ever get accepted into the academy." Peggy narrowed her eyes. "He's a good man: kind, gentle, and loving, but he isn't a brainiac. And that entry exam is quite hard to pass."

"So I've heard." Riley made a note not to mention her brother was an FBI agent. Probably wouldn't go over well . . . for a number of reasons.

"He's a noble and proud man. After several years of working for a security company in their maintenance department, he finally asked his boss about training to become a security officer. They talked and the company helped him take the necessary classes and get certified with his gun."

"So, he was a security officer?"

"Yes. He stayed at the security company for about three years after becoming a security officer, until the owner of the company sold it and moved out of state."

"What did your husband do then?"

"He went to work as a security guard for the Louisiana State Museum."

Interesting twist. Broadened the scope of the target audience.

Peggy sat straight, nearly on the edge of the chair. "He'd been working there for about eight years. They'd promoted him several times. First from night shift to day. Then from a regular guard to a supervisor. Then to assisting with private collections and special exhibits. He loved his job and was good at it. Always made perfect marks on his reviews."

Riley could feel the heart of the story about to erupt. "So, his crime was . . . ?"

"A special collection was on exhibit. Various items from multiple private collectors. All pieces from the Civil War. All pieces from the Confederacy. All priceless." Peggy licked her lips, her face drawn tight. "It was on the fourth night of the display. Someone broke into the museum and stole several of the private pieces."

Well, that didn't seem bad enough to land in Angola. After all, that was a pretty hard prison, even if the new warden had reformed it after its bad reputation.

"One of the night guards was shot as the thieves left."

Riley's mouth held no saliva to swallow. "What happened to the guard?"

"He didn't die but he's paralyzed." Peggy shook her head. "Don't you see? Armand would never shoot anyone, much less one of his own. He was trained in weaponry but he hated guns. Which is why the good Lord's plan didn't allow him to become a police officer."

There had to be more to the story. Then again, wasn't there always? Jeremy always said there were three sides to every story: each person's and then there was the story the readers wanted. She rolled the pen in her fingers. "Why would the police suspect him of involvement?"

Peggy writhed her hands together in her lap. "Because the security system had been disarmed, they were pretty sure it was an inside job."

Understandable.

"Armand was one of the guards who assisted in installing extra security cameras and stuff whenever special exhibits were shown on the third floor." Peggy sniffed. "He wasn't working that night."

The fact that he helped install security systems wasn't enough of a reason for the police to look into a person. She knew, Rafe talked about his frustrations at times. "Did your husband have an alibi?"

"Just me and the children, but apparently that wasn't good enough."

Still . . . "Was there any forensic evidence at the scene?"

Peggy's face contorted into a grimace. "Well, his fingerprints were in the museum, but so were every other guard's."

What wasn't she saying?

"But what got him arrested was the testimony of a pawn-shop owner."

"Oh?" Riley kept her face muscles neutral but held a viselike grip on the pen.

"He identified Armand as the man who pawned one of the items taken in the robbery."

Wow.

"He was mistaken, of course."

What could she say to that? Riley mentally changed the angle of her story. Something like despite the man's obvious guilt, his wife still believed in his innocence and stood by her man. Something mushy and all lovey-dovey. Maybe Jeremy would go for that.

"Mistaken? He flat-out lied."

Riley turned around to meet Jasmine's hot stare. "How do you know?" Realizing how accusatory that sounded, she quickly added, "For certain, I mean."

"I saw my dad that night. During the time of the break-in and shooting. He was asleep on the couch, just like he said." Jasmine tossed her backpack on the floor of the mobile home. "But I was too young to testify. Daddy said no one would believe me. His attorney refused to even let me give an affidavit or talk to the judge in chambers."

Jasmine wore anger like the latest fashion. "Plain and simple, my daddy was framed, and that's a fact."

• • •

"I hated to call you out on your weekend off, again, but this one . . . well, I ain't ever seen anything like this." Bob moved around the two cruisers and coroner's vehicle toward the water's edge. If the crime scene bugged out a seasoned vet like Bob . . .

Yellow tape danced on the April breeze, mocking yet beckoning at the same time. The sun touched the tips of the tree line. They'd have to work quickly before the sun disappeared entirely.

All the official vehicles were bunched in one area. Groups of officers clumped outside the official crime-scene area. Hayden picked his way carefully to the bayou. He could see what Bob meant before he reached the marshy brink.

A man hung upside down on an alligator hook in the spine. Dangling from the old cypress tree over the water, the body had been stripped of all clothes, legs bound together. Pale and grotesque.

The coroner nodded as Hayden approached. "Evening, Commissioner." He took another photograph of the body, then handed the camera to his assistant.

Lee Morrow had been a fixture in this nasty business since Hayden was a rookie. "Hey, Lee. What's the word?"

The coroner moved the body with his gloved hand. "As usual, can't go on record until I do the autopsy, but my bet is that cause of death is exsanguination."

The two officers took a step back. Hayden stiffened his back against the shudder. "He bled out from the hook?"

"Yep. Looks that way, although the bayou washed away any blood."

"Think the killer expected an alligator to come along and assist in getting rid of the body, and any evidence?"

"Maybe." Lee took a final glance at the body before stepping back and motioning for his assistant to help get the body out of the tree and onto the stretcher. "But gator season won't open for months. Most people aren't out baiting this time of year."

"You're saying the killer had the hook and hooked our vic before bringing him out here?"

"Can't be positive because the body was over water, so blood evidence is gone. That's my best estimation at this point." Lee and his assistant removed the body and heaved it onto the stretcher. "By the looks of some of the bruises on his face, I'd say he put up a pretty good fight." He zipped the bag around the body. "No ID, obviously. I'll run his prints and dentals as soon as I get back."

"Guesstimation of time of death?"

"Considering the condition of the body and taking in account the weather, I'd say within the last ten to twelve hours."

"Thanks, Lee."

The coroner nodded as he and his assistant made their way with the body to the coroner's van.

Hayden stared out over the bayou, then back at the tree. "The killer wanted to make a statement," he murmured.

"What?" Bob and one of the other officers looked at Hayden.

He nodded toward where the dead man had been hung. "You don't do something like this to somebody unless you're trying to send a message."

"What kind of message is this? Mess with me and I'll make gator bait outta you?" Bubba Fontenot, one of the newer, younger officers, spit tobacco into the bushes.

Hayden scowled. "Go back to your cruiser and get rid of that mess in your mouth. You could contaminate my crime scene."

"I didn't spit inside the taped area, Commissioner, I promise."

"Go do as I say, Officer."

Fontenot stalked off to his car. Hayden shook his head. "These younger guys . . . I just don't understand them."

Bob snorted. "What he didn't want you to know is that he vomited when he arrived on scene and saw the body. He says snuff gets that taste out of his mouth."

"Ah." Still didn't make a lot of sense to him,

but he had to focus on the crime scene staring him in the face.

Focus. Focus. Focus.

"Where's the man who found the body?"

Bob nodded at his cruiser. "I gave him a bottle of water and stuck him in the backseat. Edward Gaston is at post there. No one has questioned him yet."

"I'll do it in just a minute." Hayden glanced back to the way he'd driven in, past the vehicles. "Get the crime unit to go over the ground with a fine-tooth comb. Lee thinks the time of death is within the last ten to twelve hours, so that means since it rained yesterday. Maybe we'll get lucky and get some tire prints that don't match any of ours or the coroner's."

Bob nodded, then lifted his radio and relayed the orders.

Why here? Hayden stared across the bayou. Why did the killer pick this particular place? Was there a deliberate reason? What was the message?

He turned. "Go ahead and get the unit in here." The bayou, she had a history of stealing evidence. She kept her secrets well. "I'll go question . . . what's his name?"

"Ellington. Davis Ellington."

Hayden approached the back of Bob's cruiser.

"Commissioner." Officer Gaston stood taller and straighter at Hayden's appearance.

"Officer. Go help Officer Travis."

"Yes, sir." The younger officer scrambled across the muddy ground.

Hayden opened the door opposite the side of the witness. He sat on the backseat beside the man but left the door open. A crisp breeze chased out the stale remnants of greasy fries. "Mr. Ellington? I'm Commissioner Simpson." He pulled out his small notebook, ever present in his front pocket, and began.

About mid- to late-fifties, Mr. Ellington had dark hair with streaks of gray, heavier in the temple area. His face, tanned and lined, had a scar just over his right eye. His calloused hands trembled slightly. "I'm Davis." His voice cracked. He cleared his throat. "I found him."

"Do you own this property?"

The man nodded. "Was passed down to me by my father. He died a couple of years ago."

"Do you live here, on the property?" Hayden glanced around but saw no buildings.

"Land sakes, no. Don't know why my father had this land. We never used it for anything but fishing and hunting."

Looked like it'd be great for that purpose. But April wasn't hunting season. "What were you doing here this afternoon?"

"Came to check my trotlines." The man's hands shook harder.

Withdrawals or nerves? Hayden smiled. "You catching anything?"

Davis shrugged. "Mainly cats, but that's what my wife likes best anyway."

His mother preferred catfish too. And she could fry it so light it practically melted in your mouth.

Hayden nodded. "What time did you set out your lines?"

" 'Bout sixish or so this morning."

"And you didn't see the body then?"

Davis cocked his head. "If I did, I woulda called the police just like I did this afternoon. Soon as I saw it, I ran down the road to the gas station and called."

"You don't have a cell phone?"

"Nah, although Loretta has one. She's learning to text her sister all the dadburned time. Just another bill I gotta pay, if you ask me."

Hayden swallowed the grin. "And you arrived at what time this afternoon?"

"Around four, right after I got off work. If there were any fish, I'd have time to clean them and get home to give to Loretta to fry up for supper."

Hayden would have one of the other officers acquire Mr. Ellington's address and place of employment and verify that he was, in fact, at work today. "You didn't recognize the body?"

Davis shuddered. "No, sir. Then again, I didn't want to take too close of a look."

He didn't blame the man. Hayden closed his

notebook. "That's all for now, Mr. Ellington. I'll have someone come explain the process to you now. Just sit tight."

"Yes, sir."

Hayden stood and motioned at an officer. He didn't have much to go on with this case at the moment, but Lee would hopefully be able to identify the body. For now, what he did know was the cause of death and a window of time in which the killer had to have been here to place the body.

Time to catch a killer.

CHAPTER FIVE

"Do not follow the crowd in doing wrong.
When you give testimony in a lawsuit,
do not pervert justice by siding with the crowd."
EXODUS 23:2

Pick up, pick up.

Riley gripped the phone tighter, willing Jeremy to answer. He had to still be at his desk—he always worked straight through the weekend until Sunday night when he put the magazine to bed. It was barely eight. No question he'd be there.

"Hello, you've reached the voice mail box of Jeremy Curry, editor in chief. I'm on another

line or away from my desk at the moment, but if you'll leave a detailed message, I'll return your call right away. Wait for the beep."

He'd seen her number on caller ID and let it go to voice mail. Riley chewed her bottom lip. How long would he be furious with her?

Beep!

"Jeremy, this is Riley. I . . . well, I have a story. Actually, a series." She hesitated, exhaling slowly. "I'm e-mailing my concept and the first article to you tonight. Call my cell." She swallowed. "I think you'll like this idea, and I promise you'll get stellar storytelling if you'll just give me another chance." Blast it, she sounded like she was begging. Maybe she was. "Anyway, check your e-mail and call me."

She ended the call and stared at the prepared e-mail. The pitch sounded good—she knew that. So did the first article. She'd resisted the urge to write it as a sensationalized piece of an allegedly innocent man in prison for a crime he didn't commit, which had been her first instinct. Instead, she pulled up as much of the emotional angle as she could muster without choking.

I Lost My Daddy and Our Home . . . All in the Name of Justice

She liked the headline: It snagged the attention of the reader and would hopefully entice them to read the article. She'd written the entire piece from Jasmine's point of view, with background provided by Peggy.

After much debate over starting the series with the love story of Peggy and Armand, Riley had opted to take a different approach. Since Jasmine had been what had initially drawn her, that's the angle she wanted to pursue. Next week's article would be Peggy and Armand's story.

If Jeremy allowed her this chance.

If this story didn't prove she could write without bias toward anyone affiliated with a criminal, she didn't know what would. Reading between the lines, one wouldn't be able to tell the author gave full support to the criminal justice system and believed wholeheartedly in the incarceration guidelines.

She reread it again. Then a third time. It was good.

Her finger hesitated over the Send button. Would it be good enough for Jeremy to get over his anger and pick it up? Would he even open her e-mail? What if he just deleted it without reading it? Or what if he had been screening his calls when she left the message and now sat in front of his computer, waiting on her e-mail?

She pressed the button and the e-mail disappeared . . . flying across cyberspace to Jeremy. Her journalistic future rested in his hands.

For the first time, she prayed favor over her writing. She usually didn't want to be so vain that she asked God to bless her writing, but today . . . desperate times called for desperate measures. If she didn't impress Jeremy, she'd be out of a job soon.

A soft knock sounded on the door to the Simpson's den. "Riley?" Remington asked in a heavy whisper.

"Come on in." She shut the laptop and stood.

"Rafe and I are going to watch a movie. Want to join us?" Remington tried to befriend Riley. Maddie too. Perhaps Riley should try harder to get to know her better. Rafe seemed to really care about her. The forever-and-ever type caring. Besides, Riley needed something to distract her. She'd used up all her good brain cells writing the article. She'd gone through all her gumption reserves to call Jeremy. She deserved a mental break.

Riley smiled. "Sure. Sounds like fun." She followed Remington back into the living room and plopped on the love seat. The movie started and she struggled to focus on the television and not on the gooey eyes her brother made. This could be a really long movie.

Despite her efforts to concentrate on the comedy, her mind kept going to Monday. The parole hearing. How vital Rafe's and her testimony would be. The dread stole her energy.

Two hours and ten minutes later, the credits rolled across the screen. She stood and stretched, fighting off a yawn. "I'm calling it a night."

Remington stood and folded the afghan, laying it across the back of the couch. "Me too. I thought Hayden would be back by now, but I guess his call was something serious."

"Wonder if he needs another pair of eyes for anything." Rafe tossed the throw pillows haphazardly on the couch.

"You're a little out of jurisdiction, Agent," Remington teased.

"I didn't mean helping in an official capacity, just if he needed a little—"

"That's it. I'm going to bed." Riley smiled at Remington. "G'night."

Rafe pulled her into his arms and hugged her tight, then planted a kiss on the top of her head. "Good night, squirt."

The name he'd bestowed on her when they were kids. She couldn't explain why that caused tears to burn her eyes, but it did. Probably too much emotion over the last day or two. Suddenly exhaustion tugged on her every muscle.

She pushed away from her brother. "Sheesh. Get some rest, dude. I'll see y'all in the morning."

Yawning again, she made her way to the den and closed the door. She stole a glance at the clock—10:30. When was the last time she was this worn out so early? She barely had the energy to brush her teeth and pull on her pajamas before crawling into bed. As soon as her head hit the pillow, darkness welcomed her into its warm embrace.

What felt like a second later, her eyes popped open.

As much as she'd been worn out earlier, now Riley was as wide-awake as ever. Every sound amplified. Those tree frogs Remington had identified for her earlier. The wind brushing against the side of the house.

Why couldn't she sleep?

She checked the clock—3:00 a.m. Unfortunately this was becoming a habit for her. She turned to her side and punched her pillow. Too much adrenaline for the day.

She tossed onto her back and stared at the ceiling, remembering Jasmine's anger and pain. Too much emotion raged through Riley. Flipping over to her stomach, she pinched her eyes shut and willed herself to sleep. It remained evasive as before.

She peeked at the clock again—3:06. She let out a groan. This was ridiculous. Riley kicked off the covers and swung her legs to the side of the bed. She needed to move. Needed to clear her head, organize her feelings and thoughts. Needed fresh air.

She'd noticed earlier that there wasn't an alarm system on the house. Odd, considering Hayden was a cop. Rafe had installed systems in both Maddie's and her places. But maybe Hopewell didn't have much crime. Probably didn't have much of any excitement.

Grabbing her cell, she eased open the door to the covered patio, conveniently located off the den, and slipped outside. A soft light shone down the path toward the water's edge. A tree frog croaked louder. Crickets answered. Low clouds hid the moon and stars. The April night held a chill.

Riley shivered and tightened the robe around her. She sat on one of the wrought-iron patio chairs, blinking. How could it be so dark? If it weren't for the low light by the path, she'd be sitting in total and complete darkness. Funny how she'd never noticed how much city streetlights illuminated the night.

She pushed a button on her cell. The backlight lit up, like a flashlight. Smiling over her silliness from a second ago, she glanced at the main screen. A missed call. From Jeremy. Her heart kicked into overdrive. The voice mail icon blazed in the night.

She forgot about the tree frogs, the crickets, and the lack of moon and stars. All that mattered was Jeremy had called her back. Riley chewed her bottom lip. Good news or bad?

Surely he wouldn't call if he thought her series idea was a bust or he hated her article. Would he? Unless he planned to fire her. Would he do that over the phone? Probably. He'd sure yelled at her in front of her colleagues—why wouldn't he fire her over the phone?

Despite the chill, sweat slicked her palms. Might as well get it over with. Knowing was better than wondering. She pressed the button to check her messages and stared into the night. She'd soon know the status of her job—no, her career—because if Jeremy fired her, chances are no one in the industry would touch her.

"First message, received today, 9:04 p.m. from Jeremy Curry." The automated voice went silent, a click sounded, then Jeremy's voice thundered against her ear. *"Hey, Riley. Got your message. And your e-mail. I have to say . . . I'm impressed. I love the angle and your writing is the best I've seen since I hired you."*

A pause, just enough for her exhale.

"I'm running the article in Monday's edition. Congratulations."

Another pause.

"But I don't have to tell you not to blow this series. It's not just me paying attention. Gus is evaluating all the staff writers. So keep up the good work."

Gus was evaluating the writers? Gus Phizer owned *Life in the South*. He would be reading her series and determining . . . what?

Nerves and excitement mingled with the sweaty palms as she saved the message—who knew when she'd need a boost and the praise of the message would lift her. Obviously, with a little too much force, as the phone slipped from her grasp. The light went out as the cover popped off and the battery bounced over the paver stones. Plunged back into darkness, Riley dropped to her hands and knees on the hard patio and felt around for the phone and battery. Maybe after she found them, she could find the cover.

She crawled around, feeling with her hands and fumbling over the rough stones. The cold seeped through the robe and pajamas, snaking down her spine. Her fingertips grazed against something. She gripped it tight—her phone. Now to find the battery and cover.

Inching. Reaching farther. Stretching. There, she curled her fingers around the . . . um . . . battery and pulled it toward her.

Something furry brushed against her arm.

Hisssss!

She jerked backward and banged her head against the wrought-iron table. Something bumped her back. Something alive.

Riley sprung to her feet and, with shaking hands, struggled to shove the battery into the cell phone.

A snarl, couldn't be more than a foot from her, bounced off the patio's roof.

She fumbled with the battery.

A growl, no more than six inches.

Battery in. She powered on the phone.

The light pierced the darkness and reflected off two yellow, beady eyes. Right in front of her.

Riley screamed and dropped her phone again.

"Morning, Hayden. How was church?" Bob Travis was a good man, to be sure, but he wasn't a Christian.

But Hayden refused to give up on his friend. "Enlightening and inspiring. Want to come with me next week?"

"Appreciate the offer, but not interested." Same response given at least once a month for the last decade. "Guess I half expected you to show up despite it being Sunday and you supposed to be off all weekend."

"Not with such a murder on our hands." Hayden leaned against the filing cabinet. "Anything?"

"Lee sent us the prints, and we sent them on to IAFIS. Nothing."

Of course not. Why would he think the national fingerprint database would snag a hit? Hayden shook his head. Why would anything be easy about this case? "What else did Lee have to say?"

Bob passed him a folder. "Already did the autopsy. Said you'd probably need it sooner rather than later."

Impressive. He flipped through the report, scanning.

AUTOPSY NUMBER: BRP00009221989
DECEDENT: John Doe

Fifty-six-year-old white male, 71 inches long and 184 pounds with hazel eyes and brown hair.

Bob continued. "Lee sent John Doe's DNA to the lab. Should hear back from NDIS next week. I requested a rush if at all possible."

Wouldn't matter. In Hayden's experience, the National DNA Index system ran in its own sweet time. He nodded as he read more.

Well-developed, well-nourished male with multiple contusions on his face and neck. Multiple lacerations and perforations with irregular edges are present on bilateral forearms. Matter found under his right fingernails has been sent for toxicology and identification.

Defensive wounds. So he had put up a fight with his killer. Had he seen the hook . . . known what was going to happen to him? Had fear caused him to panic? Had he hurt his killer? Scarred or marked him in some way? Hayden skipped over the gross description details before he read on.

CAUSE OF DEATH: Exsanguination
MANNER OF DEATH: Homicide

"Lee said time of death was between six and eight, Saturday morning."

The normal two-hour window. Hayden closed the folder and plopped it back on Bob's desk, then sat on the edge of the empty desk in the cubicle. "Forensics come back with anything?"

"Still processing."

Yeah, it was a weekend and the full team didn't work on Sundays. But this was one nasty murder. Hayden hadn't been able to wipe the image of the man hanging upside down on that hook from his mind.

"Have you run the MO through the system?"

Bob nodded. "No hits. No crime scene even comes close."

True. They were dealing with one messed-up killer. "Any matches from missing persons?"

"Nothing here. We're waiting to hear back about Baton Rouge, Donaldsonville, and Lafayette."

More often than not, when a person didn't come home on a Saturday night, loved ones waited until Monday to file a report. Especially if the missing person had a social life. Hayden never understood that logic until Emily came of age, then he understood all too well.

"We're pretty much at a standstill until information comes back."

He couldn't just sit on his hands. "I'll be in my office for a bit." Hayden crossed the common area and opened the door to his office. He left

81

the overhead light off and sunk into his chair behind the desk. Sometimes he did his best thinking alone in the dark.

His mind flipped through what they knew, which wasn't much. More would come, in time, but something kept niggling at Hayden. There had to be a reason for the location. It wasn't a place someone would just pass and see—it was too far off the beaten track. Yet Davis Ellington had stated he didn't recognize the victim.

Could the location have been someplace special, personal to the killer?

CHAPTER SIX

"When justice is done, it brings joy to the righteous but terror to evildoers."
PROVERBS 21:15

"And this will run in your magazine tomorrow?" Mom passed the computer printout back to Ms. Baxter. The afternoon sun streamed through the shoddy kitchen window framed with bright gingham curtains. Even Mom's decorating touches couldn't hide how horrible living here was. Jasmine hated this trailer. Hated that she had to share a room with Mikey. Hated most of all that Daddy wasn't here.

She just wanted to go home. To her old life. To

her real life. Before Daddy got arrested and sent to jail.

"Yes."

Mom reached for her hand across the table. "Are you really okay with this? All your friends at school can see it, know all this about you. You have to be sure."

She'd be like, almost a celebrity. Kinda. Yeah, it would bite for everyone to know they'd lost their house and were broke—that part might cause a fight or two if people didn't keep their mouths closed—but if the series did what Ms. Baxter said . . . "You think starting with me and how I feel about Daddy being in jail and what's happened to us will make readers want to read more?"

Ms. Baxter nodded. Her pretty brown hair that looked so soft, like it belonged on a shampoo commercial, brushed against her shoulders. "The readers will read about you and be intrigued. They'll care. And because they'll feel invested in your story, they'll read each installment, anxious to find out what happens."

"You don't have to be okay with this, Jaz." Mom squeezed her shoulders. "You're in high school, and we all know how difficult that is. This will just add stress on you." She turned to Ms. Baxter. "I think this might all be a mistake. I didn't want to talk with you, but she was so adamant. I don't—"

"No, Mom. I want to do this. For Daddy." If there was even the slightest chance this could help the legal system see how wrong it was for him to be in jail, she'd put up with more of the prison and convict jokes—the ones she never told Mom about.

Mom's frown deepened, but she didn't say anything. Mom was really a pretty lady. Once. Back before Daddy was arrested and his trial and then his going to prison, Mom used to have smoother skin. Brighter eyes. Less gray hair. And she used to wear makeup and fix her hair. Poor Mikey. If Daddy stayed in prison, her brother would never get to see how pretty Mom could be. Even in her best church dress she still wore from this morning's service, she looked tired.

"Are you really sure, honey? It won't hurt our feelings in the least if you've changed your mind."

Jasmine needed to do this not only for her dad, but also for Mom. "I'm positive. This is what I want." She held up her hand. "Seriously, Mom, I know what can happen, what people will say, and I'm okay with it. Our story needs to be told." So maybe, just maybe, this would never happen to another family.

Ms. Baxter smiled. "It's okay to be nervous. Even a little scared."

"Do you ever get scared, Ms. Baxter?"

The composed and pretty woman shocked Jasmine by laughing. "All the time. Just last night, I couldn't sleep so I went outside to sit. A raccoon came up and scared me so badly, I dropped my phone. Almost broke it."

Jasmine grinned.

"I don't know who was more startled: me or that varmint." She winked at Jasmine, then turned to Mom. "I'll write up what I have proposed for next week's segment and run it by you tomorrow afternoon to look over, when I bring you a copy of Jasmine's article. It will focus on your husband's and your love story."

If Mom only knew that would be more embarrassing than *her* article. None of Jasmine's friends' moms and dads were still together. Some of the kids were on their second or third set of stepparents.

"That should really get the readers invested in your story. Then I'll go into the crime." Ms. Baxter tapped her pen against the notebook. "I have the name of your husband's attorney. Was there an investigator or anyone else who worked on the case that you can recall? I'd like to talk to as many people as possible."

"I just don't know." Mom shook her head. "It's been a while."

Jasmine looked at Ms. Baxter. "Would a copy of the court thing help?"

Ms. Baxter's eyes widened. "The transcript?"

"I guess. The whole trial written down?"

"You have a copy?"

"Yeah. The attorney got it right before he filed Daddy's appeal. It's in Mom's room. I'll grab it."

It was right where she remembered. Right on the bookshelf, lying under one of the gazillion Bible study books Mom had. It didn't make sense. Mom was such a devoted Christian, not just for show like some of the people she knew at church, yet all her prayers hadn't stopped Daddy from being put behind bars. On her birthday, nonetheless. What kind of God did that? A lousy excuse for one, that's who.

Jasmine shoved the Bible off the transcript, letting it shift sideways, and grabbed the heavy folder. She hurried back to the kitchen and handed it to Ms. Baxter. A sound, half cry–half groan, came from Mikey's bedroom. Already standing, Jasmine put her hand on her mother's shoulder. "I'll check on him."

She headed to the room she shared with her brother. He lay on the floor, whimpering.

"Hey, Mikey, what's wrong?"

"I'm hot."

She knelt and laid a hand on his forehead. Heat transferred to her hand. She jerked back. "You're burning up." Jasmine jerked him into her arms and stood, then rushed back to the kitchen. "Mom, he's got a fever again."

"Let me see." Mom took him from her. "Sweet boy, do your ears hurt?"

Mikey started crying. "A little."

"What can I do to help?" Ms. Baxter asked.

"He gets ear infections a lot." Jasmine ran a hand over his head. "Want me to see if we have any refills left on his last prescription?"

Mom shook her head. "That was the last one without us going back to the doctor." She stood, holding the clinging and crying Mikey. "I'm going to take his temperature." She made her way to the bathroom.

"Should we call the doctor?" Ms. Baxter asked.

Jasmine wished. "Not yet. Not unless Mom can't get his fever to come down and we *have* to get a prescription for an antibiotic." Which would cost more money than they had for the month. "He has chronic ear infections."

Mikey let out a wail. It trailed down the hall, bouncing off the walls of the trailer. It rattled down Jasmine's spine.

"They can't do anything about them? If they're chronic, they should consider doing something more permanent about it than antibiotics."

Jasmine shrugged. "They've talked about putting tubes in, but . . ." If they couldn't afford a doctor visit or antibiotics, they sure couldn't afford a surgeon's fee, hospital fee, and everything else.

Mikey cried out again, this time with a higher pitch.

Ms. Baxter cringed. "But what? They don't

think it's the best idea? Are there other tests they need to run?"

"No. The surgery is so expensive."

Now Ms. Baxter's perfectly arched eyebrows shot up. "Insurance won't cover the surgery?"

Jasmine couldn't help herself—she gave a snort-laugh. "Our insurance is a joke, Ms. Baxter. We used to have it through Daddy's job, but we couldn't keep that. The grocery store's policy is a joke. Every time the doctor recommends us going to an ears, nose, and throat specialist, the insurance claims they won't cover the additional expense. So Mikey goes back to our regular doctor, who can only prescribe antibiotics."

"What about a second opinion?"

Seriously? "I mean no disrespect, Ms. Baxter, but really? The insurance won't cover a specialist, and they sure won't cover a second opinion."

The lady reporter blushed.

Mikey cried out again. Then Mom hollered, "Jaz, can you bring me some of the children's ibuprofen?"

"Coming." She opened the kitchen cabinet and grabbed the medicine. "I'm sorry, Ms. Baxter. We gotta take care of Mikey." She moved to the hall, then froze. "But you'll still come tomorrow, right?"

Ms. Baxter slipped her notebook and Daddy's trial transcript into her black tote. "Yes. I have something I have to do in the morning, but I'll be by tomorrow afternoon. After you get home from school." She smiled. "I'll bring you your own copy of the magazine."

Wow. She would really be kinda like a celebrity.

"Jaz?"

Yeah. Sure. Right. A celebrity who was broke and needy.

"That was a delicious dinner, Mrs. Simpson." Thomas Vince, the guy Emily had been seeing for the past couple of months, pushed his black-rimmed, round glasses back up the bridge of his nose.

"You're quite welcome, Thomas." Ardy took a final drink of her iced tea. "So, tell me more about your store. I do love antiques."

The man explained, in detail, how he scoured area estate sales and flea markets to get the best antiques. Riley had watched Emily and the antique-shop owner interact all evening. It fascinated her because had she just met Thomas on the street, she'd have sworn he was—what was the word everyone was using these days?—metrosexual? But Hayden's sister was practically gushing over him, so a platonic relationship didn't seem possible.

Thomas seemed warm and genuine, even if he came across a bit prim and proper. Emily, on the other hand, glared at Riley every chance she got. Or so it seemed. Riley couldn't quite figure

89

it out. Had she done something to offend her?

"What made you decide to open a store in Hopewell, of all places?" Hayden asked Thomas.

"I wanted to get out of the New Orleans area. Too much crime." Thomas smiled at Ardy. "Seemed like every month or so one of my neighboring businesses was getting broken into. My shop got broken into five years ago, and I said enough was enough." He clapped his hands together. "I did some research on the outlying communities, found which had the lowest crime rates, and started looking for square footage to purchase. The rest," he smiled at everyone up and down the table, "is, as they say, history."

Ardy stood and grabbed her plate. "I understand. Who wants banana pudding for dessert?"

In record time, the table was cleared and everyone had coffee and pudding before them.

"How's your story coming, Riley?" Remington asked.

"It's coming." She still was a little leery about sharing her opinions. Especially when she didn't know exactly what she thought just yet. "The research is quite intensive."

"I bet." Emily sneered across the table.

Ever since Ardy had introduced them, Emily had been borderline rude to Riley.

Thomas stood, pushing the glasses back up his nose. "It was a lovely dinner, Mrs. Simpson. Thank you."

Ardy wore a startled look. "You're welcome. Are you leaving?"

"Yes. As I informed Emily earlier, I purchased an estate-sale lot that is scheduled to be delivered this evening. I must be at my shop prior to the delivery's arrival." He swayed slightly, as if he had an injured foot, then steadied.

"Oh. I see."

Emily leaned over and planted a kiss on her mother's cheek, then Hayden's, and finally Remington's. "I'll see y'all later." She didn't even bother speaking to Riley or Rafe. Maybe she had an aversion to all the Baxters for some reason.

Riley and Remington finished cleaning the kitchen, much to Ardy's argument, then Riley excused herself to her room to work.

But the den, while large and comfortable, didn't give Riley the inspiration she needed. She opened the patio door and slipped outside.

The last rays of the sun streaked across the sky. Riley sat on the patio, the transcript of Armand Wilson's trial lying open on the wrought-iron table. A breeze blew across the back of Ardy Simpson's house, lifting the copy pages. Riley enjoyed this quiet moment. It was in times like these that she felt closest to God. Right about now, she needed to feel His presence more than ever.

The door off the living room opened, and Hayden stepped onto the patio. "Am I interrupting you?"

Yeah, but she didn't mind. "Not at all. Just doing a little appreciating of God's masterpieces." She waved to the chair beside her. "Join me, if you like." The irony that she acted like the hostess when this was his family home didn't escape her.

Hayden sat and peered out at the setting sun. He said nothing, just sat with her in silence.

For the first time in a long time, Riley felt comfortable sitting with a man without forcing conversation. It was nice to share the beauty of the sunset and not feel compelled to have to say something.

Another breeze floated across the bayou. A hint of fish and wet dirt surfed on the gusts, causing Riley to crinkle her nose.

Hayden chuckled, making her realize that sometime while she'd been studying nature, he'd been studying her. She shifted in her chair.

"Sorry. Sometimes I forget not everyone is accustomed to the smell." He inhaled deeply and closed his eyes.

"You like the smell, then?" How, she couldn't imagine.

"Smells like home to me."

She smiled and nodded. Riley wasn't sure what to make of Hayden. He was handsome with that easy smile of his, that went without saying, but he also had an interesting depth to him. Something about his eyes drew a person in. Maybe because they pooled understanding and empathy. His whole demeanor was trust personified.

It almost intimidated her. Hadn't she thought Damon and Garrison were both trustworthy too? Look how those two turned out.

"Are you nervous about tomorrow?"

She jerked from her musings. "What?" Heat crawled up the back of her neck. Had he noticed her silently appraising him?

"The parole hearing. Are you nervous about speaking?" His eyes were serious now but still full of understanding and empathy.

"Not really—well, a little, I guess." Now why had she admitted that? She hadn't told Rafe when he'd asked her right after the delicious Sunday dinner Mrs. Simpson made. That woman's red beans and rice was slap-your-momma good.

"I can only imagine. I'll be praying for you and Rafe both. You'll do fine." His smile was a little crooked, now that she looked at his face straight on. His imperfection was a bit endearing.

"Oh. Yeah." She wouldn't admit she hadn't been paying close attention to what he said, but if she had to, she could probably describe his voice and the way it made her pulse respond in no less than 250 words. The blush worked its way up to her cheeks. She ducked her head, hiding in the dusky hue of orangey red.

Hayden motioned to the open transcript on the table. "Working?"

93

"Yeah. For my series." Wow, some journalist she was. Riley sat up straighter. "I'm reading the trial transcript, and already the facts seem a little . . . off."

"That's good, right? For your story's sake?"

"I suppose. But if he *is* innocent, it's reprehensible that this man has sat in prison for almost a year for a crime he didn't commit." She couldn't quite accept someone in prison as innocent.

"Although I hate it, especially in my profession, mistakes do happen."

She'd never considered something like this happening. Until now. She had always assumed if someone was arrested and indicted, he was guilty. Surely the police wouldn't arrest someone they didn't know was guilty. They had to have evidence of guilt, right? Prosecutors and grand juries didn't indict unless an overwhelming amount of evidence existed.

Maybe she was wrong. "I don't understand how such mistakes can occur."

Hayden ran a hand over his chin and leaned back in his chair, stretching his long legs out in front of him and crossing them at the ankles. "Some cops don't take the right amount of time to properly investigate. They aren't thorough. Some just flat-out make mistakes. They're human." He shook his head. "Sometimes, there's political pressure coming down, rushing them to make a collar."

"But these are people's lives. Surely due diligence should be taken, regardless of pressure or politics."

"In a perfect world, you're right." He sat up and leaned his elbows on the patio table. The light had faded so she couldn't make out his facial expression. "But we don't live in a perfect world."

Riley chewed her bottom lip.

He tapped the transcript. "Want to run some questions by me? I'd be happy to help you if I can."

She smiled in the dark. "I appreciate it. Let me finish reading the whole thing, then if I still have doubts, we'll talk."

"Fair enough." He stood, his 100-percent male silhouette hulking over her. "You ought to come on in. The mosquitoes will be out soon."

She closed the file and slipped it under her arm as she let him pull out her chair. "Mosquitoes bad?"

"Didn't you know—the mosquito is Louisiana's state bird?"

CHAPTER SEVEN

"This is what the LORD Almighty said:
'Administer true justice; show mercy
and compassion to one another.' "
ZECHARIAH 7:9

Oswald.

What kind of parents name their son Oswald? Did they despise him from birth? Before he even drew his first breath?

As a kid, he'd looked up the meaning of his name in a couple of those baby name books in the library, positive Oswald had a noble and manly meaning. It did—God's power. He'd been pretty happy to find that out. His mistake had been telling everyone at school that because of the meaning of his name, he had the power of God.

He'd survived elementary school by being the punch line in a joke . . . junior high by being the punching bag. But he'd changed all that in high school.

Oswald.

He'd been the star of his high school's track and field team. He was so good, he was awarded a scholarship. His future plans had included marrying Kelly.

So, again, he had to wonder about his parents.

What would possess them to bestow such an awful moniker on an infant? It wasn't a family name. Those library books had stated the name had a German origin. His family wasn't of German descent.

Oswald.

It just didn't make sense. With such a meaning behind it, the name should've been strong . . . masculine . . . commanding. Not . . . him. Not even in his glory track days.

But now, even with his appearance, no one would accuse him of not being commanding. No one would dare question his virility. At least not that it could get back to him. He had power now, and that was sexy in today's world. That's what brought the women to him. That's what had people lining up to be his friends.

Hadn't hurt that he'd legally changed his name as soon as he could. His mother had never known. After high school, he'd walked out the door of their shabby double-wide with orange carpet and never looked back. Why should he? He was destined for a better life. He was better than the trailer park that housed the street drug manufacturers and small-town pushers. He was smart and powerful.

He was full of God's power, if he believed those library books. And if he believed in God. But he'd stopped believing in that fictional character about the same time he stopped waiting up on Christmas Eve to catch Santa Claus. Neither had been anything but disappointments.

He'd continued in his destiny, fulfilling his fate. Even the one slipup had helped him gain insight and perspective. He was one of the most powerful names in the movers and shakers circle. Those on the outside of his group wanted to know him. Would beg just for him to look at them, really look at them. Those on the inside had a healthy fear of him. He was loved by many, feared by even more. A very real, very deadly fear.

All warranted, of course. He hadn't gotten to his level of power without learning to look out for himself first. He'd made enemies. In the business world, who hadn't? But he made sure he had the documents to back up his threats, and he made it abundantly clear that everyone knew he wasn't afraid to use whatever ammunition he had.

He sat back on the leather couch and stared out into the black void again. It'd been a long time since he'd thought of his mother . . . longer still since he'd allowed himself to remember his father. Used to be, he'd think of his mother around holidays. Sometimes on his birthday. Not so much in the last couple of years. But tonight . . . tonight he let himself wonder about what life could have been.

Kelly . . . all smiles and high school giddiness. Then her avoiding him. Not coming to the hospital. Eventually stopped visiting him all together. Not answering his calls. Then the gall to tell him she was pregnant with someone else's baby.

Oswald.

He remembered the past of his youth, after his dad left, which he hadn't allowed himself to do in a very long time.

The therapy. The prescription drugs. The crack—a poor man's cocaine. The parties. The police. The stench of sweat and vomit.

Footfalls on the floor snatched him back to the present.

The strawberry blonde opened the study door and stepped inside, wearing nothing but the silver fox fur he'd bought her tonight. "Looks like you're done working to me." She struck a pose, letting the desk lamp cast her in an attractive smoky-hue-type silhouette. She was, after all, experienced in using lighting to her advantage.

He stood and moved to his desk. "I told you I'd be up in a few minutes." He waited for her reaction, that trained pout she'd use to show her displeasure.

She didn't disappoint. "It's lonely upstairs without you."

He knew the score. She didn't care about him, only his power and what it could do for her. To her, and the many other women who sat by the phone waiting to be at his side in a moment, he was merely a means to an end—a way to get more out of life than they'd been dealt. He understood that. Strangely enough, he respected it even, on some level. It didn't bother him. Or it shouldn't.

He reached out to the laptop open on the desk. The article still blazing on the screen mocked him, causing him to grind his teeth.

"C'mon, you said you wouldn't be long." Had her voice been so whiny an hour ago when he'd brought her home? "It's been at least an hour."

He shut the laptop and faced the night, no longer interested in the woman waiting.

Because deep inside, despite the balance of his bankbook and the people who bowed to his will, he knew it could all come crashing down on him. With articles like the one he'd just read, he could be exposed. And if he was exposed, everyone would know he was nothing more than . . .

Oswald.

Riley toyed with the hem of her suit jacket as she licked her lips. The smooth linen against her fingers seemed out of place contrasted with the harshness of the prison. She straightened the scarf around her neck, despite her trembling hands.

"Stop fidgeting," Rafe whispered. He patted her hand. "It'll be fine."

How did he know? He couldn't be certain, no matter how confident he tried to act. She'd seen Simon's sister and that other woman . . . had seen the board on the monitor—there was a very good chance he could be released early.

Just the thought made her stomach knot.

The air-conditioning unit kicked on with a hum. She rubbed her arms against the chill, knowing it had nothing to do with the actual temperature of the place but everything to do with the reason for being here.

The room's setup was basically the same as when she'd been here last week, except there wasn't a chair for Simon since inmates weren't allowed to attend the hearing where victims or their families spoke. This time, three chairs sat in front of the monitor. One for her, Rafe, and Mr. Patterson. Not for Maddie, who'd refused to come, which was a whole other reason for Riley's irritation.

The door swung open and the same official stepped inside. She looked as if she wore the same shabby outfit she'd worn on Friday. But today, despite her appearance, she was all smiles as she shook their hands. "I'm Betty Mason. Are you ready to get started?"

Mr. Patterson nodded, then motioned for her and Rafe to take their seats while Betty turned on the monitor and tested the equipment.

Moving along quickly, Mr. Patterson gave a brief statement of the facts of Simon Lancaster's crime, then introduced her. They'd already determined she'd speak first, then Rafe. Mr. Patterson wouldn't be allowed to argue for or against parole at this point.

"As Mr. Patterson said, I'm Riley Baxter. Plain and simple, because of Simon Lancaster's actions, my parents are dead." She swallowed, then continued, having memorized what she wanted these people to know. "No, I'm not a child who relies on her parents, nor was I when they were killed. But there are some things that girls assume from childhood into adulthood my parents and I will never get to experience."

She licked her lips, remembering to speak slowly because when she got upset or excited, she tended to speak faster. "My father will never be able to walk me or my sister down the aisle at our weddings. He'll never be able to stand up as best man for my brother. He'll never be able to play ball with his grandchild. Or teach his grandchild how to ride a bike.

"My mother will never get to help me or my sister pick out our wedding dresses. Plan the best wedding ever." Tears filled her eyes but she pushed herself. She owed this to her parents. "She'll never be able to walk us through pregnancy, labor, and delivery. She'll never cry the first time she holds her grandchild."

Rafe grabbed her hand and squeezed.

She squeezed his hand back and let the tears spill. "My future children, and future nieces and nephews, will never know their amazing grandparents. They'll never see how generous and giving these people were.

"As a parole board, you can't bring our parents back to us. You can't undo the damage this man inflicted on my family and our friends. You can't give our future children their grandparents."

Riley stiffened her spine. "But you do have the power to stop this man from causing such destruction and pain again." She sniffed, then stared directly into the camera sitting on the tripod. "I beg of you not to let this man out and give him the opportunity to rob other families of their loved ones, and their future."

Riley ducked her head, wanting to sob like a child so badly but denying the emotions. She wouldn't let the board perceive her as merely a weak and emotional woman. Composed again, she lifted her gaze back to the camera.

Mr. Patterson addressed the satellite board and gave a quick introduction of Rafe.

Rafe nodded. "Thank you, Mr. Patterson." He smiled into the camera. "I am Rafe Baxter, the only son of Kyle and Mary Baxter. I can tell you that these were dedicated and loving parents. They were missionaries, opting to bring the good news of Jesus Christ to all areas of the world. Even when those areas were hostile. You see, our parents were willing to risk their lives to save the eternal lives of people they didn't even know. That's the kind of people they were."

He paused, and Riley caught one of the board members on the monitor making a note on her notepad.

"Our parents also gave back to their community. When stateside, they would spend their weekends assisting at the homeless shelter and food kitchens. They also lived as they preached—they tithed well over 10 percent of their income. Truly, they were some of the most selfless and generous people you could ever hope to meet.

"As far as my profession, I'm a senior agent with the FBI."

That got the board members' heads jerking up and staring into the camera, eyes wide.

"I hold the justice system in high esteem. I believe that good will triumph over evil. While recent events made me question the legal system, I do believe in it. My parents raised me and my sisters with a strong sense of not just citizenship, but a heightened sense of morality and values."

He stood, careful to stay in the camera's lens. "Therefore, I know the statistics of repeat offenders, the rate of reform failure, and the overall lack of success of alcoholics' rehabilitation."

Riley's hands shook. She clasped them tightly together in her lap.

"The facts are that Simon Lancaster got behind the wheel of his oversized pickup truck after having several-too-many shots at the local bar. He ran a stoplight and T-boned our parents' little compact, ending their lives in a single moment. He was tried, found guilty, and sentenced for this."

Rafe let out a long and loud sigh. "But these aren't all the facts. Our mother survived the impact. She made it to the hospital's emergency room in the back of an ambulance. She held on until I arrived. A damaged spinal cord and multiple, massive internal injuries made her final words just a breath, but I'll never forget them. *'Faith, hope, love . . . son.'* " Rafe's voice cracked. "And then our mother was gone forever."

New tears slid down Riley's cheeks. The dirty prison room fell away as she remembered her parents. Especially her mother. Rafe had never told her this part before. She silently sobbed for what she'd missed.

Rafe cleared his throat. "Even our mother's last words weren't about her. One day, I aspire to be as wonderful of a person as she was. That's for me to work on. For you, I ask you to take into account all the facts and deny Simon Lancaster's request for parole." He sat down. "Thank you."

"Commissioner, we got an ID on John Doe." Officer Bubba Fontenot rushed down the police station's hallway.

Hayden stopped and waited.

Nearly out of breath, the younger officer fell into step beside Hayden. "Lab came back on their

NDIS. DNA is a positive match with that of one Matthew Nichols."

Hayden took the folder and led Bubba into the large room with all the officer cubicles.

"Just heard back from sheriff's department's Missing Persons." Bob Travis pushed away from his desk and leaned back in his chair. "They have the report on Nichols, filed early this morning by his wife, who apparently has been out of town until last night. I've sent units to take her statement and bring her in for visual identification of the body." He passed Hayden a file.

"Let me know if we get anything else in." Hayden went to his office and studied the missing persons report.

The physical description matched what Hayden had seen of the victim and what Lee had put in the autopsy report. Matthew Nichols was fifty-six years old, employed with For Your Health Managed Care, married for thirty-one years, and the father of a twenty-eight-year-old son who lived in Birmingham, Alabama.

It didn't make sense. Hayden grabbed the case folder he'd left sitting on his desk and flipped it open. Setting the motive for murder itself aside for the moment, the manner of murder had meaning. The placed location of the body.

He laid out all the facts they had. Nothing even remotely made a connection. Perhaps after speaking with Mrs. Nichols, something would become apparent. They needed something to go on. Some sort of lead.

Hayden glanced at the clock hanging over his door. Time to head to his mom's. She'd made a farewell dinner for Remington, Rafe, and Riley, and Emily was scheduled to make an appearance. He sure didn't want to miss that.

Right.

CHAPTER EIGHT

"And will not God bring about justice for his chosen ones, who cry out to him day and night? Will he keep putting them off?"
LUKE 18:7

"We've gotten several calls about your article today. It seems everyone's interested in the next one." Jeremy paused. "Even Mr. Phizer."

Riley glanced at the magazine on the passenger seat, conveniently opened to her article. Her first *real* byline. She closed her eyes and rested her head back against her car's headrest. Amazement seeped into her consciousness. For her morning to have been so horrible at the prison to this awesome news—huge contrast, but she loved it and would relish every second of it she could.

She struggled to contain the scream bubbling up in her chest. "Really?" She forced her voice to remain neutral but probably failed by epic proportions. "I'm glad he's pleased."

"You'll have the next article ready to send me by Wednesday?"

As if she hadn't already written it. "Shouldn't be a problem."

"Excellent." Another pause. "I'm proud of you, kid."

"Thanks, Jeremy. I have to go now. I'll e-mail the article by five on Wednesday." She ended the call and all but bounced in the driver's seat.

They loved her article. They loved her series. She was high on the success. This was *it*—her big chance, and she'd knocked it out of the ballpark. She pumped her fist through the air, then laughed at herself. If anyone inside Ardy Simpson's house happened to glance out a window to the driveway, they'd think she was insane for sure.

She got out of the car and made her way inside the Simpson home. She knocked twice, then stuck her head inside the door. "Hello?" A mouth-watering aroma met her, welcoming her in a swirl of spicy enticement.

"Riley, come in. I told you not to bother knocking." Ardy's quick greeting from the kitchen was as inviting as the fragrant steaming pot on the stove.

Remington and Rafe sat on two of the three bar stools. Emily, with her wispy blonde hair, perched on the stool beside Remington. Thomas Vince stood next to the bar, looking strange and out of place in such a bright and sunny room.

"Hayden should be here in just a minute." Ardy darted about the kitchen. "Emily, why don't you and Bella set the table?"

Remington stood, but Emily just tossed a disdainful glare at her mother's back.

The friction made a polar bear's den seem warmer.

Riley moved beside Remington. "Let me help."

"Thanks." Remington opened a cabinet and passed a stack of plates to Riley. "Emily's having one of her moods. She's bipolar. Don't take it personally," she whispered under her breath.

Thomas hovered at Remington's side. "Please, allow me." He moved with a slight limp. Birth defect? Old injury remnant?

Hayden walked in mere minutes after the last plate and fork were set. "I smell some amazing crawfish étouffée."

His deep baritone raised the hairs on Riley's arms, not to mention his smile sent her heartbeat into overdrive. She turned her back to him. *Stop reacting like a silly little schoolgirl. Seriously, Jasmine would show better composure.*

"About time you got here. We're starving." No mistaking the condemnation in Emily's voice toward her brother.

"Nice to see you too, Em."

"Let's all sit down and eat." Ardy ladled the étouffée into huge bowls. Remington carried two at a time to the table.

Once everyone took seats around the table, Hayden offered up thanks, then the basket of bread passed from person to person. Rafe answered Ardy and Hayden's questions about how the hearing had gone. It seemed wrong that there was even a sliver of a chance that Simon Lancaster would be released early to live his life while her parents never could.

Riley focused on the delicious food. The rich and creamy étouffée sent her senses reeling with savory spices and flavor.

Ardy smiled down the table at Riley. "I picked up your magazine today. Your article is great. You are a wonderful writer."

Warmth spreading throughout her chest and not from the spicy food, Riley ducked her head. "Thank you."

Rafe nudged her. "I read it too. It's good, sis, really good."

"Thanks, Rafe. And Jeremy—he's my editor—called. The magazine's already getting responses. Even the owner of the magazine is pleased. They've accepted the series pitch. The next article will run Monday."

"That's impressive, Riley." Hayden's eyes were as soft as his voice.

Good thing she was sitting because the

butterflies flitting in her gut said her knees would be too weak to stand. Heat marched across her face. "Thank you."

"So, that's what you do for a living? Expose other people's misfortune for your own fame?"

Riley's eyes widened, and her jaw dropped.

"Emily!" Ardy scolded her daughter before offering a red-faced grimace to Riley. "I'm sorry. Emily isn't feeling very well today."

Not feeling well? The little brat needed to learn some manners. Riley plastered on a smile for Ardy. "It's okay. I understand how it can confuse those who don't understand journalism." She faced Emily. "I'm actually working with this family in an attempt to gain support for the father's next appeal."

Emily snorted. "Whatever you hafta tell yourself to sleep at night."

"That's enough, Em." Hayden's voice was low . . . steady . . . commanding. Riley could easily imagine him leading the police force.

"I was just—"

"Stop." His stare left no room for argument. "I said that's enough."

Nobody spoke. Nobody moved. Even the air went still. The hostility suspended over the room could have smothered a small child.

"Fine." Emily shoved back her chair, the legs grating against the wood floor, and stood. "I can tell where I'm not welcome." She threw down her napkin and stormed from the room. "Thomas, let's go."

Thomas, wearing a look of pure confusion, stood. "I'm sorry, everyone. Please excuse us." He slowly followed Emily into the living room, his limp a bit more pronounced than normal.

Ardy was on her feet in a second.

Remington followed suit, gently grabbing Ardy's arm. "Let me. She's either gone off her meds again or the dosage is wrong. I'll talk to her." She left before Ardy could argue.

"Ignore my sister. She uses her illness as an excuse for deplorable behavior. I apologize for her lack of manners and social graces." Hayden smiled, his eyes as dark as Hershey's chocolate. "So, will you stay in town while you write the series?"

"Oh, you have to stay here with me." Ardy sank back to her chair.

Were they kidding? After Emily's little display? All Riley wanted to do was take a long, hot, soaking bath. "Thank you, but I think it's best if I stay at a hotel."

"Oh no. I insist. Hotels are so impersonal." Ardy's concern had already shifted.

"In case you haven't noticed, we don't really have any hotels here in Hopewell. We have one motel, and I don't know that I'd recommend it for a lady."

"Hey, you let me stay there." Rafe chuckled

112

before turning serious. "But Hayden's right, Ri. It's not what you're used to."

Great, make her sound like a snob. "I'd planned to stay at a hotel in Baton Rouge. Only to be closer to Jasmine and Peggy for interviews."

"Baton Rouge isn't even twenty minutes out. Oh, please, stay with me. I so enjoy having company. Now that Emily's moved out, this big ole house is too quiet. And I love to cook and can only get Hayden to come out here every couple of days to eat." Ardy's voice rose at least an octave or two.

"Think of the money you'll save the magazine —that should make your editor really happy." Rafe nodded.

Who was her brother trying to help here?

"I'll make a deal with you." Hayden leaned forward and spoke in a stage whisper. "You stay with my mom so she'll have someone to dote over, and I'll take you out to dinner this weekend. Anywhere you want to go. And I'll give you a local cop's insight into your case."

She opened her mouth to politely decline but no words came. Her emotions seemed to hold her speechless. She swallowed, hard, then licked her lips. "How can I turn down such an offer?"

Ardy smiled, as did Hayden and Rafe.

Riley bowed her head and studied her étouffée, praying no one noticed the heat searing her cheeks.

•••

"I'm very sorry for your loss, Mrs. Nichols." Hayden sat on an uncomfortable chair in the late Matthew Nichols's home. Friday had arrived with a snail's pace, and he couldn't help feeling relieved the week was finally drawing to a close.

He had a date with Riley Baxter tonight, yet he couldn't allow himself to think about that now. He had work to do. As such, he couldn't help himself from taking inventory.

The house sat on a cushy corner lot in an upscale neighborhood. Stone and brick front, carefully cared-for lawn that screamed of a gardener in residence, and an intricately patterned stone walkway. Just a skip away from upper class.

The house's insides bespoke of an interior decorator and expensive taste. Everything Hayden could see was for show, nothing for comfort, from the prissy and ornate end tables to the hard but perfectly accented chairs.

"Thank you for your condolences." Mrs. Nichols perched on the edge of her seat, her legs properly crossed at the ankles. Her spine as straight as a rod. "How may I help you, Commissioner?"

He was pretty certain she wouldn't have entertained his visit if he hadn't been the commissioner. "I have a few questions about your husband. For our case."

"Of course." She gave a slow nod. Not a single,

carefully dyed auburn hair dared move out of place of the bob cut popular with his mother's generation.

Hayden pulled out his notebook and flipped to a blank page. "I understand your husband had been employed by For Your Health, correct?"

"Yes. Matthew was a sales representative for the company. His team's leader." The pride slipped from under her polished poise.

"I'm sorry, I have no idea what For Your Health does. Could you help me out by explaining?"

"It's a managed health-care company."

He still wanted her to explain it in her own words. He stared back at her, keeping the blank expression in place.

Her smile was reserved. "When you go to your family physician for something specific, and he can't figure out what's wrong with you, he refers you to a specialist."

He nodded.

"Some insurance companies require your physician to provide a referral number to the specialist, similar to a preauthorization."

"Right. I get that."

"Most of the time, those types of policies are indicative of a managed-care system utilized by the primary insurance carrier."

"Our police department's policy is like that."

"But of course." She flashed the dentally perfect smile. "Matthew's job was to oversee a team of three, himself included, in selling this managed-care plan to local governments. Police departments, fire departments, local politicians."

He grinned. "Ah, so he sold Hopewell's agencies on this."

"Not just Hopewell, but an entire four-parish-wide sweep, including all the little towns and communities within."

Impressive. "How long did he work for the company?"

She tapped her chin with a perfectly manicured fingernail. "A little over twenty-six years. He took a starting position right before our son was born."

Right. The son. Who lived in Alabama and according to Officer Travis's notes from yesterday, was on his way here. Funny it took him almost a week to get one state over.

"It only took Matthew five years to be promoted to team leader." She smiled like a polite politician. "He still holds the record for being the youngest to reach team leader."

"Did you ever hear your husband mention a Mr. Ellington?"

"Matthew didn't discuss business at home. He respected people's privacy, as well as abided by government regulations regarding privacy."

Interesting statement. Hayden cleared his throat. "Your husband retired not too long ago?"

Her composure slipped and a frown wrinkled her brow. "Less than six months ago."

"Do you mind me asking why he retired? He was only fifty-six—that's a bit young to retire. At least in my book."

He could tell she struggled with keeping her self-control. "He hadn't planned on retiring when he did."

Hayden inched to the edge of his chair and tightened his grip on the pencil. "So, what prompted him to take early retirement?"

"His two team members, Mack Thompson and Evan Coleman, died this year."

He waited for her to continue. Did the company plan to not give him another team? Or were they going to put him on a team, but not as a leader?

She remained as silent and stoic as a granite statue in her straight-back chair in her formal sitting room.

"I'm not exactly following, Mrs. Nichols. While horrible for his team to have died, I don't understand how that connects with his retirement."

"He just felt like it was time for him to retire after they died." Her lips pinched into a fine line.

"Were they close? He and his team?"

She lifted a shoulder. "I suppose as close as one gets when working eight hours a day with someone, five days a week."

"How long had they been a team?"

"The three of them, together. Let me think." Again, the pink nail tapped against her chin. "At least fifteen or sixteen years."

Why was she being so evasive? What wasn't she saying? "Did they ever hang out together outside of the office?"

Her prissiness returned in full force. "*Hang out,* Commissioner? Matthew didn't *hang out.* Not with Mack and Evan. Not with anyone." She stood, none-too-discreetly looking at her watch. "If that's all, I have a pressing engagement."

Her husband just died and she had plans?

Hayden stood, slipping his notebook into his pocket, and passed her his business card. "My office and cell numbers are both listed. Please call me if you think of anything else that could help us solve your husband's murder."

She took the card, holding it with her nails, as if touching the card with her bare fingertips would soil her. "I certainly will." She gestured toward the front door.

He gave her a curt nod before returning to his cruiser. At least he had his date with Riley to look forward to tonight.

But Mrs. Nichols . . . the woman was either hiding something she didn't want him to know about her husband and his colleagues or she was scared of something. Either way, he intended to find out.

He'd start by looking up the details of Mack Thompson and Evan Coleman's deaths.

CHAPTER NINE

"The LORD is known by his acts of justice; the wicked are ensnared by the work of their hands."
PSALM 9:16

Everything about Hayden Simpson spoke of his proper upbringing. Riley ate it up—his manners stood in such contrast to the last couple of men she'd dated. Wait a minute. Where had that thought come from? This was just dinner. A thank-you for staying at his mom's house. Still, she couldn't help comparing Hayden's politeness to Damon's curt attitude. Or Garrison's abusive tone.

From the moment he'd picked her up from Ardy's, Hayden was the quintessential southern gentleman: opening both the car and the restaurant doors for her, asking what she wanted to eat and then ordering for her, and standing when she excused herself to the ladies' room. She couldn't remember the last time a date treated her with such . . . respect. Had anyone ever been so courteous before?

She didn't think so. Certainly not Garrison, who'd hated Rafe so much that when she finally saw him for the abuser he was, he vandalized Rafe's house. And not Damon, who was not only a liar, but a cheater.

The restaurant Hayden had taken her to sat nestled into the edge of the bayou with a long boardwalk lining the space between land and water. The chef boasted that his restaurant served some of the best jambalaya this side of the Mississippi. His claims hadn't disappointed.

In keeping with the understated décor, the dim overhead lighting cast shadows on the fabric wallpapered walls while the flickering candle in the middle of the table radiated intimacy.

"So, you've already got the article sent for Monday's magazine?" Hayden stirred his after-dinner coffee. No creamer, one sugar. She'd paid attention.

"Yep. And my editor told me it was one of my best pieces." That was putting it mildly. Jeremy had been totally hyped over the article. And when she told him she planned to interview Armand for next week's article, he'd been beside himself giddy. She'd already thought of ways to draw out his interview over two weeks, extending her series.

She'd done it. She created the boost her career needed.

"That's really good." Hayden set down the spoon. "After reading the trial transcript, do you think he could be innocent?"

She'd gone round and round with herself on that same question. "I just don't know." Riley ran a finger absently around the lip of her cup. "I can't believe a man who loves his family so much would risk being separated from them. Not without a really good reason. And that's what he doesn't have in this robbery."

"Financial difficulty is the number-one motive I find for robbery."

"He didn't have any financial problems. At least not on paper. No credit cards, a normal mortgage . . . he wasn't behind on any payments."

"Maybe a hidden addiction or gambling problem?" Hayden took a sip of his coffee and stared into her eyes with such intensity, she had to focus on what he said.

"Nothing like that. No indication of anything amiss." She took a gulp of her coffee. It nearly scorched her throat. She blew out a puff of air. "He was in security, so he knew what the consequences would be." That, above all else, was what didn't make sense to her.

"So the motive is weak. What evidence was presented?"

"The pawnshop owner positively identified him as the man who pawned two of the stolen items. One was recovered."

"That's pretty damning."

"I know." She sighed. "But I just can't see him being that stupid." She shook her head. "He specialized in alarms. You can't convince me he walks into a pawnshop with no disguise, nothing, and sells two items he supposedly stole without so much as a by-your-leave. That's just crazy."

"That does seem unlikely. Why did the police consider him a suspect?"

"He'd helped install the alarm system that was conveniently disabled for the robbery."

"I see." Hayden rubbed his chin.

"But that's part of why I have such a problem with it all. His wife is an honest lady. She says her husband is smart. Until I can talk to him, I have to believe his wife." She crossed her arms and rested them on the table. "If that's true, then why would a smart man break into his own place of employment? Anyone with half a brain, especially in security, would know that employees and those with access would be vetted as suspects first."

Hayden nodded. "Right."

"If he figured it was worth the risk, why wouldn't he establish an iron-clad alibi beforehand?"

"Because it's hard to have an iron-clad alibi if you're guilty." Hayden chuckled.

She tented her hands in front of her. "Come on, you and I both know guilty people procure alibis that hold up in court."

"True, although I hate to admit it."

"So it doesn't make sense. If he is even semi-intelligent, weighs the risks and still agrees, then surely he wasn't stupid enough not to set a stronger alibi than his daughter."

Hayden took another sip of his coffee. "You'd

be surprised. I've seen a lot of really, really smart criminals who almost get away with their crimes. Almost. There is usually one detail they overlook. Might be big, might be small, but it kills the opportunity of a perfect crime."

He had more experience, which was true, but still . . . "I just can't see it. And then there's the whole other issue of his partners."

"Partners?" Hayden's brows shot up. "You didn't mention that before."

"The man who was shot during the robbery testified there were at least three men involved, possibly a fourth."

"Did the eyewitness identify your guy?"

She shook her head. "His testimony was it was dark and they were all wearing black. He got a look at the getaway vehicle, a dark van. No connection to Jasmine's dad was even implied with regard to the van. He drove a light-colored sedan."

The pert, pretty waitress appeared at their table, refilled their cups with the savory coffee, discreetly laid the leather pad with the check inside at Hayden's elbow, then disappeared across the lush carpet.

Hayden's gaze didn't trail behind the attractive blonde but stayed focused entirely on Riley. Her chest warmed. Damon would've been checking the girl out, would've probably excused himself to the men's room only to get caught in the kitchen trying to get the girl's number.

"What's the deal with the partners?" He smoothly slipped a credit card into the pad, not even looking at the check, and slid it to the table's edge.

"That's the thing." No matter how many ways she could get past the obvious trip ups, the fellow-robbers theory caught her. "He didn't have two close friends. His wife said so. He had one friend he hung out with, Doug Adare, who has an airtight alibi for the night of the robbery: He was in the hospital having had his appendix removed at three o'clock that afternoon. Doctors testified there was no way Doug was out of bed by that evening, much less involved in a robbery."

She took a sip of the fresh coffee. "Jasmine claims her father never had any friend over to the house except Doug. Even four of his coworkers gave statements that he only hung out with Doug."

Ms. Pert-and-Pretty whisked by and grabbed the pad without even breaking her stride.

"On the other hand, and I'm just playing devil's advocate here so don't get upset, but if he did make some new, uh, acquaintances with the intent to commit a crime, do you think he'd bring them around his home with his wife and children? His job?"

"If that were true, why *wouldn't* he bring them around his job, to case the place?" She smiled and snuggled back against the cushy chair. Sparring with Hayden was invigorating. Fun. A *lot* of fun.

"But he could have had them there, out of sight from his coworkers. He did, after all, work in security, yes?"

No wonder he was the commissioner.

The waitress returned, handed Hayden the leather pad, and smiled her full wattage at them. "Can I get y'all anything else?"

Hayden looked at Riley.

"Oh, nothing more for me." She'd devoured a bowl of shrimp soup, a salad, the special jambalaya, and topped off everything with *riz au lait* and a latte. To say she was stuffed was an understatement.

"No, thank you." Hayden gave the woman a smile, polite but not interested.

"Then y'all have a good night." The waitress shuffled to the next table.

"How about a walk along the boardwalk?"

She stood. "Sounds lovely." At least the evening wasn't ending just yet. Something about Hayden made her feel safe . . . sheltered . . . cherished. Silly, really, but that's how she felt.

He slipped his hand under her elbow and led her out the front door. Heat shot from the point of contact up her arm and into her chest. She shivered, which was odd since his touch blasted through her, but maybe she just reacted to the cool evening breeze.

The sun had nearly set across the April sky as they stepped down the stairs to the wood-plank boardwalk snuggling the bayou's edge. The scent of freshly turned soil overpowered any fish scent. The breeze tickled Riley's nose.

"Now, enough about your case." Hayden took hold of her hand. Warmth branched out from her palm. "Tell me about you."

Her pulse hiccupped. "What do you want to know?"

"Everything. About growing up. Favorite color. Favorite movie. What TV show do you watch? Everything." He gave her hand a gentle squeeze as they strolled along the creaking boards.

She laughed. "Okay. Here goes. I'm the baby of the family—adored, not spoiled—Rafe and Maddie saw to that. We were a close family who enjoyed doing things together. Our parents doted on all three of us." Her humor slipped as she realized they could hear something this next week about Simon Lancaster's parole determination. "I really miss Mom and Dad."

"I'm sorry." His thumb caressed hers. "I didn't mean to bring all this up."

"No, it's fine." Riley shoved off the melancholy mood. "Now, to answer your other questions, I don't have one particular favorite color. I love pretty much all the primary colors equally. I have two favorite movies: *Gone with the Wind* and *Casablanca*. And the television shows I DVR are all documentaries from the National Geographic and True Crime channels." She was speed talking, a sure sign of nervousness to any person trained in detecting body language.

She forced herself to slow down, grinning up at him. "And before you ask, my favorite books are the classics, but with a twist. I enjoy Hawthorne—really, and Shakespeare. I love classical music, Beethoven, specifically, and I'm a registered Democrat."

He jerked his hand free and frowned. "A Democrat? That's it. Date over."

"Ha. Ha."

He laughed and grabbed her hand again. She welcomed the return of the physical contact. *His.* "I like you, Hayden. I really like you." Did she really just tell him that? She swallowed, not believing she'd just said that aloud. Flaming heat seared her cheeks and she ducked her head.

"Well. I like you too, Riley."

She struggled to recover at least some of her composure. "So, tell me about you, Mr. Police Commissioner."

"Short story, actually."

"Really?"

"Yep, I—"

The musical notes from his cell phone interrupted.

"Sorry. Occupational hazard." He pulled the phone from his hip. "Hayden Simpson."

She glanced out over the bayou. The breeze caused the weeds at the bayou's edge to sway in a graceful ballet of nature. Gentle ripples skimmed over the water's surface.

"It'll be okay. I'm on my way." Hayden shoved the phone back to its holder on his hip. "I'm sorry, Riley, but I need to cut our date short."

"Is everything okay?" Maybe there was another story to tell in Hopewell. She could be sitting on a goldmine of opportunities.

"That was Mom. It's Emily."

One less.

Why didn't he feel more satisfied? He should.

One less enemy on this earth.

But he didn't feel any satisfaction or accomplishment, and that stunk.

Oswald waited on the balcony, overlooking the darkened woods cozied against his property line. The moon sat high in the Louisiana sky, illuminating the low-lying clouds that teased of rain to come.

More than one storm simmered on the horizon.

The anger inside continued to brew, boiling in his gut. He fisted his hands into tight balls tensed against the railing. If only things had been different. It was all their fault.

Their fault he was in the condition he was. Their fault his father had left them with nothing more than a note that read: "I'm sorry, I can't take it anymore." Their fault his mother had taken up with the man she did and exposed them both to a world of drugs and decay of the human condition. That she'd dared to give birth to a product of her union, such an inhumane act on her part . . . it was unthinkable. But he'd taken care of that little problem. SIDS had become such a wonderful excuse for unexplained infant deaths.

One less problem.

He unclenched his fists and grasped the railing. A splinter stabbed under his skin, but he just gripped the wood harder, letting it embed deeper into his flesh.

It was nights like tonight that made him miss what he'd lost. What they'd stolen from him. Normalcy. Family. His future.

Taking over the family business, robbed.

College scholarship, robbed.

Marriage, robbed.

Future as a track star, robbed.

Every single milestone of his adult life, robbed. They'd stolen everything from him. The promise of a future. Generational support. All without an apology.

No remorse. No regret. No restitution.

If he'd ever believed in good and evil, heaven and hell, God and Satan, then they were truly the spawn of Satan. They destroyed families, eating the children and spitting them out into an unwelcome world where they could barely survive, much less thrive.

Like thieves of the human spirit, they stole in

under the guise of being helpful, of being concerned, and sucked the life out of people, leaving nothing but decayed and withered shells of broken promises.

They snatched the dreams of children and adults alike, tossing them into a fiery pit to be devoured and lost forever.

Like the burning hell they represented.

The splinter festered in his palm, burning the flesh and turning the skin red. Oswald left the balcony and headed to the bathroom for his tweezers and antibiotic cream. No sense getting an infection when it could be easily prevented.

That's what angered him all the more: What they'd done to him could have been so easily prevented. A simple *yes* instead of an automated condition of repeated *no*'s.

He dug out the splinter, holding it up with the tweezers. No more than a sliver of wood, but left alone, it would have festered and become infected.

Like what they did. They festered his life with their vile lies and *policies* and infected him with anger and bitterness. Parasites.

His heartbeat raced faster. Blood pumped through his veins as if a dam had burst. He willed his heart to slow. His pulse to calm. His anxiety to still.

He returned his first-aid supplies to the medicine cabinet, then sat in front of his computer. He stared at the special-interest article still lit up on his monitor.

With the article, this reporter had picked at the scab covering his fragile control. She'd touched on his exposure. Left him raw.

And this was just the beginning? A start to a series?

His breathing came in pants. He closed his eyes, focusing on the oxygen moving in and out of his body.

She had opened the floodgates on his restraint. On his anger. On his pain. On his loss. She'd poured salt in the wounds he'd endured from them.

She had become one of them.

A problem. *His* problem.

She needed to be stopped. To be silenced. To become . . .

One less.

CHAPTER TEN

"See what this godly sorrow has produced in you: what earnestness, what eagerness to clear yourselves, what indignation, what alarm, what longing, what concern, what readiness to see justice done. At every point you have proved yourselves to be innocent in this matter."
2 CORINTHIANS 7:11

"She won't let me take her to the emergency room." His mother's face was a couple of shades paler than when Hayden had picked up Riley for their date. "But I think she needs stitches."

"Where is she?"

"The living room."

He moved past his mother. The soft murmurs of Riley's voice soothing as his mother followed him into the living room.

Emily lay on the couch, an ice pack wrapped inside a towel against her cheek. "I told her not to call you."

"Shut up." He sat beside her. "Let me see."

"It's nothing. I told her I'm fine."

If that were true, she wouldn't have come home. He gripped his hand on hers and pulled the ice pack free. Blood stained the towel a bright, bold red, but it was her face that rendered him momentarily speechless.

A gash approximately two inches long and about a fourth of an inch deep jagged down the right side of her face. It started at the top of her cheekbone and ran diagonally toward her mouth. He wasn't a doctor, but that wound would need ten stitches, if not more.

She pressed the pack back against her wound. The pain had to be horrible, but she didn't show it. "It'll be fine."

"You need stitches."

Emily narrowed her eyes. "I don't. It's okay."

So she wanted to be difficult. "How'd it happen?"

She shrugged. "Me and a friend were messing around, goofing off at my place. It's an accident."

Like he would accept that? "How, exactly, does your face get slashed while you're goofing off with a friend?"

"Stop being a cop."

"Stop being a brat."

She glared at him, then threw her scowl behind him. "What's *she* doing here?"

Hayden peeked over his shoulder. His mother and Riley had entered silently and stood by the doorway. He focused back on his sister. "That's not important. How did you get the cut?"

Ignoring him, she continued to stare at Riley. "Emily!"

His sister gaped at him with such loathing . . . "I told you, it was an accident."

"Don't try my patience any more, Em."

Mom rushed to the end of the couch and stroked Emily's hair. "Honey, we're trying to help."

"I just want to be left alone." She pushed to her feet, swayed, then plopped back onto the couch.

Mom moved to hold her. Hayden held up a hand to stop her.

"No, you don't. You want sympathy or empathy or maybe just attention—I can't say for sure, but you definitely don't want to be left alone. Otherwise, you wouldn't have come to Mom's."

"Hayden," Mom whispered.

Emily's eyes widened.

"You need something, Em. What is it? A place to crash? Someone to make you take care of yourself?"

Moisture filled her eyes, shimmering under the lamp's glow.

"Don't even try. Your crying stopped having an effect on me years ago when you started using the waterworks as a way of manipulation."

And just like that, her eyes went dry and hard. "I don't have to stay here and listen to this." She stood, wobbling, but sturdier than a few moments ago.

He stood as well. "Then go." He waved toward the front door. "Go ahead. No one's stopping you."

"Hayden!" Mom shot to her feet. "Emily is more than welcome here. This is her home."

"No, Mom, it's not. She moved out. This is your home and she's here at your leisure, not the other way around. If she's going to stay, she needs to abide by your wishes, which are for her to seek medical attention." He crossed his arms over his chest. "Isn't that why you called me? Because she needs to go to the emergency room?"

"Well, yes." Mom begged Emily with her eyes. "Honey, I just want you to be okay. I think you need stitches."

"I do as well."

Emily returned to scowling at him. "Who asked you?"

"Mom did. When she called and asked me to come immediately. To check on you." He softened his tone. "And I came because you're my sister and I love you. We want to help you, but you have to help us, Em."

She ducked her head and her shoulders shook as she sobbed in silence. Real or for show? Who knew? It could be either. But at least she wasn't as hateful as before.

"Sit down." He helped her sit on the couch for the third time. Mom sat on her other side. "Now, tell me the truth. How did you get the cut?"

"Me and a friend really were fooling around. We had some bottoms of those old Coke bottles —the really, really thick ones. We were holding them up like glasses and laughing at how distorted everything looked through them." The ice in the pack shifted, splitting the tense silence. "I don't know if I moved or he did, but somehow, the edge of the broken glass slipped across my face."

He? Every muscle in Hayden's body went taut. Some *guy* was playing around with his little sister and sliced her face? "Who? That Thomas Vince fellow?" He couldn't imagine the guy being strong enough to do damage to anyone.

Emily shook her head. "That's why I didn't want to tell you. I knew you'd be more concerned with the who than the truth. It wasn't Thomas. He'd already left."

Playing around with thick Coke bottles like glasses . . . were they making fun of Thomas?

He ground his teeth. "Either way, you need stitches." He stood. "Come on, I'll drive you to the emergency room. Mom and Riley can follow."

"No." She shook her head. "I don't want to go to the hospital."

And then it occurred to him. "Have you been drinking, Em? Taking anything?"

She gave him a dirty look, but she didn't answer him.

"Em?"

"We had a couple of beers, no big deal. It's not illegal."

He ground his teeth harder. *Lord, I could sure*

use a little help here. I'm not Emily's father, but Mom looks to me in helping with her. I need some wisdom.

"Oh, Emily." Mom's frown cut deep into the lines in her face.

"See! That's why I didn't want to say anything. Always the same thing. Disapproval and condemnation."

He grabbed her by the arm and helped her to her feet. "Regardless, you need stitches. I'm going to take you to the hospital."

She jerked her arm from his grasp. "They'll want to ask my friend questions. I don't want him to get into any trouble. It was an accident."

He'd have to relate to her vanity. "You have to get it looked at, Em. Do you want a big, ugly scar down your face? That'll happen if you don't get stitches and this gets infected. It could be really, really ugly."

From the horrified look she wore, he'd scored.

Mom jumped to her feet. "Wait here until I bring my car around to follow y'all. I had parked it behind the shed so Bella would have room. Won't take but a minute." She moved faster than he'd seen in a while. Probably scared Emily would put up another argument if they didn't get her into the car quickly.

He left his sister staring blindly into space and joined Riley across the room. "Sorry about all this."

She smiled. "No worries." She nodded toward

137

the couch. "That *accident* sounds like it could be domestic abuse. Especially when drinking is involved."

"Who asked you?" Emily shot off the couch and stomped toward them, her eyes glazed like some psycho.

Hayden recognized the anger flickering in her eyes. Anger flamed by alcohol on top of medication for her bipolar disorder.

He stepped in his sister's path. "Em, she has a valid point."

She froze, the hatred in her look shooting at him. "Oh, so now you're listening to her. Over your own flesh and blood?" Em paused. "Well, half of your flesh and blood. We don't share the same father, do we, *half* brother?"

Well now, she'd extended her claws all the way out. Hayden's chest tightened. It hurt enough that he'd only recently learned the man he'd idolized and loved all his life wasn't his biological father. It hurt even more that his mother hadn't told him until she'd had no other choice. Remington had known as well. Since both kept the secret from him, he had trouble trusting. Emily knew how much pain it caused him.

"But you, Ms. Big-Shot Reporter, you need to mind your own business and keep your opinions to yourself." Her words were a bit slurred, as if she'd taken something and it was beginning to kick in.

Had she taken any drugs on top of drinking? On top of her prescription medication? That would explain why she didn't seem to be overly affected by the pain from the gash.

"That's about enough, Em. Have you—?"

Emily swayed. Her eyes rolled back in her head, then her entire body went lax. Hayden caught her just before she fell, Riley helping support her. He swooped Em into his arms. Riley rushed to the front door and swung it open for him. She ran down the steps and opened the passenger side of the car. He set Emily down, then connected the seat belt.

"Do you mind riding with Mom? Telling her what's going on?"

"Sure. Of course."

He shut the car door and faced Riley. "Sorry our date ended like this." She had no idea how sorry. He wanted to get to know her better. Just being around her did strange things to him.

"Me too." Her eyes lit.

Mom's car rumbled in the drive behind his. "We'll have to do it again. Without this part." He held his breath, waiting for her response.

"Sure."

Hayden walked around and slid in behind the steering wheel. Soon. He'd take Riley out again. Right after he figured out what to do about his sister.

Buzz! Buzz! Buzz!

Keeping her eyes closed, Riley felt around the

table beside the bed for her cell. It vibrated again. She grabbed it and pressed the earpiece against her head, still buried under the covers. "Hello?"

"Good morning, Riley."

She whipped the covers from her head and squinted at the clock. "Jeremy. What's wrong?"

"What's wrong? Nothing. Not a thing."

Then why on earth was he calling her before eight on a Monday morning? Ahh . . . Monday morning. Her article. "Getting any response to my article?" She sat upright in bed, chewing her bottom lip.

"Any response? Luv, we've been bombarded with calls since the switchboard opened, and our voice-mail boxes are full with messages from before we answered the phones."

Her mouth went dry. Had to be good news . . . he'd called her *luv,* which he'd never done before. "People like the story?"

"They're loving it. Eating it up. Can't get enough."

She smiled. Euphoria was better than any drug on the market—legal or not.

"So much so, I'd like to send a photographer over there. Take some shots of this Peggy and Jasmine and little Mikey. The house they used to live in and the trailer they live in now."

Sending a photographer? This *was* big. "I'll meet with Mrs. Wilson and ask her permission." And set up some other angles to work for future parts of the series she hadn't even pitched to Jeremy yet.

"You do that. I'm moving next week's article up to the front page of the section."

F-f-front page? Seriously? This was bigger than big. This was epic. "I'll call her this morning." If only she could get the prison to let her interview Armand. So far, each of her calls to Angola officials had yielded no progress. But if Jeremy was going to send a photographer . . . maybe she could use some persuasion with the warden.

"Let me know as soon as you do." Voices muffled behind Jeremy over the connection. "I have to go now. You're doing great, luv. I'm proud of you."

Riley ended the call and tossed the phone on the bed, then stood and stretched. Still smiling, she looked out the window. No sign of the sun. Dark clouds clumped all across the sky. Ominous. Fore-boding.

The weather didn't matter. She could walk through a hurricane right now and not feel the wind.

She grabbed the phone and dialed Peggy's number. She would've been up some time ago getting Jasmine and Mikey off to school.

One ring.

With any luck, Peggy would have some time to talk with her before or after work today. If she could get permission, Jeremy could have a photographer up here by tomorrow morning.

Second ring.

Perhaps she should go see Hayden and ask for his assistance in gaining access to Armand at the prison. He was, after all, a police commissioner. She'd try the warden one more time, and if she still didn't get the interview request granted, she'd ask Hayden for help.

"Hello?"

"Mrs. Wilson? It's Riley Baxter."

"Oh, hi. I haven't seen the magazine yet. I'll grab one at the store this morning."

"There's something I'd like to discuss with you. Do you have any time for us to talk today?" She held her breath and crossed her fingers.

"I'm only working until two today. Why don't you come by the house around two thirty?"

Riley smiled. "That sounds perfect. I'll see you then."

She wasted no time showering and getting dressed before joining Ardy on the patio for a cup of coffee. "It's so beautiful and peaceful out here."

Ardy nodded. "Even with the approaching storm, I love it here."

"How's Emily?"

"In therapy." Ardy set her cup on the iron table. Lightning flashed through the darkened sky. "Emily's a good girl. She took her father's death very hard and then got diagnosed as bipolar."

Spoken like a mother. Riley sipped her coffee to avoid saying anything that could insult her host.

"I know most people can't see it, but Emily has a heart of gold. She's just a bit rough around the edges."

That was putting it mildly. "What did the doctors say about scarring? She's so pretty, I wouldn't want there to be a big scar."

Ardy smiled. "Unless you know where to look, you shouldn't be able to see nothing more than a faint line. That's what the doctor said."

"That's good." Riley would be devastated if her face got cut like that. Sure, it sounded superficial and vain, and perhaps it was, but it was the truth. She stood and grabbed her cup. "Well, I'd better get—"

"Don't break his heart."

"What?" Her pulse pounded in her ears.

"I can tell Hayden really likes you." Ardy's eyes were full of emotion. "I know it's none of my business, but I'm asking you not to break his heart. He's a good man and deserves happiness." She stared out over the bayou. "I've caused him quite a bit of pain this past year. I want him to be happy."

What was she supposed to say to that? "Um, Mrs. Simpson, I really like Hayden. I have no intention of hurting him."

"He's struggling to regain his footing. It's a long story, but you need to know I'm the reason he might have trust issues. Because I lied to him all his life about who his father was. The deception nearly undid him."

"Mrs. Simpson, I don't—"

"He worshipped my husband. Thought his dad was the best man on earth, and he was right." Tears floated in her eyes. "I took all that away from him. When your own mother lies to you, how can you trust anyone?"

Riley leaned over and patted Ardy's shoulder. How was she supposed to respond? She wasn't good with these types of situations. Maddie was the one who handled emotional things.

Ardy sniffed. "So you can see why I want him to be happy."

"You raised a good man, Mrs. Simpson. I don't know about his pain, but I can tell you Hayden is kind, considerate, and the most honest gentleman I've ever met."

She smiled. "Thank you, Riley. You're a sweet girl. I can see why Hayden's taken with you."

Riley nodded, not daring to speak. There wasn't anything to say.

CHAPTER ELEVEN

"Do not pervert justice; do not show partiality
to the poor or favoritism to the great,
but judge your neighbor fairly."
LEVITICUS 19:15

Electrocuted?

Hayden stared at the report Bob had handed him minutes ago with the disclaimer, "You aren't going to believe this one."

Evan Coleman had been electrocuted in a freak bathroom accident five months ago.

Details were even sketchier: Evan Coleman, age forty-six, divorced with three children he did not have custody of, lived alone in a second-floor apartment just outside Port Allen, in West Baton Rouge parish. Sheriff deputies were called by the apartment manager who had received reports from the tenants in the same building as Coleman's that their electricity had gone out suddenly, as if a fuse had blown. The manager sent maintenance to replace the fuse, and power was restored. Hours later, the tenants in the unit directly below Coleman's called to report water leaking from their ceiling.

Upon entry into Coleman's apartment, the manager noticed a foul smell and heard water running. He entered the bathroom and found Coleman in the bathtub full of water and over-flowing, the shower curtain loosely wrapped around his body, and a MP3 home station still plugged into the wall lying in the tub.

Hayden flipped the report to the next page. Coroner Lee Morrow ruled the cause of death was electrocution. The sheriff department investi-gators found no evidence of foul play. It was their report that Mr. Coleman was in the shower, somehow got tangled up in the shower curtain, and lost his footing. In his attempt to regain his balance, Mr. Coleman reached for the towel rack, just above the shelf holding the MP3 home station, fumbled, and knocked the electronic device into the tub with him.

Hayden shut the file and stared at Officer Bob Travis. "You're right . . . I don't believe this. A freak accident?"

Bob leaned back in the chair sitting in front of Hayden's desk. "These kinds of things do happen. Sometimes."

"Are you serious? You believe this was a freak accident?" He needed some antacids. The shrimp po'boy he'd had for lunch now caught in his chest, burning.

"I don't know. On one hand, because of Nichols's method of death, I say no. But on the other, the investigators found no evidence of foul play."

He couldn't help but wonder how hard they'd looked. If they had no reason to suspect anything but an accident, would they have given any other consideration?

Hayden handed the file to Bob. "Check with the investigators. Find out what their impressions were. If they noticed anything odd about the scene. Find anything you can."

"Yes, sir." Bob shut the office door behind him.

Accidental bathroom electrocution. It was just too out there for him to buy. Not on the heels of seeing Matthew Nichols's body hanging from a hook in a cypress tree.

A knock jerked his attention to his office door. Officer Edward Gaston handed him a file. "The file you requested on Mack Thompson."

"Thank you."

Edward exited as quickly as he'd entered while Hayden opened the folder. If Thompson had died from something as freaky as electrocution . . .

Not quite as freaky, but close.

According to the police report—this one from Brusly PD—Mack Thompson, forty-eight, married, no children, had been out walking his dog eleven months ago and was struck by a vehicle, killing him instantly. The accident was a hit and run. The vehicle was never found, the driver never identified. He was survived by his wife, Ethel, and their poodle, Silly.

The case remained open at the Brusly Police Department.

Hayden shook his head and shut the file. The case details swarmed his mind for attention. Eleven months ago, Thompson killed by a hit-and-run accident. Five months ago, Coleman died in freaky accident. Last week, Nichols was murdered and left for gator bait. Each death more gruesome and odd. Each escalated from the previous.

Three coworkers, the only men on their team. Nichols had felt something was wrong with his teammates' deaths. So much that he'd taken early retirement.

But that hadn't saved him.

Thompson dead in his own neighborhood, on the street where he and his wife lived. Coleman dead in his own apartment. Nichols dead . . .

Why Davis Ellington's land?

Hayden flipped through the case file on his desk. There was no connection between Matthew Nichols and Davis Ellington. But what about the land?

He turned to the notes from his conversation with Ellington. There. He'd inherited the land from his father who died *a couple of years ago.*

Hayden buzzed Bob's extension and spoke as soon as Bob answered. "Davis Ellington. Get the name of his deceased father, date and cause of death." He hung up, his blood rushing.

Same feeling he got every time he was about to get a break on a case.

His intercom buzzed. "Yes?"

"Sir, there's a lady out here to see you." Officer Bubba Fontenot's breath hissed against the phone. "A Riley Baxter."

Riley? Here to see him? "Bring her back." He closed the files scattered across his desk and placed them in a neat stack in the corner. Was something wrong with Emily? His mom?

He stood as the door opened and she stepped inside his office. "Riley, how nice to see you." He nodded at Bubba, who looked disappointed to be sent away.

"Come, sit down." Hayden guided her gently by the elbow. He caught a whiff of her perfume as she passed him. Tangy. Fruity. Gut tightening.

"I'm sorry for just dropping by like this."

"No, that's perfectly all right." More than all right, it made his whole day. "You look lovely, by the way."

She blushed in that cute way of hers. "Um, thanks." She tucked a lock of hair behind her ear as she studied the floor.

"Is everything okay?"

"Everything's great. Well, I have a little problem I'd hoped you could help me with."

"Sure, if I can." He moved to his chair. "What is it?"

"The warden at Angola. He's denying my

request for an interview with Jasmine's father."

"Does he say why?"

"I'm not on some list or something."

The visiting list. "Upon incarceration, each inmate submits a list of people he'd like to visit. The prison does a check on everyone listed. Once approved, only visitors listed on his current approved visiting list are allowed to visit."

"But I didn't know him when he was incarcerated, so he couldn't submit my name on any list." She wrinkled her nose.

Riley looked cute when she was annoyed. Hayden thought it best to keep that observation unsaid. "You can ask his wife to tell him to request your name be added when she visits."

"How long does it take to get approved?"

"Usually a couple of weeks, on average."

"I need to interview him this week for my article."

"Did you mention to the warden you're press?"

She nodded. "He wasn't impressed."

Hayden could imagine. "I bet not."

"So, I was wondering, and I understand if you don't want to and if you don't, I promise there'll be no hard feelings, but I'm just asking if you could maybe call the warden and put in a good word for me?" She looked like an angel sitting there, smiling at him.

How could he say no?

"I promise he would only take shots you tell him that he can." Riley sat at the rickety kitchen table in the Wilsons' shabby-but-neat trailer, all but begging Peggy to allow her to bring a photographer for some candid shots.

The rain beat down on the tin roof, sounding out an interesting rhythm. *Tap. Tap. Tap-tap.*

"Mikey's too young. I can't allow him to be exploited like that."

She'd been afraid the single mother would balk at that. "Okay, even though we could photograph him from behind so no one could recognize his face, I understand. Just you and Jasmine."

"She's so young." The indecision ran the curve of Peggy's face.

Riley shook her head. "I disagree. She's been very mature in all her dealings with me. It's her story that initially grabbed the hearts of my readers." Wow, that had a nice ring to it—*my* readers.

The rain continued to pelt the mobile home. *Tap. Tap. Tap-tap.* Thunder rattled the kitchen window.

"I feel like I'm failing at protecting her. Like I'm using her to help my husband."

"Jasmine wants to help her father. That's why she's doing this. She said so." If Peggy didn't let a photographer come around, Riley would have to do some serious persuading to keep Jeremy from sending someone on the sly. She had seen him employ such tactics before.

If he did, and Peggy figured it out, which she would as soon as Jeremy ran the photographs, Riley's series would be dead in the water.

Lightning lit up the stormy sky. A clap of thunder shook the trailer. *Tap. Tap. Tap-tap.*

"I don't know . . . it feels wrong to me. Like I'm a bad mother."

"You aren't a bad mother, Mrs. Wilson." What was it with the women in this area second-guessing their parenting? First Ardy and now Peggy.

"Thank you for saying so."

The front door of the trailer opened.

Peggy reached for a towel. "How was school today? Come on in and get dry." She passed the towel to Jasmine, who still had the hood of her Windbreaker over her head. "It's really coming down. If it doesn't stop storming soon, we'll have to pick Mikey up from the bus stop."

Jasmine turned, shrugged out of her jacket, and hung it on the rack beside the door. She rubbed the towel over her head.

"Honey, Ms. Baxter came back to ask our permission for her magazine to take some photographs of us to use with the articles. How do you feel about that?"

Riley chewed her bottom lip.

"I think it's a great idea." Jasmine faced them and lowered the towel.

"Oh, merciful heavens, what in the world happened to you?" Peggy was on her feet and to her daughter in a flash.

"It's no big deal, Mom. Don't freak."

"Don't freak? Have you seen your face?"

Riley couldn't blame Peggy. Jasmine's left eye was nearly swollen shut. Already, the skin under her left eye socket to the cheekbone had turned a deep purple. It was ugly and would get uglier.

"What happened?" Peggy opened the freezer and grabbed a bag of frozen peas and carrots. She slapped it on Jasmine's face and shoved her into one of the kitchen chairs.

"A girl at school and I disagreed." Jasmine shrugged as she held the bag of vegetables against her eye.

"You got into a *fight?*" Peggy fisted her hands on her hips.

"*Fight* is such a harsh word. More like we had a minor altercation." Jasmine grinned at Riley from the edge of her mouth. The edge Peggy couldn't see. She winked with her nonswollen eye.

Riley pressed her lips together. She had to admire the girl's spunk and gumption.

Wind gusted outside the cheaply insulated walls, shoving and rocking the trailer. *Tap. Tap. Tap-tap.* Peggy ignored the weather. And Riley.

"Jasmine Jean Wilson, don't you be cute with me." Peggy gripped the back of the vinyl kitchen chair. "I would suggest you tell me exactly what

153

happened before I call the principal and ask him."

The girl ducked her head. "He sent home a note."

"A note? You get in a fight with another girl at school, and the principal sends me a *note?*"

Riley could feel Peggy about to explode but was powerless to do anything more than watch. A silent observer.

"More like a suspension notice."

Peggy turned and threw the towel on the counter. "Suspended. Like I need to deal with this right now. Jasmine, what were you thinking? How could you act so immaturely?" Her face had gone beet red.

Jasmine's shoulders straightened and her head came up. "It wasn't like I went out looking for a fight, Mom. The girl started it."

"I raised you better than to fight like a common thug. Your father and I taught you to walk away from violence."

"I said I didn't start it."

"Even so, why didn't you just walk away? Would that have been too difficult?"

Jasmine shot to her feet. The chair scraped against the bubbled linoleum and crashed to the floor. "Yes, it would have. She called us trash. Said you and Dad were sappy and stupid. Said my daddy should rot in prison. So, yeah, Mom, it would have been too difficult for me to walk away."

Riley went as still as a corpse.

"This girl read the magazine article?" Peggy's tone was level.

Riley wanted to warn Jasmine, but she couldn't. All she could do was pray Jasmine would weigh her response.

Jasmine must have recognized her mother's tone as well. She locked gazes with Riley over the table.

The rain didn't slack up. *Tap. Tap. Tap-tap.*

"This is all because someone read these stupid articles and confronted you."

Jasmine didn't answer.

"I warned you this would happen. That people would know all about you and your feelings. I told you they'd make fun of you."

"I don't care if they make fun of me, Mom. I care that they made fun of you and Daddy." Jasmine lowered the peas and carrots. Her eye was still swollen, but at least she could open it a centimeter or two.

Peggy turned to Riley, shaking her head. "I knew it. I felt this was a bad idea, but I ignored my gut."

Her stomach tightened into a tight ball, squeezing her insides.

Another flash of lightning popped against the black sky. The air crackled outside the trailer.

"No. No photographer. No pictures. No more

interviews. No more articles. We're done with all of this."

"You can't mean—"

"Mom, don't do this. We have to help Daddy. Please."

Peggy shook her head even harder. "No, this doesn't help him. Seeing you like this . . ."—she gestured at Jasmine's face—"doesn't help him. This will only make him worry." She looked back at Riley. "I'm sorry, but no more."

"Mrs. Wilson, please—"

"No, that's it. I'd like you to leave. Now."

Riley stood, unsure what to say. She'd never had someone ask her to leave before.

"Mom, don't do this."

Peggy snapped. "Jasmine Jean, go to your room. And keep that bag on your eye. I'll deal with you in a moment."

Jasmine shot Riley an apologetic look, then stomped down the hall.

Peggy faced her. "Again, I must ask you to leave. We have nothing else to say to you. It's nothing personal, but I must insist that you not run another article where me or my daughter are the subject."

Riley stepped out into the raging storm but didn't so much as feel a raindrop. All she could feel was her career crashing around her feet.

CHAPTER TWELVE

"If you see the poor oppressed in a district, and justice and rights denied, do not be surprised at such things; for one official is eyed by a higher one, and over them both are others higher still."
ECCLESIASTES 5:8

It'd been one of the worst days she'd had in . . . well, since Simon Lancaster's parole hearing. Her muscles tensed just to think of his name.

More pressing at this moment was that she now had no choice: She had to get an interview with Armand or her series was dead. If it was dead, her career at the magazine ended, and she'd have to start all over again.

Riley flipped onto her side, placing a pillow between her knees. Her eyes settled on the clock—11:00.

She tossed onto her back, pulled the covers up under her chin, then peeked at the clock again—11:48. She pinched her eyes closed and willed herself to fall asleep. Visions of standing in the unemployment line haunted her.

Midnight.

Her muscles tensed. She mentally attempted to make each body part relax. 12:17. Counting sheep? Not hardly.

She crunched herself into the fetal position on her right side and punched the pillow under her head. 1:10. Where was the relief? Peace? Rest for the weary?

Popping her knuckles, she rolled over onto her back. 1:33. Her eyes began to grow heavy.

Plop. Plop. Plop.

Riley jerked into a sitting position. What was that noise? What had awoken her from her hard-to-come-by sleep? If some stupid tree frog had robbed her of slumber . . .

Plop. Slurp. Plop.

There it was again. It sounded like footsteps in the mud outside. In the flower beds lining the patio.

Maybe she'd imagined the whole thing. Like a dream that cusped on reality just enough for belief. She strained to hear the sound again.

Slurp. Plop. Plop.

The sound definitely came from along the patio. Her heart raced. Faster and faster. She slipped out of bed and crawled across her floor to the door. Easing herself into the hallway, she crept along.

Creak. Scrape.

Was that somebody opening a window in the living room?

She had to move, had to check on Ardy. Riley tiptoed across the hallway until she reached Ardy's bedroom door. With the stealth of a cat burglar, she lifted a shaking arm toward the doorknob.

Creak-creak.

Fear welled in her throat. She had to hurry. Turning the knob as silently as she could, Riley eased open the door. From her kneeling position, she could see Ardy lying on her bed, facedown.

Swoosh.

Was that air coming in through an open window? She needed to get help. Now.

She crept forward, pulling Ardy's door closed behind her. She rushed to the bed. "Ardy. Ardy."

Hayden's mom bolted upright. "Who's there? What?"

"Shh. It's me, Mrs. Simpson. Riley."

"What's wrong?" Ardy reached to her bedside table, fumbling with the lamp.

"No, leave the light off. I think someone's outside—or maybe inside now."

"The house?" Ardy grabbed a scrunchie and wound her hair into a makeshift bun while slipping out of bed at the same time.

"Yes, ma'am." She hoped she hadn't imagined the whole thing. She'd be beyond embarrassed if it was just the wind. Or that stupid raccoon.

The way her day had gone, it probably was the raccoon.

"My gun's in a safe in the closet." Ardy headed to the closet.

A gun? Well, her son *was* a cop.

"I'll see if I can hear anything." And make sure it was more than a varmint set out to scare her on a regular basis. Even though the critter was a nuisance, Riley would hate for Ardy to mistakenly shoot an animal.

Outside the door, she paused, trying to discern any sound from inside. Moments passed. Silence. She trembled as fearful images built in her mind.

Carefully, she continued down the hall and slipped into the den. She fumbled around in the dark until she reached the bedside table and grabbed her cell. Just in case it wasn't a raccoon.

Swoosh.

The air dropped by at least ten degrees. Her pulse raced. No animal could open a window.

Holding the receiver tightly, she punched in the numbers for Hayden's cell.

A chilly, black silence surrounded her heart.

He answered on the second ring. "Hayden Simpson."

"It's Riley. I think someone's here—in your mother's house," she whispered.

"Is Mom awake?" His voice was calm.

She answered quickly, trying to drown out her choking, beating heart. "Yes, she's okay. She's grabbing her gun out of the safe."

"Look, I'm on my way. Go back to Mom's room. Tell her not to play Annie Oakley. You both wait in her bedroom until I get there. Do you understand?"

Creak. Creak. Creak.

"Riley? Did you hear me?"

160

"Yes." She'd never had fear hold her in its icy grip so tightly before.

"Then go. I'm already in my car and will be there as soon as I can."

"Okay." She headed toward the hallway again.

Creak. Creak. Creak.

"Hayden?" she whispered.

"Yes?"

"Please hurry."

Lord, please let them be safe. Keep Mom and Riley under Your veil of protection. Let me get there in time. Please, God, watch over them.

Hayden punched 911 into the cell phone and informed Dispatch to get a unit to his mother's house immediately, then closed his cell phone.

Thank goodness it was the dead of night. Little to no traffic meant he could get to them faster. *Just let me get there in time, God.* His heart raced inside his chest as he switched lanes to get around a compact car. Protectiveness seeped into his very bones.

His tires nearly hydroplaned over puddles in the road from the storm. The moon still hid behind the clouds. Lightning threatened as it lit up the sky.

Thoughts tripped over each other in Hayden's mind. Somebody was in the house? How did that happen? Who? Why?

Whipping his cruiser into his mother's driveway, he registered the scene: front porch light on as usual, no motion detector lights on from the rear or side of the house, and no strange vehicles in the vicinity. Hayden slammed the gear into Park. He didn't even take the time to remove the key from the ignition as he withdrew his 9mm Beretta and crept toward the house.

Crouching low, he circled the front and went toward the back of the house. Nothing. He continued his circling, every muscle in his body on alert, until he reached the front door. He looked right and left. No movement. He used his key and unlocked the front door.

With a practiced eye, Hayden glanced around the living room. Nothing moved or seemed to be amiss. Right hand armed with his handgun, he spun around to face the kitchen area. Nothing out of order there either.

He crept down the hall toward the bedrooms, stopping to check out the bathroom. Nothing unusual. He made it to the master suite. He pushed the door open all the way and entered. "Mom? Riley?"

The end of a snub barrel met him at eye level. Then Mom lowered her weapon. "Did you find anything?"

"Nothing outside. I wanted to check on y'all first before I went through the whole house."

"We're fine. Go see." His mother shoved his arm.

He caught sight of Riley over his mother's shoulder. While strong—she'd have to be as the sister of an FBI agent—her face drew pale and her chin trembled for a moment. He wanted to comfort her but had to check out the rest of the house. "Be back in a minute. Stay here."

Slowly, he walked through the house until he made it to the den. With his toe, he pushed open the door standing ajar and slipped inside. The smell of Riley permeated the room. He didn't know what perfume she wore, but the scent filled his senses in an intoxicating way. *Back to business, Simpson.* Hayden looked over her room but found nothing amiss. He stopped when he glanced at her bed.

The covers were wadded up on the floor, as if she had literally fallen out of bed. The imprint of her head remained on the pillow, along with a single strand of hair. For a moment he was tempted to reach out and take it. Just being in this woman's space had a strange effect on him. He shook his head, about to leave, when he spied it.

A leaf. Wet. Muddy. Fresh.

Hayden tightened his grip on the gun and inched the patio door open with his foot. He whipped onto the patio, holding his stance with his firearm extended. The motion-detector light now blazed from the corner of the house, illuminating the backyard clear to the bayou. Someone had definitely been out here since he'd pulled up.

The wail of a siren pierced the chorus of the night.

Focused on the darkness, Hayden refused to leave his spot. The intruder had to be close if he'd slipped out of the house after Hayden had arrived on-site. Close and brave, or very stupid. Just one little movement, he'd be all over the intruder, if he could just see . . .

Lights strobed, blue flashes clashing with lightning popping across the sky. Sirens howled as a cruiser sloshed and splashed down the driveway.

Hayden held firm, waiting . . . watching . . . praying. Just one little movement. One indication someone was still out there.

"Commissioner?" The call came from the patio. Officer Gaston.

"Don't step out here. Protect the den. It has evidence we need to retrieve. Call the crime unit out."

"Yes, sir."

Still not budging, Hayden considered scenarios. Was someone targeting his mother's house because of his investigation? Did they think he had put information here? The perp had to be long gone by now, but Hayden couldn't make himself move. Not yet. Not until he'd made sure no one crouched behind the front row of trees.

"They're on their way, sir. I've also cordoned off the den."

"Good. Have you double-checked the house?"

"Yes, sir."

At least his mother and Riley were safe. "Get some floodlights out here."

A crash of thunder boomed. Lightning split the skies. A raindrop plopped on Hayden's arm. Another. Two more. Four. Eight. Too many to count.

And then the clouds opened, dumping rain. So much for preserving possible evidence for the crime unit.

The bayou had, once again, taken what she wanted.

Failure.

It had been many years since he'd had to swallow that particularly bitter pill. He hadn't liked the taste in his younger days; he certainly didn't enjoy it now.

He rolled an executive pen between his thumb and forefinger as he stared at the phone set to speaker. "You believe you did the right thing in frightening her? Weren't you instructed to locate and eliminate her?"

The weasel's voice cracked. "I needed to verify I had the right person. You wouldn't want to be responsible for the wrong woman's *elimination,* right?"

Had this imbecile gone stupid? Using sarcasm

. . . with him? Who did he think he was? He would be eliminated as soon as he completed the assignment.

If he completed the assignment.

"I, uh, confirmed it's positively her." Back-peddling little son of a . . .

Failure.

He tossed the pen onto his desk. "In getting caught, you've put her on alert." He sat forward, glaring at the phone. "In addition to encouraging her to be more cautious, you involved the local police."

"How was I supposed to know she was staying at the house of the police commissioner's mother?"

It took all his willpower not to raise his voice. He wouldn't allow that. Losing self-control would imply he wasn't in command.

Failure.

"Now that you are aware, you'll have to make adjustments to complete your assignment in a timely fashion."

"About that . . ."

"Yes?"

"Well, uh . . . now that the police are involved . . . uh . . . we need to discuss my fee. Renegotiate."

"Are you out of your mind? They're only involved because of your inability to follow simple orders."

"But there are risks now, you know. Ones that

weren't there before. I have to take more preventive measures because of the dangers of getting caught."

"Because you created them!" He'd done it—lost his composure.

Failure.

"That's not the point."

Not the—"Listen, you little puke, I hired you to—" He stopped. Took a slow breath in through his nose, then exhaled with a long hissing over his teeth. "I hired you to do a job. You've already failed in your objective once. Don't make that mistake again."

He pressed the button, disconnecting the call, and then sat back in his leather chair.

The nerve! Lowlife.

He should have hired a professional. He hadn't because they were harder to dispose of when tying up loose ends. But they were less inclined to fail since their reputations were on the line.

Too late now. He'd deal with the situation as best he could.

His gaze fell on the magazine lying open on his desk. On *her* article. If only she hadn't poked her nose where it didn't belong. Digging up ghosts who should stay buried and chained in the tomb.

If she continued writing about this, somebody would take an interest. If that happened, some-body could piece together the inconsistencies.

The chance of exposure was possible. No way could he allow that. He trembled as rage washed over him.

Epic failure.

CHAPTER THIRTEEN

"You are always righteous, LORD,
when I bring a case before you.
Yet I would speak with you about your justice:
Why does the way of the wicked prosper?
Why do all the faithless live at ease?"
JEREMIAH 12:1

"Has the crime unit reported anything from last night?"

Officer Fontenot scrambled to sit up straight, failed, and stood instead. "Uh, no, sir. Not yet. I'll call for a status update right now."

"Do that." Hayden nodded, and biting his lips to hold in the chuckle, he entered his office and flipped on the light.

A new folder sat on his desk, wearing a yellow sticky note that read: "Research you asked for on Davis Ellington's father."

Hayden slipped into his chair and woke up his computer, then opened the folder. According to the file, Robert Ellington died two years and four months ago due to congestive heart failure.

He had been diagnosed with heart disease nearly three years ago. No indication of foul play in his death.

Buzzz!

Hayden reached for the phone and answered the intercom call. "Yes?" He continued reading about Robert Ellington, who had served on the Louisiana Health Care Commission.

"Line one is a Riley Baxter for you." Greta, the dispatcher, always had a cheerful tone to her voice, no matter the circumstances.

"Thank you." He pushed the button and lifted his pen, flipping his notepad to a clean piece of paper. "Riley, what's wrong?"

"Nothing. I'm sorry, I didn't mean to alarm you."

After last night's episode, he had no idea what to expect. But if nothing was wrong . . . "It's okay."

"Did you find out anything from last night?"

Direct. He liked that. "We're waiting on the crime unit's report. As soon as I know something, I'll pass it on to you and Mom." Which would give him a legitimate excuse to call her.

"I appreciate that."

Her hesitation was heavy. "Riley, is something else wrong?"

"I just wanted to ask . . . to remind you . . . about Angola. My interview." Her stammering tugged the corners of his mouth into a smile. "I don't want to bug you, but could you please call them and see if you can help me get in and conduct the interview with Jasmine's father?" Her words tripped over one another.

"I have the note on my desk." He grabbed the note stuck sideways on his calendar and squinted to read his own handwriting. "Armand Wilson, right?" The name sounded familiar to him. Wilson . . . Armand . . . Armand Wilson . . .

"Yes, that's right. I really, really appreciate this, Hayden. I know you're busy being the commissioner and all, so I'm so grateful for you making the call." Again her sentences ran together as she spoke in one breath.

He grinned, able to clearly visualize her face filled with the animation present in her voice. "I'll phone the warden as soon as we hang up."

"Thank you. I'll talk to you later. Bye."

Shaking his head and chuckling, he accessed his computer and found the phone number for Angola State Penitentiary. He dialed the number and opened a search engine while he waited for the call to connect. Armand Wilson . . . why did the name sound so familiar? He'd do a search as soon as the—

"Warden's office, how may I help you?"

"This is Police Commissioner Hayden Simpson over in Hopewell. Is the warden available?"

"Hold, please."

A rap sounded at the door. Hayden glanced up

170

just as Bob stuck his head inside, waving a folder. Hayden motioned him inside.

"How may I help you, Commissioner?"

"Good morning, Warden. I need a favor."

"What's that?"

"I have a journalist friend who has been interviewing one of your inmate's family members. She'd like to interview the inmate but hasn't been cleared for visitation. I was wondering if perhaps there was a way to speed up the process."

"Who's the inmate?"

"Armand. Armand Wilson."

"Hang on a minute."

Hayden covered the mouthpiece and looked at Bob. "Whatcha got?"

"Crime unit's report." He tapped the folder.

"And?"

"Nothing of use."

He'd been afraid of that. "What about the prints on the patio door?"

"All accounted to your mother, sister, you, or Riley Baxter."

And it'd been too wet outside to gather any evidence the rain hadn't washed away. For now, the case was—

"Commissioner? Sorry to keep you waiting. I had to look up the inmate."

"No problem. I appreciate you taking the time, Warden."

"Armand Wilson's not on any restricted visitation and is an exemplary inmate. I'll authorize this visitor. A lady, you said? What's her name?"

"Riley Baxter."

"Riley?"

"Yes, Riley. R-i-l-e-y."

"Got it. When will she be here?"

He hadn't asked her, but from her call a few minutes ago and the eagerness in her voice . . . "How about tomorrow morning?"

"Fine. She'll need to be here before one thirty because that's the latest the bus makes its final departure to the visiting areas."

"Great. I'll let her know." He jotted down the time on the corner of his notepad. "Thank you, Warden. I owe you."

"Not a problem. I'll make sure the right people are notified."

Hayden hung up the phone and took the folder Bob handed him. As Bob had said, no forensic evidence was recovered at the scene. Whoever had been in his mother's house was either very smart, or very lucky. He shut the folder and plopped it on the edge of his desk. "I just can't figure out why someone would target my mother."

"Maybe her house wasn't a target, per se, but was accessible." Bob leaned back in the old chair facing Hayden's desk.

If only he could consider that. "In a rainstorm. In the middle of the night." He shook his head.

Convenience or opportunity weren't considerations either.

"I took the liberty of scheduling routine patrols by the house."

Mom wouldn't appreciate it, but safety was paramount over what she wanted. "Thanks."

Bob nodded toward the other folder on the desk. "Anything interesting in Ellington's file?"

Actually . . . he flipped through the papers and found what niggled against the edge of his subconscious. "Ellington's father, Robert, served on the Louisiana Health-Care Commission." He pushed the folder to Bob. "I'm not exactly sure what that commission is, but Nichols was in the managed health-care business. I can't believe that's just a coincidence. Do some digging and see if you can find a connection between the two, will you?"

Grabbing the folder, Bob stood. "I'll get right on it." He paused at the door. "Don't forget to call Ms. Baxter back." He gave a rare grin before ducking out of the office.

Hayden lifted the receiver and punched in Riley's number. She answered and his heart kicked. Just at the sound of her voice.

He was in trouble.

Riley toyed with the laminated edge of her press badge clipped to her jacket. The smooth plastic against her fingers seemed out of place contrasted with the harshness of the prison. She'd opted for jeans, a simple cotton blouse, and a lightweight suit jacket. Professional, yet not overbearingly so.

"Remember, a guard will be in the room the whole time." The seasoned guard's stare washed over her. He smiled wide, the crow's-feet deepening as he patted her shoulder. "You'll do fine."

She didn't know what Hayden had said, but the warden had personally met her upon her arrival, informed her that he had arranged for her to interview Jasmine's father in a private room, and gave her the sweet guard as a personal escort. Totally different than when she went for Simon Lancaster's appearance. She didn't know whether to be alarmed or impressed to rate an escort.

Cha-clink!

She jumped when the sound echoed off the quiet walls, her spine stiffening as the electronic door of bars disengaged and slid apart at an agonizing snail's pace. Her heart skipped a beat as the door clicked into an open position. A whoosh of frigid air blasted against her face, kissing the errant strands plastered against her cheek.

The guard touched her shoulder again and gestured toward the long hall. She dragged in a long, ragged breath, let it out slowly, and proceeded. Her pulse hammered despite her attempt to self-calm. Riley discovered her feet were reluctant to move, as if she were the prisoner condemned, not the man she was set to interview.

"You just head on down this hall until you get to the end. On the right, another guard will be waiting to show you to the interview room." The old guard patted her shoulder again. "You'll be okay."

"Thank you." Taking slow, sure steps down the icy corridor, she ignored the creepy feeling spidering up her spine. Unlike the wing where the parole hearings had taken place, the air in this area reeked of urine and feces, masked only by the overbearing odor of cheap disinfectant. She swallowed against the urge to turn and run.

Cracks streaked along the dank, dismal gray floor in a repetitive pattern, causing a strange sense of normalcy to invade her perception of the unexpected. The dreary, yet foreboding atmosphere overpowered her senses more than the stench.

She lifted her eyes, keeping them focused on the hall stretching out in front of her. Each step took her closer to her meeting. Her mind raced with the questions she had to ask, the answers she needed to know.

As she neared the end of the hall, Riley took in another deep breath. This was her big break. She set her jaw.

The other guard, this one younger, met her at the corner, smiling as his eyes quickly took her in like a starving man.

She flashed the guard her practiced benevolent

smile. "I'm here to interview Armand Wilson." She brandished her ID.

The guard leered, sending the hairs on the back of her neck to full attention. "Well, ain't you a piece of candy I'd like to—"

"I don't have much time." She cut him off, shoving down her annoyance. She forced her facial muscles to relax before grimacing at the young man. "The warden said I needed to report here."

The guard continued to ogle her with such appreciation that made her skin crawl and had her memorizing his name and ID number. Finally, he took the time to direct her to a closed door off the main hall.

In an attempt to still her quivering hands, Riley firmly grasped the cold metal doorknob. Her palm left marks of condensation. She crossed the threshold, a death grip on her father's old briefcase. Thankfully, after a thorough contents check of the worn leather accessory, the warden had granted her permission to keep it with her.

She blinked several times as she entered. The room was stark and void of furniture, save for a desk and a few chairs on either side. Like the parole hearing room, this one boasted no windows —no chance of sunlight, or hope, to pierce the stagnant atmosphere. Musty air hung like a cloud of death. She swallowed, her heart blanketed in doom and gloom.

Forcing her feet to uproot, she took rigid baby steps toward the desk. Riley pulled out the chair. A screech grated against her eardrums as metal slid against worn and battered concrete. She sank down against the frigid metal with no seat cushion, squaring her shoulders and keeping her back straight.

The guard posted at the door gave her a cold stare, then pulled the door closed. He flopped onto the chair beside the door, wearing a look of disinterest and disdain.

Fear snaked up her stomach, holding her a terrorized hostage. What had she been thinking? She couldn't do this. Wanting nothing more than to bolt from the room and run to the comfort and security of her own apartment back in Tennessee, she hesitantly set her satchel on the desk and withdrew her supplies.

Lining up her pens and pencils gave her hands something to do. *I'm a professional. I can do this.* She repeated the phrase over and over, as if that would help calm her frazzled nerves.

Sure, she knew Jasmine and Peggy . . . knew they were lovely people undergoing a very trying season in their lives. But what did she know about Armand, really? Only what a daughter and wife had told her. What if they were wrong, clinging desperately to the belief of the man they loved as innocent? Could he be dangerous?

She rearranged the tape recorder, as well as the

empty notebook on the desk, then moved them back to their original position. The telltale rattles of keys echoed from an adjacent room. Her heartbeat quickened as her stare locked on the door in the opposite side of the room. In just a minute, she'd be face-to-face with Jasmine's father. A man convicted of a crime his family swore he didn't commit. A man who could make her career.

Riley tried to mask the fear she knew rested across her features. What if he truly was guilty, despite Jasmine's strong protest? Hadn't a jury of twelve convicted him?

She shook her head as a guard led Armand Wilson into the opposite side of the room. He shuffled in, a smile on his face and a brightness to his eyes, nothing like she'd expected. Visions of a Pulitzer prize danced before her eyes, bringing her smile back, only this time the gesture felt genuine. With a deep breath, Riley set about doing the job she loved.

Determining if Armand Wilson was the inno-cent man his wife and daughter claimed.

Chapter Fourteen

"Do horses run on the rocky crags?
Does one plow the sea with oxen?
But you have turned justice into poison and
the fruit of righteousness into bitterness."
AMOS 6:12

"You were right. It's not a coincidence."

Hayden sat back down in the chair behind his desk. So much for an early lunch. "Come on in, Bob, and have a seat. Tell me what you found out."

As instructed, Bob sat. Instead of his normal relaxed posture, this time he sat on the edge of the chair. "So you know, the commission examines all health policies developed by the state's Department of Insurance. The commission itself makes recommendations to the commissioner of insurance on such policies as well as recommendations for reform of the health-care and health-insurance systems in the state."

"Sounds complicated."

Bob lifted a single shoulder. "Well, it gets more complicated."

Maybe he should take a couple of antacids before he leaves for lunch. Or maybe he should just skip lunch altogether today. And it'd been a pretty decent morning too, despite everything.

"Robert Ellington served on a subcommittee to the commission. This one was tasked with researching one of the causes of rising medical costs: too many tests and treatments by independent doctors."

Hayden rubbed the bridge of his nose.

"Basically, they were supposed to figure out if people were seeking out specialists to get second opinions and if the insurance companies were paying for all this."

"That makes sense." He leaned back in his chair.

"So, this subcommittee does very little research on its own, but from what I could find out, that's fairly common. Subcommittees seem to get different *experts* to come in and give a spiel, and then the subcommittee members discuss and vote on their recommendation to the commission."

Why'd it have to be so convoluted? Couldn't anything be simple anymore?

"In every instance I researched, the commission voted to adopt whatever policy each subcommittee recommended."

That sounded a little . . . wrong. "So, essentially, whichever expert puts on the best presentation gets the state policy written in his or her favor?"

"Simplifying, but, yes. Basically."

More than a little wrong. This setup was all kinds of wrong. "Lots of room for corruption."

"Maybe." Bob sat back in the chair and crossed an ankle over a knee. "It gets better."

"Hit me. I can't wait."

"So, this subcommittee Ellington sat on . . ."

The blood rushed in Hayden's veins, the old familiar feeling of being onto something. "Yeah?"

"One of the *expert* teams they brought in presented that insurance companies were paying double costs for a second opinion. That often doctors could handle the patients' illnesses and specialists weren't needed. They proposed if there was a central system in place, one entity that would compile and approve every procedure, visit, and treatment plan for each and every patient—"

"A managed-care company."

"Right."

"Like Nichols's company, For Your Health."

"*Exactly* like For Your Health."

"Let me guess: Nichols and his team were the ones who pitched the idea of managed care to the subcommittee."

"Yes, sir. According to the records."

"How long ago?" The blood kept rushing.

"This is where our connection gets weak." Bob frowned. "Almost twelve years ago."

"What?" There went his theory. "A dozen years?"

Bob nodded. "That's why it took me a bit of digging to get the records."

He'd been so sure this connection would pan

out, be the lead they'd been searching for. But twelve years . . .

Bob must have read his mind. "I know, I know. But just in case, I looked up the name of one of the other subcommittee members who signed the recommendation Ellington did."

"And?"

"Jason Vermillion."

Images shot through Hayden's mind: Memories of his rookie days as an investigator. His first real case. Some images he'd love to wipe from his mind. But couldn't.

Jason Vermillion. Freak fishing accident. Out in his johnboat in the bayou, setting trotlines. Somehow or other—no one really ever came up with a workable theory on the how—Jason got tangled up in the thirty-two feet of trotline. Over thirty hooks imbedded all over his body. Wrapped up tight, he fell overboard. Unable to use his arms and legs because of the line binding him, Jason drowned.

Hayden hadn't believed his death an accident back then, and now he sure didn't. Could the unexplained death that haunted him have a connection to the Nichols case a dozen years later? The similarities couldn't be denied. "Who else was on that subcommittee?" The blood was rushing again.

"As the subcommittee chairs, only Ellington and Vermillion signed the recommendation to the commission. I've already requested a full list, as well as the minutes from the meeting where Nichols and his team pitched. Recommendation reflects there were three other committee members."

"Stay on it. This is our best lead." Their only lead at the moment.

"Yes, sir." Bob stood and ambled out of the office.

Hayden stared after him, his thoughts jumbled. If the crimes were connected, why such a long time lag? It didn't make sense. Nothing about the case made sense.

To top it off, he'd lost his appetite.

Armand was thirty-five, but honestly, had Riley not known that fact, she would have never guessed his age. Standing about five eleven and weighing about a muscular 170 or so, Jasmine's father had wide shoulders and a trim waist. He smiled as he approached the table. "Ms. Baxter, I'm told?"

She returned the smile. It'd be hard not to as he oozed charm. "It's a pleasure to finally meet you."

He frowned but sat. "Finally?"

"I'm sorry, I should have explained." She lifted the pen and clicked.

Armand smiled wider, showing white but slightly crooked teeth. "They told me you were a reporter of sorts and wanted to interview me?"

"I'm a journalist. I met your daughter and wife

here a couple of weeks ago. I've been inter-viewing them."

"Peggy? Jasmine? Are they okay?"

She found herself drawn to the love in his voice as he said their names. It was almost a caress. "They're fine. Lovely ladies. And Mikey . . . well, he's quite the little charmer."

"Praise the Lord." His relief shone on his face, in every line of his expression and in each blink of his brown eyes. "You've interviewed them?"

As briefly as possible, Riley explained the series. When finished, she held her breath, waiting for his response. If he didn't agree to be interviewed . . .

"Why are you doing this, Ms. Baxter?"

She hadn't anticipated that question. "I don't exactly understand."

"I just want to be sure we're both aware of the expectations. I know what this could mean for my case and my family, but I want to know what's in it for you. What's your motivation?" He crossed his arms over his chest and studied her.

To become as well respected as Barbara Walters? "Honestly? I need the series to succeed to prove myself to my editor."

A minute passed, a very long sixty seconds for Riley. Then Armand grinned. "I can appreciate that. I like your candor." He leaned forward, resting his elbows on the table. "So, let's get started. What do you want to know?"

She pressed the Record button on the recorder and lifted her pen. "Did you do it? Did you rob the Louisiana State Museum?"

"No."

"How do you explain the pawnshop owner's positive ID of you?"

He shook his head. "I can't. Maybe it was someone who looked like me. Maybe he made a mistake. All I can tell you is the truth, and I've never stepped in that pawnshop in my life."

Fair enough. "Did you have any financial problems? Hidden addictions? Owe money to anyone?"

Armand laughed. "Nope. I didn't have any financial problems. I don't drink, don't use tobacco, and certainly don't do drugs." The smile slipped away. "I'm a Christian, Ms. Baxter, a God-fearing man. I do my best not to lie, I don't steal, and I certainly don't try to kill."

After having gotten to know him through his wife and daughter, Riley believed he honestly was a Christian. Unlike Simon Lancaster's so-called prison conversion to Christianity. "Then this doesn't make sense." Now more than ever she couldn't believe they'd gotten a conviction off the purely circumstantial evidence.

"I know." His expression was as gentle as his words. "I've gone over the facts of the case a million times, I promise you. There's no explana-tion. I don't know who broke into the museum and stole those artifacts. I most assuredly don't know who shot the independent security man. I—"

Wait a minute. "Independent security man?"

"Yeah. The man who was shot didn't work at the museum."

"I don't understand."

"There was a special exhibit on display that night. Private collectors. All Civil War artifacts. All from the Confederacy. The owners of the stuff hired their own security as backup."

She hadn't read any of this in the trial transcript. "Was that common?"

"Sure. Happened all the time. I imagine it still does. Private collections usually have independent security. The museum won't add any extra men to guard over special exhibits or anything."

The prison guard stared openly at them, no sign of disinterest in his demeanor now. He pushed back the sleeve of his uniform and inspected the watch on his wrist.

She clicked her pen. Again. Again. "The items stolen . . . were they part of the private collection?"

"Yeah. Confederate artifacts."

Interesting. "And the guard shot, you didn't know him?"

"No."

"Tell me what you think happened."

"Whoever did this, they knew the layout. Knew where security would be. Knew how to work inside the museum."

"An insider, which is why you were a suspect."

He shook his head. "I don't think it was an insider. They knew a lot, as I said, but no more than what someone who frequented a museum would know."

"Like a patron?" She hadn't been to many museums in her life, but Riley didn't think she could break into one just by visiting often.

"We have a handful that come in at least once a week. A couple of them know it so well that we joke with them that they could be tour guides." He rubbed his chin. "And there is the group. The money and important people."

She paused in her note taking to stare at him. "Money and important people?"

"The museum gets a set amount of funding from the state, yes, but a lot of the money for the museum comes from private donors. The Friends of the Museum group meets monthly at the museum. They hold fund-raiser exhibitions and dinners, receptions, all kinds of stuff. They have money and power."

In her experience, a dangerous combination. "Like?"

He wiped his hands on the prison pants. "Like certain politicians and their, uh, female friends."

"Mistresses?"

He shrugged. "It's not my business, Ms. Baxter. The good Lord doesn't like gossip."

Riley nodded. "So, these people . . . members of

the Friends of the Museum . . . they're in the museum enough to know about security and so forth?"

"Yes, ma'am."

The guard shifted in his chair, checking his watch.

Who knew how much time they'd allow her? "Who? Give me some names." She poised the pen over the notebook.

"I can't do that."

She let out a long breath. "I'm trying to help you, Mr. Wilson. If you think any of this group might know something . . ."

"I appreciate that, Ms. Baxter, I surely do, but you'll have to get their names elsewhere. I signed a confidentiality statement when I hired on."

A confidentiality . . . what? "Is that normal? In the security industry, I mean?"

"I suppose. I don't rightly know for certain. I just know at the state museum, all employees had to sign one."

It was something to go on. "What about other employees of the museum? Curators? Receptionist? Office staff?"

"Not many people worked there on a daily basis. Maybe five or so."

The guard stood and stretched. He checked his watch again, then stared at them.

"Do you have any suspects in mind? Any theories?"

The guard straightened his chair.

"I've had time to think about it, and I still don't have any idea, and I don't want to theorize without facts. I don't want to put anyone through what I've experienced."

Admirable, but not the smartest thing. She couldn't help contrasting Armand's motives and actions against Simon Lancaster's.

"It's time to go, Wilson." The guard approached.

Armand stood. "It's been a pleasure talking with you, Ms. Baxter. Please give my love to Peggy and the kids. Tell them I miss them, but I'm so proud of them for being strong with you. Ask them to keep the faith for me."

She struggled to her feet. The guard shook his head. "Please be seated, ma'am, until the prisoner has exited."

Riley dropped back to the chair. "I will, Mr. Wilson. I'll be back, too, if I can."

The guard led Armand from the room. Riley turned off the recorder and slipped it into the attaché case. She stared at her notes and lifted her pen. Across the bottom of the page she wrote a single word . . .

Innocent.

CHAPTER FIFTEEN

"Here is my servant whom I have chosen,
the one I love, in whom I delight;
I will put my Spirit on him,
and he will proclaim justice to the nations."
MATTHEW 12:18

Great. Emily's voice trailed throughout the house.

Riley shook her head. She shouldn't think like that. This was Ardy's home. Too bad her sweet disposition hadn't been passed along to her daughter. Well, that wasn't exactly a nice thought either. Riley just couldn't help herself. Something about her and Emily was like the bayou mist and Mercedes-Benz.

Maybe she should stay in her room until Emily left. She'd slept in this morning because she spent the better part of the night working on the next segment in her series and sending it to Jeremy. Armand's interview. As she'd reviewed her notes and written the article, her belief that Armand Wilson was innocent grew stronger.

Now what to do about it?

Bright sunlight, a contrast to the skies of the past few days, shot past the curtains and filled the room. A glare blazed off the top of her laptop sitting on the table.

She couldn't sit idly by and allow an innocent man to stay in prison while his family struggled. They were genuinely nice people. Jasmine and Mikey deserved having both their parents around, working together to raise them. Riley would figure out something to do to help. Maybe she could send her series to some lawyers and ask them to work on Armand's case pro bono. Maybe Hayden could give her some suggestions.

After a hot shower with plenty of her favorite vanilla-scented suds, Riley felt more alert. She quickly dressed and headed into the kitchen. A cup of coffee would be the final piece of her wake-up puzzle. She'd love to go work out—it'd been over a week since she'd seen the inside of a gym. Somehow, she didn't think Hopewell would house a chain of fitness centers. Coffee would have to do.

"Well, well, well . . . good morning, or is it afternoon already?" Emily's rudeness only took second place to her sarcasm.

Riley ignored Emily hovering by the bar, keeping her focus on the coffeepot on the burner. The alluring aroma of the strong chicory scent had her mouth watering. She poured herself a cup and glanced out the kitchen window. Where was Ardy? No sign of her, but the police cruiser Hayden had assigned crept by the house. At least she felt safer.

"Mom said to tell you she had to run to the

grocery store but would be back soon." Emily's disdain was as apparent in her voice as the stitches on her face.

Riley tilted her head toward the injury. "Does that hurt much?"

"It's fine." Emily turned away from her, holding steady to the back of a bar stool. "And none of your business."

Maybe it was because she hadn't yet finished her first cup of coffee. Maybe it was because no one was around to act as buffer. Maybe she was sick of Emily's whining over nothing when Jasmine had nothing and didn't whine. Or maybe Riley had merely grown weary of guarding her tongue. She wasn't sure of the reason, but she stopped filtering her response. "Oh, I know. You've made that abundantly clear. Not just to me, but to your brother and your mother as well. Nothing you do is anyone else's business, until you need something."

Emily spun, raw fury blazing in her eyes. "Just who do you think you are? You come up here, stay in my mother's house, and act like you have a right to pass judgment on any and everyone? I don't think so."

Riley set her cup on the counter. Perhaps it was a very good thing the kitchen bar separated them like a partition. "What is your beef with me, huh? I haven't done a thing to you but try to be nice, and all you do is snap my head off."

"Why are you here?"

"I came for a parole hearing and—"

"No, not here in town. *Here.* Staying at my mother's house."

Oh. "You know. You were here the night she asked me to stay."

"Why did you? Weren't you staying at some hotel in Baton Rouge before your brother came?"

"Yes. But your mother practically demanded I stay with her when I tried to leave."

Emily's laugh came out only half sarcastic. "That's just her southern manners and hospitality."

The coffee tasted burnt on her tongue now. "Is this what your attitude is all about? Because I'm staying here with your mom?" And then realization slammed full force against Riley. "You're jealous."

Emily snorted. "Don't be silly. Why on earth would I be jealous of you?"

She chewed her bottom lip as she struggled with what to say. She took a deep breath and lightened her tone. "Because your mother is an amazing woman and she loves everyone. You're afraid I'm taking some of her attention from you."

Emily opened her mouth, but Riley cut her off. "And I don't blame you. I'd feel exactly the same way if I were you."

Snapping her mouth shut, Emily slumped to one of the bar stools. Riley leaned over the bar. "I can't tell you how jealous I'd be of anyone who got close to my mother, if she were still alive." She swallowed, letting the emotions she normally kept in check, flow freely. "I'll tell you a little secret: I was always jealous of Maddie. She was the first daughter. More refined, like Mom. More interested in things Mom was interested in."

Emily blinked but kept quiet.

Riley pushed past the pain simmering in her stomach. "And Rafe . . . well, you can understand how jealous I was of him." She remembered his voice thick with emotion when he shared their mother's last words. How she addressed her *son*. Tears burned Riley's eyes. "If I'm being honest, I have to admit I'm still jealous of him. Jealous that he got to see Mom a final time. Got to hear her voice a last time. Jealous that he gets to carry the knowledge that her last words on this earth were directed entirely to him."

The intense pain threatened to consume her. Riley bent her head and let the tears fall. Let the ache spill out. Let the anger dissipate into grief. As she sobbed, she realized someone patted her back. Comforting. She lifted her head and, through the tears, caught Emily crying with her.

"I'm sorry. I didn't realize." Emily sniffed. "I'm sorry for being so mean. I am jealous. I moved out to prove a point, but I miss Mom. I lashed out at you when I shouldn't have. It's my fault things aren't right between me and Mom, not yours."

"It's okay. I totally understand. But please, please know that I'd never do anything to try to drive a wedge between you and Ardy. And take it from someone who can't just drop by to visit her mom . . . stay close. If I still had my mother, I'd be visiting all the time. Doing stuff *she* wanted to do, not just what I wanted."

Emily nodded. "I'm going to go back to the therapist and shrink. I think they need to adjust my medication again."

"That sounds like a good plan. But I really don't want to come between you and Ardy. Matter-of-fact, I'll pack up and head to the hotel tonight."

"Don't you dare." Emily sniffed again and dabbed her nose with her sleeve, then laughed. "Mom would get on to me for that."

"I won't tell her." Riley wiped her face, then poured herself a fresh cup of coffee. "But seriously, I don't mind going to the hotel." She'd probably get a lot more work done without the distractions of food and visiting, but she'd miss Ardy.

And Hayden dropping in as he'd started doing the past few nights.

"Don't be silly. Mom told me about the break-in. You're safe here. Mom's a crack shot with that gun of hers." Emily grinned.

"I don't doubt that."

"And there's Hayden." Emily waved toward the front window. "He has that cop driving by here at least every hour."

Riley chuckled. "I've noticed."

Emily propped her chin in her hands, elbows dug into the counter. "Speaking of Hayden . . . were you on a date-date with my brother the night Mom called him to take me to the emergency room? A real date?"

Heat flooded her face.

Emily laughed. "Oh. By the color of your face, which is as red as a fire engine, I'd say it was a real date."

Riley laughed as well, touching her burning cheeks.

"So, how's *that* going?"

"We've only gone out that once. Your brother is a perfect gentleman." What else could she say to his little sister? That she'd never been so attracted to a man before? That he made her pulse spike when he walked into a room? That the sound of his voice caused her heartbeat to hiccup?

"That's it? All you can say is he's a perfect gentleman?" Emily laughed louder. "Wow, I'll have to talk with my brother. I didn't think he was so boring. Maybe that's why he's never had a serious girlfriend before. And all this time, I thought he just had too high of standards."

"No! Hayden's not boring. Not in the least. He just isn't all hung up on himself. He's terribly exciting. And kind. And charming. And—"

Emily cackled. "That's more like it."

Riley clamped her mouth shut. Her face burned hotter than hot.

"Me thinks thou protests too much." Emily laughed harder. Riley couldn't help it, she joined her new friend. Truth be told, Emily was actually quite funny. Riley had a feeling if she had the time, she and Emily would become close friends. But she lived too far away. The thought grieved her. Not just because home meant far from Emily.

Home meant far from Hayden.

How many dead ends did he have to hit before they came up with something? Anything? Just one, solid lead . . . that's all he needed, but Hayden would take whatever he could get. Any break in the case—either of them—would be more than welcome at this point. Investigative work could only take them so far.

God, we need help.

Hayden closed his eyes and rubbed them. He'd passed tired at least two hours ago but refused to give up and go home. The weekend loomed too close.

Still nothing on the break-in at his mom's. The patrols had been uneventful over the last twenty-four hours. He should be grateful for that, but they didn't have a single thing to go on. Not a suspect. Not a motive.

Nothing.

Seemed like that was the MO for all his cases lately: the break-in at Mom's. Nichols's murder. Jason Vermillion.

The last two were connected, Hayden still felt that way. He just had to prove it.

"Got it." Carrying a manila envelope, Bob stormed into the office without knocking and sat.

"What?"

"The other subcommittee members."

Hayden stretched his arms over his head. "Give 'em to me." He turned his notepad to a blank page and grabbed a pencil.

"Curtis Goins, deceased."

Name didn't ring a bell. "Cause of death?"

"Car accident. Hit-and-run over in Baton Rouge. Messed him up pretty bad, from the coroner's report."

"When?"

Bob flipped pages. "Four years ago."

"Ever catch the driver?"

"Nope."

Big surprise. "Who else?"

Bob turned to the next page. "Allen Boyce, also deceased."

This was getting way too obvious. "Cause of death?"

"Stabbed. Multiple times." Bob shook his head. "And before you ask, it was three years ago, over in New Orleans, where he retired four years ago. No arrests ever made in conjunction with the case."

As if he expected anything else at this point. "This is crazy."

"I know." Bob scratched the stubble on his chin. "Because the times are so spread out and the crimes, while similar, are different MOs."

"And the last one?"

"Lisa Manchester."

He hovered his pen over the paper. "Cause of death?"

"Hayden, she's still alive. Retired from local politics, including her work for the Louisiana Health-Care Commission about twelve years ago and dropped out of sight."

The blood stirred, starting to rush. "Where?"

"Baton Rouge."

"Got an address for her?"

Bob handed him a piece of paper. "Took me a while to track it down. Apparently, this woman doesn't want to be easily located."

Like she was hiding from something or someone? Hayden grabbed his keys. "Come on, let's go."

The drive to Ms. Manchester's residence took less time than Hayden had to work out some theories in his mind. After years of working together, Bob understood Hayden's methods, which included his wallowing through the facts of a case while he drove.

He pulled the cruiser up the driveway and stared at the house at least two hundred yards down the private drive. "Are you sure this is the right address?"

"Verified it myself."

"Where did she work outside of the commission?"

"She didn't. Her only job outside of the home was the commission."

Apparently Hayden was in the wrong arm of the local government, or she'd married well. "Is she married?"

"Never married. No children."

Hayden parked in the circular drive in front of the house. A six-foot fountain in the center of the circle drive cascaded water over granite. Despite what Bob said, the woman definitely wasn't keeping a low profile. "Does her family have money?"

"No indication of that."

Stepping onto the red brick driveway, Hayden studied the house from over the cruiser's roof. "Then how did she afford this place?"

At least three stories, the house replicated Southern plantation in style and grace of days of old. Hayden half expected to see Clark Gable and Vivien Leigh spill out onto the veranda at any minute.

"Good investments, maybe?" Bob asked.

Hayden snorted. "If that's the case, I need to

find out who her broker is." He led the way up the front steps. He didn't even get a chance to ring the doorbell or use the large brass lion's head knocker before a man swung the door open.

Bent and gnarled, the man had to cock his head to the side to look at Hayden. "May I help you?"

"We're here to see Ms. Manchester."

"The lady doesn't receive visitors this late. Especially gentlemen visitors." The censorship echoed in Quasimodo's tone.

"It's okay." Hayden flashed his badge, holding it down so the hunched little man could see clearly. "We're here in an official capacity only."

"Oh. Well. Madam isn't dressed. She's already retired to her room for the evening. You'll have to make an appointment and come back tomorrow."

Hayden checked his watch—5:45. And she'd gone to bed? "I'm afraid we have to insist. I need to speak with Ms. Manchester. Now."

The man hesitated, then stepped aside to let them enter. He showed them to a formal living room housing the most uncomfortable-looking chairs Hayden had ever seen.

"Wait here. I'll see if Madam can see you for a moment."

Yeah. Do that.

"I'll be right back." He gave them a final stare, as if he were afraid they'd destroy the place before he returned, then disappeared, shutting the door as he left.

"Creepy," Bob whispered.

Hayden nodded. Everything about Lisa Manchester was odd. Where and how she lived, hiding but flashing of wealth . . . the only subcommittee member still alive. It was time for answers.

The blood rushed through Hayden.

CHAPTER SIXTEEN

"When the islanders saw the snake hanging
from his hand, they said to each other,
'This man must be a murderer; for though
he escaped from the sea, the goddess Justice
has not allowed him to live.' "
ACTS 28:4

"I thought I was clear. Did you not understand that I meant for you to stay away from all my family, and that included my husband?" Peggy leaned against the doorjamb.

A breeze pricked the bumps on Riley's arms. The thunderstorms from yesterday had lowered both the temperature and the humidity. The sun had already set, letting a chill seep into the air.

The chill had nothing on the iciness of Peggy Wilson's greeting.

Riley's defenses crumbled on the inside, but she couldn't show that. She squared her shoulders.

"I'm sorry, Mrs. Wilson, but I really do want to help."

"Help who? Me? My kids? Armand? Or do you want to help yourself, Ms. Baxter?"

Ouch.

But if she were in the same position . . . funny how that seemed to be a common thread in her life recently. First with Emily, now with Peggy. "I deserve that. I'm not gonna lie to you, this series has launched my career. I'm getting a weekly byline on the front page of my section, and I've never had that before."

Riley held up her hand before Peggy could reply. "But that's not all. I want to help your family. I don't understand why it has to be one over the other when both purposes can be fulfilled by the same action." She shook her head. "I believe your husband is innocent, Mrs. Wilson."

Moisture pooled in Peggy's eyes as she opened the door and moved aside. "Then come on in and let's talk."

Riley crossed the threshold and stepped into the living room. "How's Jasmine's eye?"

"A lovely shade of purple today." She motioned to the couch and dropped onto the threadbare love seat. "Have a seat. Sorry the house is a mess, but Mikey's ears are infected again and Jasmine and I have been taking turns staying up with him. They're both sleeping right now."

Because of the medical problems of Rafe's

goddaughter, Riley had an idea of the problems with surgical procedures and insurance companies. It seemed as if the two entities couldn't agree on what was best for the patient. "I'm so sorry. Is he any better?"

"On yet another round of antibiotics. At the rate we're going, the co-pays at the doctor's office and pharmacy are going to fill our out-of-pocket maximum." Peggy exhaled forcefully, sending the curls resting on her forehead out of her eyes. "But the good Lord will take care of us in His way." She smiled. "Armand said he likes you. He's impressed with your tenacity."

Riley liked him too. But more importantly, she *believed* him. "I've reviewed his trial transcript too many times to count. And after talking with him, I can't believe the jury didn't find him not guilty."

"I agree. When the foreman read the verdict aloud, my heart and stomach flipped places. I tried really hard to be strong for Armand, but I couldn't keep my gasp silent." She shook her head. "I'd been positive they'd find him not guilty. When they didn't, I crumbled all the way to my foundation."

Riley could relate. If Simon Lancaster had been found not guilty . . . interesting how she would have felt the same over a not-guilty verdict as Peggy did over a guilty one.

"I'll be the first to admit that guilty verdict not

only knocked me out, but it also chinked away at my faith. How could God have let my innocent husband go to prison? What had we done so wrong to be ripped apart? How was I supposed to bear all the responsibility for our family on my own? I'd never been anything but a housewife and mother."

Words wouldn't form in Riley's mouth. She, too, had questioned God's wisdom when her parents were killed. All because of one man's addiction. Senseless.

"Me and God . . . well, let's just say that I didn't hold my temper or my tongue very well." Peggy chuckled. "Good thing our heavenly Father doesn't wash our mouths out with soap without giving us the opportunity to apologize first."

Riley couldn't help grinning. There were many times in her struggles with her grief that she'd yelled out to God. Screamed *at* Him. "I think God expects that, don't you? Just like you know when you make a decision Jasmine won't like because she can't see past the here and now, she's going to be angry. Stomp to her room. Slam a door."

"Or curse me under her breath." Peggy nodded. "Yes, I think God does expect that. I also think He *wants* that. For us to bring Him our every emotion, the good and the bad. Isn't that what a relationship built on love is all about? Sharing everything?"

She'd never thought about it quite in those

terms, but Riley realized Peggy had a valid point.

"I got mad, but then realized I couldn't be bitter. Not if I wanted to be there for Jasmine and Mikey. I didn't have the luxury of staying angry. My children needed me to be calm and peaceful, so that's what I determined to be. And only God can provide peace and calm in the most terrible of storms."

The strength of this woman amazed Riley. With Peggy's permission, her faith would be the focus of the next article in the series. She already had the headline: A Testimony of Faith—One Woman's Walk Through the Storm of Life. She'd have to push the envelope with Jeremy, who didn't like any piece focused on religion, but she couldn't write about Peggy Wilson's strength without telling about the underlying support of it. Since the series had only continued to gain followers, Riley had an idea she could hold her ground with her editor.

"I'd like your permission to speak to your husband's attorney."

Peggy rolled her eyes. "If you can get him to return your calls, more power to you."

"He won't return your calls?"

She shook her head. "He only answers Armand's because he has to. We've been waiting on him to file some additional paperwork for Armand's appeal. And he hasn't been to see Armand in months."

"Have you spoken with someone at the court about this? It's obviously some form of misconduct on his part. He's a court-appointed attorney, right?"

"Yes. He didn't impress me during the trial. He talked Armand into refusing to let Jasmine testify." She glanced over her shoulder toward the bedrooms before leaning closer to Riley. "I think Jasmine carries a burden she shouldn't because of it. She thinks if she'd been able to testify and tell the jury that she saw her daddy here at home during the time of the robbery, he wouldn't have been convicted."

Maybe that would have made a difference to a jury. Cute little girl on the stand telling them she saw her daddy in her living room.

"I don't know if it would've changed anything, but she so wanted the chance. To be told she couldn't by that attorney, and then confirmed by Armand . . . well, it really cut her to the quick."

"What reason did he give Mr. Wilson to get him to agree to not let her testify?"

"He said the prosecutor would rip Jasmine to shreds on cross-examination. That no one would believe a child trying to keep her daddy at home and that the jury would think less of him because he'd resorted to exploiting his child to save his own hide."

Well, that did sound like a legitimate explanation.

"Armand thought he was doing the best thing for Jasmine and himself. I agreed at the time, but now . . . well, I often wonder if we made a mistake."

"They say hindsight is twenty-twenty, right? You could only do what you felt was best at the time."

Peggy sighed. "You're right. I think Jasmine knows that, deep down. She's just at that age where she really needs her daddy, you know?"

For the advice on boys. For the sense of security no one else could ever provide. For the warmth of being Daddy's little girl. Yes, Riley knew all too well. "Yeah." She had to shove the word over the grief. She felt a true kinship to Jasmine Wilson.

If she could find a way to help the situation, Riley would do whatever it took. No matter what.

"The only mention of her name in the press I'll accept is in conjunction with her obituary."

"Yes, sir." The new hire seemed to get the point.

"Today."

"I'm on it right now."

Oswald liked that. Much better than the previous one. "Did you take care of the other problem we discussed?"

"Already handled as you requested." A minor break in the phone connection crackled. "You'll never hear from him again."

This one understood his place. Maybe he'd keep this one around. "I'll call you in the morning to ensure the assignment has been completed. Don't disappoint me."

"No, sir. I have everything under control."

He hung up the phone, suddenly craving a cigarette. It'd been a good five years since he smoked. Sometimes he truly missed the habit. After a good meal. After sex. Now.

On his best days, he managed to avoid thinking about the undesirable tendencies he had to leave behind when he left prison. Smoking, drinking, drugs . . . while he still enjoyed a nightcap, now he poured a high-price, labeled scotch rather than putrid cheap wine that would leave him with a headache the next morning. He'd quit the habits now. Habits were signs of weakness. Of someone who allowed cravings to dictate his life.

No more.

Just as he'd left behind the name his mother had saddled him with and the mess of a life she'd stuck him in. He'd left behind the signs of weakness and never looked back.

He never would.

His office phone rang. He ignored it. That's why he had an assistant—to screen his calls, among other things.

"Sir?"

"Yes?"

"A Johnny Smith is on the line for you."

He'd wondered how long it would take for the weasel to get around to contacting him. Had taken him long enough. Had he even made the connection, or was this call for an entirely different reason?

In the event the idiot had actually used his brain and made a connection, the situation needed to be under control. Tomorrow.

He smiled at his secretary. "Tell him you tried to catch me but couldn't. Assure him that you'll have me call him in the morning."

"Yes, sir." She backed out of the office, pulling the door closed.

He grinned. He'd truly left the past behind. The days when he couldn't manipulate. When he waited at the mercy of politicians and game changers. When he couldn't do anything more than survive. When he had to live by everyone else's rules.

No more.

He hadn't been expecting her to be so . . . young and healthy.

And beautiful.

Hayden stood as Lisa Manchester entered the formal sitting room. From the attitude of her butler, doorman, whatever he was, Hayden had assumed she was elderly or handicapped. He should know better. She couldn't be older than his mother and moved with a ballerina's grace.

"Please, sit down." She waved him and Bob

away. "Charles said this couldn't wait, so please get on with whatever you need to see me for. I'm very tired and need my rest."

It took all types. "We're investigating the murder of Matthew Nichols."

Her expression never changed.

"Did you know him?"

"I don't believe so." She stood. "Is that all?"

"No, ma'am." Hayden refused to stand, no matter how rude. "What about Mack Thompson or Evan Coleman?"

She sighed and sat, keeping her posture perfectly straight. "Those names aren't familiar either."

"What about Robert Ellington?"

Her eyes widened, just for a split second, but it was enough that Hayden caught it.

"You knew Robert Ellington?" Apparently, Bob had caught her reaction as well.

She had a strange way of turning to look at you without moving. It was the oddest thing—only her eyes moved, but they didn't dart from subject to subject. They kind of . . . rolled, then shifted to the next object. She did it again to focus on Bob. "I'm sure you gentlemen are aware I served on a committee with Mr. Ellington." She frowned. "Of course I knew him."

"What about Jason Vermillion?"

"Of course. Same reason."

Hayden drew her attention. "Curtis Goins and Allen Boyce?"

"Of course. We served on committees together through our positions at the health-care commission." She gave an almost undetectable tilt of her head. "But you already know all this. You went through quite a bit of difficulty to find me. Why don't you ask the questions you came to ask?"

Hayden tapped his notebook. "Why don't you explain to me about that difficulty?"

"What about it?"

"You built layers upon layers of corporations and aliases to mislead and misdirect in the event anyone looked for the owner of this place." Bob stretched his legs out in front of him, narrowly missing the coffee table. "Why is that?"

She shrugged. "You found me. Obviously."

"We're the police. We have resources the ordinary person doesn't." Hayden met her icy stare.

"All of my corporations and holdings are registered and filed properly. Each layer, as you call it, is legal."

"But why?" Bob leaned forward, his discomfort as obvious as hers.

"That's my personal business." She turned her frigid glare on Hayden. "Is there anything else?"

"Yes. Why did you retire from the commission so suddenly and seem to disappear?"

"Again, that's my personal business."

Now Hayden placed her name. "You retired right after Jason Vermillion died, didn't you?"

Funny, now that he recalled the case, he realized she looked exactly the same. As if she hadn't aged at all.

"I did." Her posture remained perfect.

"I talked with you back then. You lived in Baton Rouge."

"I did." The tip of her tongue peeked out from between her lips in the middle of her mouth. "That's not a crime to move, I hope." But she didn't smile.

"No." This was like pulling eyeteeth. "I have to ask, Ms. Manchester, how do you afford this place?"

"That's rather personal, isn't it?"

Bob stood suddenly, causing her to suck in air. "According to records, you paid cash for it. How'd you manage that?"

She looked from Bob to Hayden. Then sighed. Glanced at the floor. The wall. Out the window. Then back at Hayden. "You aren't going to let this drop, are you?"

"No, ma'am. Not until I get some answers. I'm working at least one, possibly more murders."

"You can't keep digging in my records. I've been careful to keep my tracks hidden. If you keep on, you'll lead him to me." Her chin quivered.

"Him?" What in tarnation was she talking about? The woman's facade crumbled like a week-old coffee cake.

She nodded, her face beginning to take on a hint

of expression. "After Jason died, I received a package. Almost a million dollars in cash and a letter."

Hayden's blood rushed faster than it had in a long, long time. "A letter?"

"A million dollars in cash?" Bob asked.

"Yes, in cash." She did that annoying eye-roll-shift-focus thing again and looked at Hayden. "The letter said: 'I know you're not to blame. This is your chance to leave unscathed. Disappear, or you'll suffer the same fate as Jason. And the others to follow.'" She shook her head. "I've never forgotten it. Nor will I."

"So, you did what when you got the package?" Hayden had to ask the question, even when the answer was obvious.

"I did as warned. I disappeared. Quickly sold my home and car, moved here. Set up dummy corporation after corporation, then bought this place. I kept myself alive and safe."

Some life. The woman wasn't eccentric as Hayden had first thought—she was terrified and a prisoner in her own home. Granted, a beautiful home, but a prison nonetheless. "You didn't tell the police? Anyone?"

"No. I knew better. This was the week after we buried Jason. I wasn't going to stick around to see if whoever bluffed." She let out a quick breath. "Besides, one million dollars in cash is quite the persuasive device."

Hayden could only imagine.

"What weren't you to blame for?" Bob asked.

She turned to him, still not moving anything but her eyes. "I don't know. I didn't then, I still don't." She swallowed, and that's when Hayden noticed the scars just under her chin. This woman had had plastic surgery. Quite a bit, if what he saw was any indication. No wonder she was like ice—she probably couldn't move her features.

"Did you keep in touch with anyone?"

"No." Her gaze bored into Hayden's. "Why would I? The letter told me to disappear, so I did. I didn't know who I could trust. I couldn't take a chance."

He knew all about not trusting. "And you have no idea why everyone else on the subcommittee and the three team members of For Your Health were murdered and you weren't?"

"No. For all I know, everyone else received a similar package and didn't act on it."

It was a consideration.

"Is there anything else? I'm afraid this discussion has upset me and I need to compose myself."

More like take some valium so as not to feel anything that would cause her to move her face and maybe crack it. "That's all for now, Ms. Manchester."

She stood. "Charles will see you to the door. And please, for my safety, do what you can to protect the details of my location."

She won for callousness of the year. "We will."

"Good evening, gentlemen." She turned and opened the door.

Charles waited in the foyer.

"Oh, Ms. Manchester?" Hayden called out to her.

She turned her entire body. "Yes?"

"We might need to ask you a few more questions. Please don't leave town without notifying us. I'll leave my card with Charles."

For the second time, her composure shifted and she frowned. She recovered just as quickly as before. "Of course."

He and Bob were silent until safely ensconced in the cruiser.

"What a whacko," Bob blurted out, as if he'd held it inside so long that it nearly erupted.

"She's a nutcase all right." Hayden started the car and steered it down the long, lonely driveway. "Sad too."

"Whatever. Give me a million dollars cash and I'm gonna go farther than half an hour away."

"But she's a woman alone . . . and it was twelve years ago. Things were different then."

"I suppose. What do you make of her story?"

"I dunno." Hayden turned back onto the road. "But most important, we need to figure out what she wasn't to blame for and why someone held everyone else involved responsible."

CHAPTER SEVENTEEN

"Does God pervert justice?
Does the Almighty pervert what is right?"
JOB 8:3

"Riley."

She knew that tone. Riley pulled over to the side of the road and tightened her hold on the cell. "What's wrong?" Her brother didn't call at eight at night using that tone unless something was wrong. "Is it Savannah?" Last she heard, his goddaughter was doing well with her latest heart surgery, but that could change suddenly. It had on several occasions.

"Savannah's fine. Where are you?"

"Just leaving Jasmine and Peggy's place and heading back to Ardy's." Oncoming car lights shone in her eyes. If it wasn't Savannah . . . "Is Maddie okay?"

"Maddie's fine, last I talked to her a couple of days ago. Says you never call her, though."

"Then what's up?" Maybe the connection was bad or she imagined his tone. She slipped the car back into gear.

A large pickup passed her.

"Why don't you call me when you get back to Mrs. Simpson's?"

She jerked the car back into Park. "Rafe, you're scaring me. Just tell me what's wrong."

"We got word today."

"Word about wh—?" The parole hearing. "And?"

"Riley, they granted his parole."

Every beat of her heart echoed in her ears, drowning out all else and pounding out a cadence. *Parole-parole-parole.*

"Riley? Riley!"

"What?" She nearly choked.

"Are you okay?"

What kind of stupid question was that? "Yeah." About as stupid as her answer.

Parole-parole-parole.

"I knew I should've waited till you were at Mrs. Simpson's. How far are you from her place?"

"I'm fine." That could very well have been the biggest lie she'd ever told in her entire life. "I mean, I'll be okay."

Headlights blinded her as she stared blankly out the windshield.

Free-free-free.

"I can call Hayden and have him come get you if you tell me where you—"

"When?"

"What?"

"When will he be let out?"

"Mr. Patterson indicated it could be as early as Monday."

Parole-parole-parole.

Days. The man who murdered her parents would be free and on the streets in four days. Four days and he'd be able to hug his sister. Kiss that phony fiancée. Start his arranged job.

"Riley, let me call Hayden."

"No. I'm not that far from Mrs. Simpson's. I can make it." But she didn't want to go there. She didn't know what she wanted except to crawl into bed and pull the covers over her head and pretend like none of this was happening.

But she couldn't do that.

"Are you sure?"

"Yeah. I'm not a child, Rafe."

Free-free-free.

"I know. It's just, well, the news . . ."

Her emotions were so tangled into a knot, she couldn't discern one from the other. "I know."

Silence hung over the connection.

"Are you sure you'll be okay?" Rafe's voice was barely a whisper.

Riley blinked away the tears as best she could. "I said I'll be okay. I'm going to go to Mrs. Simpson's, take a hot shower, and let her make me a cup of that hot tea of hers."

"Okay. I love you, Ri. Drive carefully. I'll call you tomorrow."

"I love you too." She pressed the button and ended the call, then threw the phone into the console.

Fresh grief raked against her raw heart, burning her chest. Stark as the night her parents died.

She laid her head on the steering wheel, sobbing. She was alone, no one to see, so she abandoned herself to the grief. She missed her mother and her father. Missed not being able to pick up the phone and call whenever she just wanted to hear her voice. Missed Mom telling her everything was going to be okay and reminding her that God was always in control.

God, where's the justice in this? Where are You now? Oh, God, I miss them.

How could the board have let him out? Didn't they listen? Didn't they understand how wrong it was for him to be out, walking around with the upstanding citizens?

Honk!

Riley jumped as the diesel sped past. She caught a glimpse of her reflection in the rearview mirror. She looked like death.

Grabbing a napkin from the fast-food place on the edge of town, she wiped the tears from her face. She still looked splotchy and red, but she'd take a long, hot shower as soon as she got to Ardy's.

She put the car in gear and eased back onto the road. Maybe if she concentrated on something else—anything else—she could make it home without incident.

Gaining speed, she headed toward the interstate.

Peggy had finally agreed to let her go with the faith element for the next article. Since Jeremy would be opposed, Riley would wait until the last minute on Wednesday to submit the article. Oh, the argument would come, but perhaps with less time, he'd give in quicker.

She slowed as she passed an abandoned vehicle on an overpass.

Her heart raced. Riley struggled to breathe. *Think about something else.*

Jasmine got up in enough time to talk with Riley. As Peggy had said, her eye was an attractive shade of purple. Jasmine joked that it looked like she'd been playing in her mom's makeup.

Riley remembered playing in her mother's makeup. Mom had caught her but hadn't been mad. Instead, she'd sat down and applied eye shadow all over her own face so Riley wouldn't feel bad.

Bile burned the back of her throat, threatening to gag her.

One more exit to go.

Something else. Jeremy had said he loved the article for Monday. Said the mail room had to start storing some of her mail in overflow bins.

She exited, then took a right. Drove four miles, then took a left.

Her limbs trembled. Her stomach felt like she'd just ridden the tallest roller coaster in the world.

Think about anything else!

She glanced heavenward. The moon blazed high in the sky, full and bright—something she hadn't seen the past few days with all the crazy storms. Stars twinkled, as if winking at her. Was there some cosmic secret she'd missed? A joke she wasn't in on?

Two headlights shot out from the darkness, causing her to squint. She gripped the steering wheel tightly. Only a mile or so more until she reached the final turnoff. Maybe she should ask Ardy for something to help her sleep. Somehow she didn't think a nice cup of decaf tea would do the trick.

She rounded a corner . . .

Yellow lights flashed. A white truck sat on the edge of the road, but not completely clear of passing traffic. Door open. An infant car seat sat on the road beside the truck.

Riley slammed both feet on the brake and jerked the wheel to the left. She skidded to a stop, about two feet shy of the car seat and door. *Oh, mercy. The baby!*

Her heart shot to her throat. Her hands trembled. *Mercy, mercy, mercy. Let that baby be okay.* Nausea roiled.

What kind of an idiot put a baby in the road on a dark night?

She grabbed the door handle and stepped on the pavement. Her knees nearly gave out, but she steadied. "Hey!"

No one answered.

Riley strode toward the open door. "Hey, are you okay?" She glanced inside the truck: It was empty. As was the car seat.

Very odd.

Her skin prickled in the night air. No one around?

"Hello?" Perhaps a woman traveled alone with a baby and hid in the woods along the road. But without the car seat? "Hello? Is anybody there?"

If help had come, surely they would've moved the truck, or at least the car seat, and shut the door.

Suddenly, Riley felt very exposed . . . very vulnerable.

She spun, rushing to her car.

Pop!

Riley couldn't move. The world looked like it'd gone slow motion. A vibration hummed in her ear.

Air wouldn't enter her lungs. Heat filled her chest. Burning.

So hot.

Her knees hit the pavement. Her hands went to her chest.

They came away wet. Red. Blood.

Car lights split the darkness. She blinked against the brightness. Falling. Burning.

Her face smacked against the asphalt. Pain

radiated down her neck. Hot. Her chest con-
stricted.

Blackness consumed.

The daily recap of the day's Masters flashed on
the screen.

Hayden chewed a potato chip as the golfer
made an eleven-foot putt for a birdie. Beautiful
shot! The greens were smooth and fast.

He couldn't help but be envious—it'd been
weeks since he'd looked at a club, much less
played a round.

His cell phone vibrated against his hip. Hayden
put down the oyster po'boy he'd picked up on
the way home. He couldn't even sit down and
enjoy a sandwich in front of ESPN without
interruption. He grabbed the phone and glanced
at the caller ID, then quickly flipped it open.
"Hayden Simpson."

"Sir, I'm on scene of a shooting," Officer
Edward Gaston said. "Victim was taken to the
hospital via ambulance after 911 was dis-
patched."

So much for a quiet dinner and catching up on
the day's sporting events. Hayden pushed off the
couch and carried his tray to the kitchen. "Where
are you?" He took a swig of iced tea before
setting it in the sink. He wrapped his sandwich
back in the waxed paper and shoved it in the
refrigerator. Would probably taste nasty

reheated, but if he was starving when he got home, it'd be better than nothing.

"That's just it, sir. Officer Fontenot called it in. He found the victim as he was headed to do the scheduled drive-by at your mother's. Shooting occurred on Bayonnette."

His stomach clenched. The road his mother lived off of. "Who is the victim?" He paused at the counter. *Lord, please not Mom or Emily. Please.*

"Not your family, sir. Um." The sound of papers rustling crinkled over the line. "Riley. Riley Baxter."

The air vacuumed out of his lungs. He balanced himself against the wall. *Oh, dear God . . .*

"She's at the hospital now. We don't have an update. Officer Fontenot says she was shot in the upper body and unconscious when he arrived."

Hayden charged out of the house and stormed to his cruiser. Shot . . . "I'm on my way to the hospital. Secure that crime scene and don't leave it until you hear from me."

"Yes, sir."

Hayden flipped on both the light and the siren as he whipped out of his driveway and gunned down the road.

Lord, please let her be alive. Let her be okay. Please, God.

Chapter Eighteen

"Learn to do right; seek justice.
Defend the oppressed. Take up the cause of
the fatherless; plead the case of the widow."
ISAIAH 1:17

"I don't know what else to tell you, Commissioner. The doctor will be out soon to speak with you." The nurse spun on her slip-on shoes and left the nurses' station.

Hayden returned to his pacing. And praying. He'd been alternating between the two for the past forty-five minutes since he'd arrived at the hospital. If someone didn't let him know what was happening with Riley soon . . .

His phone vibrated. He snatched it free. "Hayden Simpson."

"Hey there." Bella—Remington's voice soothed his nerves. "Sorry I didn't get your call earlier. We were in the middle of a movie. What's up?"

"Is Rafe with you?" He moved to the waiting-room area, stepping into a corner away from the handful of people waiting.

"Yeah. After the day he had, we decided a comedy was needed."

The day he had? It was about to get a whole lot worse. "What's wrong?"

"Uh . . . didn't Riley tell you?"

"Tell me what?"

"The board elected to parole the drunk driver who killed their parents. She didn't tell you?"

"She didn't have a chance." He swallowed, staring at the door the nurse had told him the doctor would enter from. "I need to talk to Rafe in a second, but first, are y'all in the car?"

"No. We're in the parking lot. Why? What's wrong?"

"Just let me talk to Rafe."

"Here he is." Mumbling sounded before Riley's brother got on the phone. "What's going on?"

"Riley's been shot. I'm at the hospital, but the doctor hasn't been out to talk with me yet."

"Shot? Where?" His voice echoed with confusion. Hayden could only imagine. He'd be crazy if Emily was shot in another state and no one could tell him about her condition.

"A couple of miles from Mom's. I don't have details yet, only that one of my officers drove up very soon after the shooting and called for an ambulance. Initial report is gunshot wound to the upper body. She was unconscious when EMTs arrived." Rafe needed to hear all available details, even though it would worry him.

"Report from the hospital or EMTs?"

"Just that she was unconscious when she arrived."

"I'm calling the airport now. I'll let you know

227

my flight information. Call my cell as soon as you hear anything." The line went dead.

Hayden took a moment to whisper a prayer for Rafe.

"Commissioner Simpson?"

He turned as a man in blue scrubs approached the waiting room.

His heart raced. "Yes?"

"Are you here about Riley Baxter?"

Hayden's mouth went dry. He nodded.

"She's resting comfortably now. The bullet went straight through her shoulder. Clean in and out."

Hayden could barely breathe. *Thank You, Lord!*

The doctor smiled. "If she had to get shot in the upper body, the angle and path it took was perfect. Minimal damage, all temporary."

He still couldn't speak. All of a sudden, he felt extremely light-headed.

"She suffered blood loss, as well. We've debrided the wound and sutured it, put her arm in a sling, started antibiotics, and checked that her tetanus immunization is up-to-date. We're going to keep her overnight for monitoring, but unless she gets an infection or a complication arises, she'll be discharged in the morning." The doctor shook his head. "She's one lucky woman. An inch to the left and the bullet could have nicked the top of her lungs or pierced her heart."

Luck had nothing to do with it. Only the

merciful Lord had protected Riley's heart and lungs. "Thank you." The knot holding Hayden's voice hostage finally untied itself.

"They're getting her settled in a room upstairs for the night." The doctor motioned toward the elevators. "Fifth floor. Check in at the nurses' station there in a few minutes and you should be able to see her."

His training and professionalism kicked in. "You said the bullet went straight through. So, you didn't recover a bullet?"

"No bullet. Entry from the back, at about a thirty degree downward angle."

"Thank you."

The doctor nodded, then rushed away, his slip-ons not squeaking on the tiles.

Hayden dialed Rafe's cell on the way to the elevators. As soon as he answered, Hayden gave him the good news of Riley's condition. Rafe and Remington were on their way to the Arkansas airport, a friend of Remington's on standby with a personal plane to fly them out tonight. He hung up, stepped onto the elevator, then dialed his mother's number.

"Hello?" Emily answered on the second ring.

Hayden groaned inwardly. He didn't need to deal with Emily tonight, on top of everything else. Especially if she was in one of her moods. He forced his tone to be light. "Hi, Em. What're you doing at Mom's?"

She giggled. "Helping Mom organize some of our baby pictures. You were such a chubby baby, Hay."

Good. She was in a good mood. "Thanks a lot, Em."

"I, on the other hand, was born beautiful."

"Yeah, I know." That should be enough to pacify her. "Hey, let me holler at Mom for a minute."

"Okay."

"Hi, Hayden. I made fried chicken for supper. You should've come by."

"Mom, I'm at the hospital with Riley. She's okay, but she's been shot." He stepped off the elevator and ducked to a corner.

"Shot?!"

"Yes. The doctor just said she'll be fine, most likely released in the morning."

"Oh, sweet Jesus. How did she get shot?"

That's what he wanted to know. "I'm going to see her, make sure for myself that she's okay, then I'll head to the crime scene. I don't know much more than that."

"We'll be up there in a minute."

We? "Mom, Rafe and Remington are on their way. They have a friend flying them in. I'm sure they'll need a place to stay. Why don't you ask Em to get the rooms ready?"

"We'll get sheets changed and then head that way."

No polite way to ask her to leave Emily at home

230

without causing a huge brouhaha. "Be careful on Bayonnette. I have units there."

"She was shot that close to here?"

"Yes, ma'am. Please be careful."

"Don't you worry, honey. We'll be there soon."

Hayden hung up and slipped the phone back into its holder on his hip, then approached the nurses' station. "Which room is Riley Baxter in, please?"

The nurse clicked on a keyboard. "They're finishing up with her now. She'll be in 507. That's down that way," she pointed to the right, "about six doors down. You can see her in about ten minutes."

"Thank you." Hayden headed back to the quiet corner.

He'd spend the next ten minutes talking to his Father—thanking Him for His grace and mercy and keeping Riley alive.

Man, but she hurt. She'd never been so sore in all her life.

Riley leaned forward as the nurse used pillows to prop her arm in the most comfortable position to take the pressure off her shoulder. They hadn't been able to give her morphine because of her allergies, and what they'd just put in her IV drip wasn't working worth mentioning.

"There. Better?" Betty, her nurse, stood back and smiled.

Better? She'd been shot. She ached all over. What kind of sadistic person asked such a stupid question considering everything? Riley refrained from replying. Probably wouldn't be a good idea to tick off her nurse. Who knew if she'd ever get her pain medication if she did? "Thank you."

The nurse smiled wider and pressed buttons on the IV control panel. "We'll be back to check on you in a bit." She patted Riley's foot. "You get some rest, sweetie."

Yeah. As if. Her mind raced. Shot. She'd been shot! She still couldn't quite process it all. Everything had happened so fast. But slow at the same time.

It didn't make sense.

A knock sounded on the door, then Hayden's head poked in. "Hey, can I come in?"

Her heart kicked up a notch. "Sure."

He came and stood at her bedside, staring at her with such intensity she grew uneasy. He must have noticed because he looked away, grabbed the chair and pulled it closer, and sat. "How're you feeling?"

"Like I've been shot." She offered a weak grin. Finally, the pain meds were beginning to take the edge off the sharpness. That, or Hayden being here made her feel better.

He grinned back. "Ha. Ha." He pulled out his notebook but didn't open it. "The doctor said you were very lucky."

"That's what he told me."

"It wasn't luck. It was God keeping you safe."

"Yeah, well, I wish God would have told me to keep on driving and not stop for the truck."

He flipped open his notebook. "Tell me about it."

She nodded, then told him everything that happened—the flashers, the truck, the car seat in the road. "And then everything went black and the next thing I knew, I woke up here, with doctors and nurses surrounding me."

He looked up from his notepad. "Can you hang on just a minute?" He lifted his cell phone before she could respond and took a couple of steps away from the bed. "Officer Gaston, it's Hayden. Describe the crime scene to me, please."

He flashed her a weak smile. "Okay. Yeah." Pause. "Yeah." Another pause. "Right." He shut the phone and returned to her bedside.

"What?"

"The truck and infant carrier are there. A police cruiser came as you fell, so no one had time to remove anything from the scene."

"The headlights." She remembered that. "I saw headlights coming straight for me just before I went dark."

"Did you see anyone at the scene?"

"No."

"Hear anything strange?"

233

If only she had. "Not that I remember." A tornado spun in her stomach.

"It's okay. Don't stress over it. It could come back to you when you least expect it."

Right.

"The crime unit is there gathering forensic evidence. There's a good chance whoever shot you planned to remove the truck after shooting you so he wasn't careful and left behind evidence."

There was that. She could hope.

He hesitated.

She recognized that look. "What?"

"I hate to ask, but I have to."

"Go ahead." Her brother was, after all, an agent. She knew all about questions and answers and reports. "Shoot. Not literally, of course."

He grinned, then turned serious again. "Do you know of anyone who would want to hurt you?"

Like someone who would try to kill her? Shoot her and leave her for dead in the middle of a dark bayou road? "No one I can think of."

"You're a journalist, Riley. Surely you've made an enemy or two."

Now it was her turn to grin, even though her shoulder throbbed and burned, which the doctor had told her was perfectly normal. More like perfectly painful. "In case you weren't paying attention, this series I'm working on are the first bylines I've had at the magazine."

"Right." He focused on his notebook. "Sorry."

"It's okay." Or was it? Didn't matter. "So I don't think I've made any enemies with my articles."

"Are you sure?" He lowered his notebook to his lap. "I mean, someone broke into Mom's house. In the room you're staying in. And now you've been shot."

It did seem like someone had targeted her. "I don't know. It's a little too coincidental, isn't it?"

He nodded.

"I wish I could remember more. I'm not much help." Frustration mixed with the pain medication, burning the back of her throat.

Hayden took her right hand. "Hey, it's okay. Don't get yourself worked up. Rafe and Remington are on their way, and if you're stressed out, Rafe will have my head."

She forced herself to smile. "You know, Hayden Simpson, I really like you. As a matter of fact, I like you a lot. A whole lot."

He smiled, sending her pulse into such over-drive, she could hear it thrumming in her ears. "Well, Riley Baxter, that's a good thing, because I happen to really like you too. A lot. A whole lot."

Even her tummy oozed warmth throughout her body. "So, what are we going to do about this liking each other?"

That easygoing smile of his flashed across his chiseled face. "I think we should follow through on the feelings . . . see what we uncover."

"Is that your professional opinion, Commissioner?" She suddenly felt woozier.

"As a matter of fact, it is."

Everything shifted in and out of focus. She blinked. Again. And again, but she still couldn't get focused.

"Hey"—he rubbed his thumb over her knuckles — "I'll find him."

Her pulse spiked as his touch warmed her.

"I promise you that—I'll find whoever shot you and see him punished."

And she had no doubt Hayden Simpson was a man of his word.

CHAPTER NINETEEN

"The LORD within her is righteous; he does no wrong. Morning by morning he dispenses his justice, and every new day he does not fail, yet the unrighteous know no shame."
ZEPHANIAH 3:5

"Crime unit's about done gathering what they can." Officer Gaston gestured to the technicians closing suitcases. "They've called for fresh eyes and more lights to search the area for forensic evidence from the scene, but they're impounding the truck and that infant car seat to go over it with a fine-tooth comb."

Hayden nodded as he surveyed the area lit up by standing flood lights blazing against the black backdrop. He tightened his grip on the handle of his police flashlight. Various official vehicles parked at odd angles—his cruiser, Officers Fontenot and Gaston's, the crime-scene unit, and . . . local sheriff?

"Who's here from parish?" He motioned to the out-of-place car.

Officer Gaston shrugged. "Introduced himself as a deputy sheriff. Don't know him. He's talking with the crime-unit techs."

Great. A probable jurisdiction battle. Technically, it was a gray area and the lines were blurred. Usually in cases like this, first on the scene took the case. Officer Fontenot had arrived before Riley even hit the ground. Hayden's team should get the case.

He'd make sure of it. The deputy would probably be grateful not to have to fill out any paperwork. Then again, he'd come even though Hopewell PD was already on-site.

Hayden turned, inspecting the scene.

The white truck sat on the shoulder. An infant's car seat on the road beside it. Her car almost sideways in her lane. Just like Riley had described.

"Have they recovered the bullet?"

Gaston shook his head and kept his flashlight beam on the ground. "No, sir. And the techs have looked. I've looked. Nothing."

"Keep looking. That bullet's here somewhere."

"Yes, sir. Crime unit has called in more techs and better lights."

Hayden had to steel himself against flinching as he stood beside the taped outline of where Officer Fontenot had found Riley. He glanced over his shoulder shining his flashlight, then down the road, then to the outline. "She said she got a funny feeling, so she was walking back to her car when she was shot."

Gaston remained silent but nodded.

"She was shot in the back, which means the shooter had to be over in that area." He spun and peered into the wooded area separating the road from the bayou. "According to the doctor, the wound came from the back and at an angle." He gauged about thirty degrees and pointed. "From about the height of those old trees there."

"I'm on it, sir." Gaston sprinted in that direction with his flashlight, calling out to one of the technicians to join him.

The uniformed sheriff's deputy closed the distance between them with his hand extended. "Deputy Max Ingram, West Baton Rouge Parish sheriff's office."

Hayden shook his hand and introduced himself. "Little surprised to see someone from parish here since we called it in on-site."

"Normally, we'd leave it alone, but we have a

couple of recent homicides we're hoping foren-sics will connect to this one."

"Really?"

"Yeah. Two guys were taken out by high-powered shots from over four hundred yards. Both chest shots. Both on isolated roads. At night, but not overly late."

Sounded similar enough that Hayden would check it out too, if he were the sheriff. "But your victims were male?"

"Right. And they were both killed on impact."

Which Riley probably would have been, had she not turned slightly because something creeped her out. That bullet could have easily entered her chest, killing her. Chills crept up the back of Hayden's neck. "Did you recover any forensic evidence at either of your scenes?"

"Not much. We got the bullets. Our estimate of distance and angle of shot is consistent with both homicides, which according to what I see here, looks to be about the same as yours."

"We haven't recovered a bullet yet."

"Your crime techs are good. Heard they called in more lights to scour the area around where the body was found." The deputy straightened. "You stand a much better chance of getting evidence with the truck and infant seat. Who knows, might be the killer's MO and he had time to clear the scenes before we got to ours. But you got here too fast for him. If the bullets match . . ."

Then there was a good chance they'd catch the guy. If that was the case, the two departments would have to work together. And then there was Rafe.

"I should warn you. The victim, Riley Baxter, her brother's an FBI agent and on his way."

"New Orleans office?"

"Nope, Little Rock."

"A little out of their area, but they're feds and can do what they want. Think he'll pull the case?"

"They could, but I know him. He's a friend of a friend . . . of sorts." The relationship dynamic was too complicated to explain. "He won't be shut out, that's for sure, but I think he'll be okay with me working the case."

As if he wouldn't. This was Riley. She might be Rafe's sister, but she was Hayden's . . . what? He didn't know, but it scared him to think he might not have had time to figure it out had the bullet been an inch off.

"Well, until we rule out there's a connection to our homicides, I need to work the case too."

Normally, Hayden might make noises about calling jurisdiction from the get-go. But this was Riley, and he wanted any and all resources available to catch her shooter. Federal, parish, local—it didn't matter as long as someone was brought to justice for nearly killing her.

Just the thought had Hayden fisting his hands.

"No reason we can't work together, right?" He

peered at the deputy. "Maybe get all three cases solved."

"I think we're on the same page."

"Good." Hayden walked back and forth between the truck and Riley's car. He liked to try to get into the head of the perp. He retraced the steps back to the truck. Back to the car. Again. Once more.

This was planned . . .

The flashers, attention getter. The truck, the big blockade. The infant seat, the guarantee stop for a woman. All carefully planned to get Riley out in the open to get a shot.

Why? Was it just a shooter's MO, or was this one different? Personal?

Hayden stared into the night illuminated by the stand of lights and his own flashlight. Why would someone want to kill Riley?

He didn't know, but he was certainly going to find out.

"Really, Ardy. There's no need to go to any trouble."

"Nonsense. I want to do this." Ardy glanced at her daughter. "*We* want to do it, right, Emily?" She poured water into the cup and set it on the adjustable table at Riley's bedside.

Riley's new friend winked at her. "You might as well tell Mom your favorite dessert and let her make it for you, otherwise she'll make about twenty and you'll have to eat them all. You'll get fat and then my brother won't fall madly in love with you." She grinned wider as she crossed her arms over her chest.

"What's this about Hayden falling in love with my sister?" Rafe blew into the room, Remington on his heels.

A fresh wave of heat shot across Riley's face. Why did Rafe have to hear Emily's teasing? "She's just picking on me, trying to make me laugh." She held out her hand to him. "You didn't have to rush back. I'm fine. Doctors say I'll be released tomorrow, probably. I hate that you wasted the time."

"Wasted my time?" He took her head, bent, and kissed her forehead. "Silly girl. Coming to see my baby sister who's been shot isn't a waste of my time."

"Nor is it mine," said a familiar female voice from the door.

"Mads! You're here." Happiness bubbled inside.

"Of course I'm here. Where else would I be with my sister shot?" She moved Rafe out of the way, leaning down and hugging Riley one-sided. She pressed her lips to Riley's temple. "I love you, goofy."

Tears snuck into Riley's eyes, but she blinked them away. "Well, although unnecessary, I'm glad you're both here."

Remington gave a little cough. "Ardy and

Emily, this is Rafe and Riley's sister, Maddie. This is Hayden's mom and sister."

The polite exchanges went around the room, then moments later, Ardy patted Riley's feet hiding under the covers. "We're going to head on to the house." She smiled at Remington, Rafe, and Maddie. "We have rooms set for all of you, so we'll see you back at the house whenever you're ready."

"We can stay at a hotel, Mrs. Simpson," Maddie said.

Riley chewed her bottom lip. Would Maddie fare any better with the same argument as Riley had?

"Nonsense. I insist you stay with me. It's settled."

Riley locked stares with Emily, and they both giggled.

Maddie looked at Riley. "What's funny?"

Both Riley and Emily laughed even harder, until pain radiated down from Riley's shoulder. She sobered immediately.

"Are you okay?" Remington asked.

"Just really sore." She shifted against the pillow. "I keep forgetting not to move my shoulder."

"We're gonna head on out, honey. We'll see you tomorrow." Ardy patted her feet again. "You feel better."

"Yeah, take it easy." Emily smiled before following her mother.

"Mrs. Simpson?" Maddie called out.

"Yes?"

"Chocolate pie."

"Excuse me?"

"That's Riley's favorite dessert."

"*Merci*, my dear." Ardy and Emily left.

"Do you need any more pain medication?" Maddie asked.

"No. It's okay now."

Rafe went agent on her. "What happened?"

Yet again, Riley retold the story. Maybe she should just record it and play it back for anyone who asked. Finally, she reached the end. "And Hayden left to go to the scene. That's all I know."

Rafe nodded. "I think I'll head over there. See if I can help."

Remington grabbed his arm. "I think I'd better go with you. To remind you it's Hayden's case. Not yours. Stop you from trying to take over."

He shook his head, then kissed Riley's again. "Okay, squirt. Try to stay out of trouble."

She chuckled. "I'm already shot . . . what more can I do?"

"Maddie, we'll come back for you as soon as I'm done at the scene."

"No rush. I want to catch up with Riley anyway."

In moments, she was alone with her sister. "I can't tell you how terrified I was when Rafe called." Maddie pulled the chair up close to the bed and held her hand.

"Hey, I'm okay." But Riley couldn't help loving that her sister was here now, like this, with her. "Doctor said I'm going to be back to 100 percent in no time."

"I know." Maddie sniffed. "But it made me scared all the same. You and Rafe . . . since Mom and Dad . . . y'all are all I have."

"Mads, we all have each other."

"Rafe has Remington now." Maddie grinned. "I think he'll pop the question before the end of the year."

"Really?" But she wasn't surprised. The way the two of them interacted . . . Yeah, she could see them married. They'd be happy together. "I'm happy for them."

"Me too."

"So, what's new back in Tennessee?"

"Nothing, really. Kinda boring with you visiting here."

"Ha." Riley rolled her eyes.

"Seriously." Maddie leaned back in the chair and propped her feet on the base of the hospital bed. "I've got a new case."

"Tell me." It'd been a long time since Riley had seen her sister this excited about anything to do with work.

"I can't. Yet." Maddie smiled. "You know how these cases can be."

"I do."

"I'll tell you as soon as I can. But I have to tell

245

you . . ." Maddie sat up straight and gave Riley's uninjured arm a little shove. "I've been reading a real kicker of series in *Life in the South* magazine. By some chick named Riley Something-or-other."

Riley laughed.

"All kidding aside, it's really good, Ri. I mean it. The first article, with that girl . . . man, I cried. I so feel for her."

"Me too. She's what made me even come up with the series idea."

"And how's it going?"

"Good." She shifted, easing her shoulder to a more comfortable position. "Good thing I have until Wednesday to turn in the next article."

"What's the next one about?"

"The next one is about Peggy Wilson, his wife. And her faith."

"I thought you said your editor didn't allow religious pieces."

"I think I can sway him on this one."

"Well, good."

"Yeah." She'd been thinking about what would come next while they'd been giving her stitches and she'd decided she would expose the lousy legal services Armand had received. Especially if his attorney still refused to return her calls. Maybe a better lawyer would take the case and file an appeal.

Maddie plopped her feet to the floor, pulling Riley out of her thoughts. "Now, tell me about this brother of Emily's she says is falling madly in love with you."

Fire filled her cheeks, but she was glad Maddie had brought up the subject. "Hayden. He's the police commissioner here."

"And?"

"And he's kind and charming and handsome as all get-out." Her face burned hotter, if that was possible.

"But?" Maddie leaned closer. "I hear a *but* in there."

Funny how her sister knew her too well, even though it'd been months since she'd hung out with Maddie—ever since Maddie had declared she didn't want to speak at Simon Lancaster's parole hearing. That made Riley so mad, she hadn't wanted to be around her sister. Now, Riley couldn't help but wonder if Maddie had spoken, would parole have been denied?

"Ri?" Maddie jerked her back to the present.

"But we've only been out once. On a real date. So I'm not sure if he's really interested."

"What's not to be interested in? You're beautiful—which runs in the family, by the way—and smart and a gifted writer. I'm sure he's as smitten with you as you obviously are with him."

Then why hadn't he asked her out again? He'd had opportunity after opportunity. "I don't know. His mom seems to think so."

"And apparently his sister, from what we overheard."

"Maybe."

"Well, I'll just have to judge for myself when I meet him tonight." Mads sat up straight, arms crossed over her chest.

Uh-oh. Ever since their parents had died, Maddie felt the need to act as mother hen. This could be bad. Very, very bad.

CHAPTER TWENTY

"But about the Son he says, 'Your throne,
O God, will last forever and ever; a scepter of
justice will be the scepter of your kingdom.' "
HEBREWS 1:8

Un-freaking-believable.

Why wouldn't she die?

This woman was not indestructible. She wasn't Wonder Woman in some invisible jet. She wasn't protected by the Secret Service.

She was a woman, human. Flesh and bone. She bled when cut and shot, just like everybody else. Just like Kelly.

Then why wouldn't she die?

Just like Kelly.

He muted the local news that had continued after the report of the attack on Riley Baxter. Fear mixed with anger in his gut, boiling, burning.

There was nothing that could link the attempt on her life back to him. All the devil's spawn he'd eliminated—none of them linked to him. Just like changing his name years ago, he'd covered his tracks well. Prior to his incarceration, he'd gotten justice from four people. Since his release, he'd removed five people from this earth. All without getting caught.

And people said there was no such thing as a perfect crime. Showed what they knew. He'd gotten away with the perfect murder nine different times. Perhaps he was just smarter than the rest.

But this woman . . . this Riley Baxter . . . she was quickly becoming a festering problem for him.

Why wouldn't she die?

She'd stumbled upon the one subject that could link him to everything. The one connection he hadn't permanently eliminated. Why bother when the man sat in prison for a very long time?

Now, the man he'd thought would succeed at the assignment had failed, just like the weasel. What was it about this woman? It was as if the hand of God covered her, protecting her.

But he didn't believe in God.

Why wouldn't she die?

His life would be so much easier if she'd never started digging. If she had just stayed in Tennessee. But no. She'd come to Louisiana to testify at some stupid parole hearing and got bound and determined to write her series.

Wait a minute . . . maybe that was his ace in the hole.

Prison had taught him many things. Hadn't that been the way he'd gotten his pardon, by learning the governor's weakness? One of the precious things about time behind bars was learning information, information he had used to his best advantage.

Since the man had failed at his assignment, perhaps he'd jump at the chance to redeem himself. Perhaps that parole hearing would glean some type of advantage over her.

If, as it seemed, no one could kill her, perhaps he could make her wish she'd just die.

"You okay, Hayden?" Bob stuck his head in the office door.

Hayden glanced at the clock—8:15. "Yeah. I'm just glad it's Friday." But they both knew their jobs weren't nine-to-fivers.

"It has been a long week." Bob slumped into a chair. "But we got a break." He tossed a folder on Hayden's desk. It landed with an echoing plop. "That's the report back on all the sub-committees Ellington, Vermillion, Goins, Boyce, and Manchester served on together. Only two."

Hayden opened the file and read aloud. "Health Care Cost Analysis and Containment."

He turned the page. "And Managed Care Review."
His blood rushed.

Bob grinned. "The minutes from all the Managed Care Review subcommittee meetings are in there. Also the recommendations they made to the Insurance Commission."

Hayden turned the page to find the recommendation.

LHCC Health Managed-Care
Review Subcommittee Minutes

Members present: Robert Ellington, Cochairperson Jason Vermillion, Cochairperson Allen Boyce, Curtis Goins, and Lisa Manchester

Staff present: Vanessa Dykes and Carlton Powers, MD

Interested parties: For Your Health Managed Care representatives Matthew Nichols, Evan Coleman, and Mack Thompson

Cochairperson Jason Vermillion began the meeting at 2:05 p.m.

Mr. Vermillion discussed the goals and objectives of the subcommittee and made the suggestion to move forward with recommendations addressing health care cost issues and managed care to present those recommendations to the Louisiana Health-

Care Commission (LHCC) for review, discussion, and action at the next regularly scheduled LHCC meeting.

Mr. Robert Ellington discussed health cost as outlined in the National Conference of State Legislatures Health Cost Containment and Efficiencies Study. He reported a strong indication for control of these high costs in use of managed care. He suggested that the subcommittee pay careful attention to the presentation provided by For Your Health managed health-care group to see if that plan would work best in Louisiana.

Mr. Matthew Nichols, Evan Coleman, and Mack Thompson presented a visual presentation reflecting an average annual savings to companies of 1.8 million dollars by utilization of For Your Health.

Subcommittee members discussed the implementation of partnership with For Your Health for all governmental insuring policies. Following a question and answer session, the representatives from FOR YOUR HEALTH were dismissed from the meeting. Further discussion by subcommittee members followed.

A motion was made by Jason Vermillion to recommend the partnership effective immediately. This motion was seconded by Curtis Goins. Cochairperson Robert Ellington called for a vote on the motion. Motion passed by majority vote: Jason Vermillion, aye; Curtis Goins, aye; Allen Boyce, aye; Carlton Powers, MD, aye; Vanessa Dykes, aye; Lisa Manchester, nay.

Recommendation is made to the LHCC for immediate partnership with For Your Health managed health care for all governmental insuring policies, effective immediately.

Meeting was adjourned by Cochairperson Jason Vermillion at 4:49 p.m.

Well, that was interesting reading. Hayden set down the folder and rubbed his burning eyes. "We have the explanation for why Lisa Manchester was given the money and sent on her way."

"Her single nay vote. It saved her life."

Hayden glanced at the report again. "What's the status of Carlton Powers, MD and Vanessa Dykes?"

"Powers was shot between the eyes twelve years ago. Dykes was stabbed forty-seven times in the chest. Also twelve years ago. Both in Baton Rouge. Both still open cases."

Hayden flipped through his notes, then grabbed a pencil and a blank notepad. "Let's make a timeline." He passed his notes to Bob. "Read me the names of the staff, subcommittee members, and For Your Health team."

Bob read them, one by one.

Hayden scribbled their names on the blank page. "Okay, now tell me how long ago each one died."

Again, Bob read off Hayden's notes.

When done, Hayden studied the page. "So we have three people killed twelve years ago. Same time, Lisa Manchester was given money and told to leave." He tapped the end of the pencil against the notepad. "Then nothing for eight years, at least nothing we've found in connection to any of this. No murders. No money. Nothing. But four years ago, we have murders start up again. Three years ago. Eleven months ago. Five months ago. Now."

"If everything is connected, and I agree they are, why the eight-year silence?"

"Regrouping?" Hayden rubbed his chin. "Gathering funds? Resources?"

"Maybe."

"If someone's motivated enough to kill nine people, starting twelve years ago and keeping up with it, I would think he or she would have resources and funds or means to get what he needed."

"True."

"In jail?"

Bob nodded. "Probably the best guess."

"Let's start there." He handed Bob another notebook and pencil. "Do a search for people incarcerated twelve years ago and released four to six years ago."

Bob wrote on his page.

"And start the search on any claims denied by policies using For Your Health. Start from the time the managed-care system went into effect and go through thirteen years ago." Hayden closed his eyes and pinched the bridge of his nose. "Something was the inciting incident that got this guy mad enough to start a killing spree. I want to know who this guy is."

"I'm on it." Bob stood. "By the way, thought you'd like to know Caleb Montgomery withdrew his charges against Emily."

Now that was a shocker. "Why?"

Bob grinned. "Can't really say for sure, Commissioner, but I believe he was helped to realize that pressing charges just might not be in his best interest."

Hayden shook his head. He didn't even want to know. "Will you please ask Gaston to come here? I need an update on Riley's case."

With a quick nod, Bob headed out the door. Moments later, Edward Gaston entered. "Bob told me you wanted an update on the Baxter case?"

"Where are we? Anything?"

"Ballistics is rushing their report on the bullet we found this morning. Deputy Ingram is back this morning. He's brought in the reports on the bullets used in his homicides to compare as soon as our report is complete."

"Good."

"And, uh, Agent Baxter is still down in the lab. Well, they kicked him out, but he's pacing the hall, so I hear."

"I'll take care of Rafe in a bit." Despite everything, Hayden chuckled. "Anything else?"

"Forensics was in early. They're running everything they pulled from the scene evidence."

"Have you found out who the truck is registered to?"

"Yes, sir. Registered to a Milton Turnkey, who reported it stolen three weeks ago in St. Martinville."

"Pull a report on him to see if anything suspicious pops up. Then call the police over in St. Martinville to see if anyone remembers talking to Mr. Turnkey on this report. Find out if anyone had an impression."

"Yes, sir." Gaston rushed from the office like a man on fire.

There had to be a break soon. Had to be. But for now, he needed to go down to the lab and save the techs.

From Rafe Baxter, Agent at Large.

"I wasn't shot in the leg. I can walk just fine." But Riley let Maddie help her up the steps into Ardy's home.

"Yeah, yeah . . . I've heard it all before." Maddie eased them through the foyer. "Rafe will be here any minute, so be glad it's me and

256

not him. He'd carry you and really irk you."

True. It'd be embarrassing. Especially since they'd already told her Hayden would come for lunch and bring Rafe.

The wonderful aroma of spices filled the air, making Riley's stomach growl. The hospital food, while edible, wasn't Ardy's. Riley estimated she'd probably already gained ten pounds in just over a week of eating the woman's cooking. So much for keeping her figure. That train of thought reminded her of Emily's comment about her and Hayden, which made her cheeks burn.

She chewed her bottom lip as Ardy and Emily greeted her. They helped Maddie and Remington escort her through the living room.

"How are you feeling?" Thomas asked.

"Better." She gritted her teeth as Maddie turned her, jostling her shoulder.

"We're all so relieved you're okay." The man gushed a bit, which left Riley hiding a grin. What *did* Emily see in him? No matter how hard she tried, she couldn't wrap her mind around the idea of wild child Emily with Mr. Prim and Proper.

"Let me find a pillow for you to sit on." Remington shrugged out of her hold on Riley.

This was getting ridiculous. "Y'all, I'm not an invalid. I can get up and around easily enough." She just had this stupid sling and cast to contend with.

"You were shot, remember? You know, with a

gun. Bang-bang." Emily made shooting movements.

"Emily!"

She turned to her mother. "What? She *was* shot." Emily put her hand over her mouth and widened her eyes, but not before giving Riley a quick wink. "Were we supposed to keep it a secret from her? She doesn't know she was shot?"

For a moment, silence filled the house. Then Riley couldn't hold it in any longer. She burst out laughing, followed immediately by Emily and Remington, then finally Maddie and Ardy joined the chorus. Thomas remained staring as if they'd all grown second heads.

"Oh, but it feels good to laugh." Riley shifted to take pressure off her shoulder. "Thanks, Em. I needed it. The hospital was way too stuffy and formal."

"I remember. When I was in the hospital, the staff had no sense of humor. It was downright depressing."

Riley smiled at Emily, noticing the gash on her face had begun the healing process quite nicely.

"I've got lunch all ready. Red beans and rice with hot water cornbread." Ardy eased Riley into the kitchen to a seat at the already-set table. "And chocolate pie for dessert."

"Boy, did we time that perfectly or what?" Hayden grinned as he and Rafe stomped through the back door. He planted a kiss on his mother's temple. "Smells great, Mom."

Ardy's cheeks pinked. "Oh, you. Come on, everyone, let's sit down and eat before it all gets cold."

As soon as everyone was seated and Hayden offered up grace, the bowls were filled and baskets of cornbread slathered in real butter passed. Conversation halted around bites of the delicious meal.

Riley cracked the silence. "Any news on my case?"

Hayden and Rafe both stopped eating. Their gazes locked across the table, an entire conversation passing without anyone else being a party to it.

"Hello? I didn't think that was a difficult question." She straightened, even though the pain medication had begun to wear off and her shoulder was beginning to throb. "It is *my* case, right?"

"Yeah, she was the one shot, remember?" Emily interjected.

Everyone else remained silent, waiting for Hayden's reply.

"Well." He took a sip of his iced tea, then set down the glass. "We retrieved the bullet early this morning. Ballistics did a great job getting their report turned around. It matches the same type of bullet, distance, and angle as two recent homicides in the parish."

She looked from Hayden to Rafe, then back to Hayden. "That means what?"

He gave Rafe a brief nod. "One theory is that the victims are all random. There is no connection to each other, to the shooter, just someone who enjoys killing."

At least it wasn't personal. "But that would mean until he's caught, no one is safe in the parish, right?"

"Very perceptive." Hayden smiled at her, but it was grim, not his usual charm, and her stomach closed off for a very different reason.

"So the police should let the public know to be careful. That's easy enough." Thomas took a sip from his mug. He couldn't abide by cold tea, as he repeatedly informed everyone who asked. A little like a priss, but who was Riley to judge?

"Another theory is that the shooter is a professional in the area." Rafe kept his stare on Riley as if he were trying to bore a hole in her.

"A professional? As in an assassin?" Riley laughed. "Why on earth would someone hire an assassin to kill me? That's the most absurd thing I've ever heard." No one else, not even Emily, laughed with her. "What? Y'all can*not* think that's the case. Come on, be serious."

"This is very serious, Ri." Rafe looked at Hayden, then back at her. "We're running down forensics to identify him, but right now, that's the theory we're working from."

"We? Don't tell me the FBI is involved now. Come on, Rafe . . . that isn't necessary. Hayden and his men can handle this." Great. She'd heard Remington warn Rafe not to step on Hayden's toes, yet here he was, pulling FBI rank.

"Actually, his help is valuable. He can access more databases than I. Or at least do it a whole lot faster." Hayden's smile warmed her from the inside out. "But thanks for being concerned about jurisdictions. Especially now that there are three levels involved: city, parish, and federal."

"Well, don't you feel special?" Emily teased.

"That's a whole lot of attention for one lady." Thomas took another sip of his hot tea. "You should feel extra safe now."

Actually, she felt more scared now than before. Who could hate her so much they'd hire someone to kill her?

"Honey, you've gone twenty shades whiter than my lace tablecloth." Ardy brought everyone's attention right back to Riley.

"I th-think the pain meds have worn off. My shoulder's getting really sore." She blinked several times, trying to absorb everything, but she couldn't. And the pain grew worse. "I think I need to lie down."

Maddie, seated beside her, had her up in a flash.

"Y'all, please finish eating." Riley forced a smile at Ardy. "It was delicious and I'll have my pie when I get up." She let her gaze flit around the table. "Please excuse me."

Maddie helped her to the den and got her settled

before bringing her a glass of water and her medication. "Can I get you anything else?"

"No. Thanks. I'll rest for a little bit and then feel better."

Her sister kissed Riley's forehead. "Okay. I'll be right outside if you need something. Holler."

"Thanks, Mads. I love you."

"Ditto, squirt." She pulled the door closed.

Riley shifted, getting comfortable, but her mind wouldn't relax. What had she done that was so awful someone would try to kill her? And here in Louisiana? Even worse was her next thought . . .

If Hayden and Rafe were right, he'd already tried twice. Would he try again?

CHAPTER TWENTY-ONE

"Praise be to the LORD your God, who has delighted in you and placed you on his throne as king to rule for the LORD your God. Because of the love of your God for Israel and his desire to uphold them forever, he has made you king over them, to maintain justice and righteousness."
2 CHRONICLES 9:8

"Are you hiding out here, wanting to be alone?" Hayden held two cups of coffee as he stepped onto the patio.

Riley smiled. "Just enjoying the cool morning."

"Mom told me how you take it." He set one of the cups in front of her. "Mind if I join you?"

"Sure." She reached for the coffee, noticing it was nicely colored. "Thank you." She took a sip. Perfect, as if she'd made it herself. His attention to details important to her . . . well, it meant a lot to her. A whole lot.

"How're you doing?" He lowered himself to the chair beside her. "I know last night's discussion was a lot to assimilate."

"About an assassin?" She shrugged with her uninjured shoulder. "I still don't think that's the case, but we'll see."

He stayed silent, sipping his coffee.

"And I know I'm safe here."

Hayden chuckled. "Yeah, because Rafe has requested a special reassignment from the bureau and isn't leaving until you do."

She sighed. "I hate when he does that. Goes all big-brother-protective on me."

"Hey, it's a big brother's right. I know." He smiled, but there was seriousness, toughness, behind it.

Her pulse pounded, having nothing to do with the coffee's caffeine. She stared out over the bayou.

"So, if it's not being shot that's bothering you, what has you looking so alone and bereft on a beautiful Saturday morning?"

"Work." For one.

"Your series?"

"I still can't grasp how Jasmine's dad is in prison." She shook her head. "I've read the trial transcript over and over. I can't see how a jury could convict him. Except for the pawnshop owner's testimony." She gestured toward her arm in a sling. "As soon as I can, I'm going to talk with him. See if I can find out something."

"I don't know if that's such a good idea, Riley."

"Why not? It was his testimony that sealed the conviction. The attorney who defended Armand didn't really do an adequate cross-examination." She took a drink of coffee. "I could've done a better job. He didn't even ask for a photo lineup, nothing. A cut-and-dried case of mistaken identity."

"What makes you say that?" There was no argument or defensiveness in Hayden's tone, only curiosity.

"The questions he asked. Or didn't ask." She let out a frustrated breath. "He never asked if the witness wore glasses or contacts and if he had them on the day the item was pawned in his shop, supposedly by Armand. Or how long it had been since he'd had his eye exam and his prescription adjusted."

"What if he already knew the man didn't wear glasses, so it was a moot point?"

She smiled. "That would be interesting if there weren't a copy of the man's driver's license in the file Mrs. Wilson gave me. He's wearing some mighty big, old glasses in that picture." She chuckled. "I won't accuse anyone. I just want to ask the questions that should've been asked earlier."

He nodded. "If you'd like me to go with you, I'll see if I can arrange that. If you'd like me to, that is."

Too bad it was morning so the dark couldn't hide the blush she knew had to be flashing on her face. "I would. Thank you."

A long silence ensued.

Hayden stretched his legs to prop his feet in the chair on the other side of the round iron table. "Anything else on your mind?"

How to voice what she felt? She took another sip of her coffee. "I guess you heard about Simon Lancaster getting parole?"

"Yeah, Remington told me. I'm really sorry, Riley."

"It's not fair."

"I know."

Riley closed her eyes and rested her head against the back of the chair. "Sometimes, I forget what their voices sounded like. I have to think so hard to remember. Each year, the memory fades a bit more." She let out a slow breath. "I can still see them, alive. Smiling. Laughing. But I can't hear their laughter anymore."

His hand took hold of hers and squeezed.

She kept her eyes closed. "I can remember the

smell of Mom's perfume on her skin, which smelled differently than the perfume in the bottle. As a young girl, I never understood that. Mom explained that the scented oils of perfumes changed a slight bit when mixed with the natural oils of the body. Since each person's oil is unique, the mixture of each person's with the perfume would truly make each woman's scent exquisitely her." She smiled. "I always liked that thought. No matter if we all wore the same perfume, we're all still unique."

"That is nice."

She sat up, pulling her hand into her lap. "I remember when I first started dating, Rafe was such a freak of a big brother, traumatizing and threatening any guy who came to pick me up. But Dad figured out why I stopped getting asked out and did something to help me. My prince. He would give Rafe a chore or something that had to be done around the time my date was due to pick me up. Rafe would never disappoint or disobey Dad, so guys eventually started asking me out again."

Hayden chuckled. "Sounds like a good father."

"He was." Yearning for what could never be thickened her throat. "I miss them both so much. It's not fair they were taken from us."

"No, it's not."

"It's wrong that they let him out, Hayden. Wrong."

"I know."

Tears burned her eyes. "It's offensive that they let out someone who confessed to taking our parents from us yet keep Armand Wilson in prison away from his family when he's innocent. Where's the justice in that?"

"I don't know what to tell you, Riley."

"It's not justice." She wiped the tears on her face on the sleeve of her uninjured shoulder. "We don't have a justice system anymore . . . we have a legal system. The two are not the same thing."

"Some might argue with you."

Riley twisted to face him. "What about you? Which camp do you pitch your tent in on the issue?"

He stared out over the bayou for a long moment. "I think it depends."

"On?"

"Each case. I think each situation has to be determined on the facts of that case and that case only."

She snorted. "Spoken like a true cop."

"It's not that. Is our system perfect? No. Is it flawless? No." He ran a hand over his hair. "But by and large, I believe our system is the best we have and we all must do our part to make it work."

That wasn't good enough. "Too diplomatic. How do you really feel about the system, overall?"

He was very quiet. Birds chirped. The wind blew, tickling Riley's nose.

"I think, overall, the system works. I'm sorry, but I do." He held up a hand. "That's not to say I don't believe mistakes are made, ones that should be corrected."

While she understood he needed to believe in the system considering his career, as Rafe did overall, she just wanted someone to commiserate with her.

"I'm not saying the parole board should have let Lancaster out, Riley." His voice came out soft, a breath of a whisper. "I work really hard to make cases against people I know are guilty. We follow the proper chain of evidence, we follow every policy and procedure, code and law—we get everything we can so the prosecutors can present all the evidence at the trial."

She knew all this . . . had helped Corey Patterson pile up the evidence against Simon Lancaster. So did Rafe and Maddie. They all had ripped their hearts out to get whatever was needed for the trial.

"It kills me when we do everything by the book and then the prosecutor messes up and something gets thrown out or they have to dismiss charges. It's not about all our hard work for nothing, but all about a criminal being out on the street."

He stared her straight in the eye. "It makes me even madder when we do everything right and the prosecutors do and the judge and jury, only to have a parole board that doesn't listen to the victims and lets people go free who haven't proven rehabilitation. Yes, it pisses me off."

"Sorry." He glanced out over the bayou, his face red. "I know prisons are overcrowded and that's a major problem. I agree criminals with crimes that had no victims should be punished in another manner. And that people who committed non-violent crimes should possibly go the halfway-house route."

"I can understand all that." She wasn't upset with him any longer. In fact, she needed to share something that had been on her heart for years. "Hayden, how do you balance your beliefs regarding the criminal system and your Christian faith?"

Wasn't that the million-dollar question?

Over the years, Hayden had asked himself that numerous times. Each time he had to mislead a suspect in order to get to the truth. Each time he had to withhold information to play a hunch. Every time he had to sit and swallow a known lie or bite his tongue to keep silent.

"I don't mean to get into a deeply personal issue, it's just . . ."

He knew. And understood. "You want to know about your feelings toward Lancaster in general, not just his parole?"

She nodded. "I know, as a Christian, I'm supposed to forgive my enemies. Forgive those who have sinned against me. So I know I'm supposed to forgive Simon Lancaster." She rolled those penetrating blue eyes of hers. "And I've tried. I promise I have. But I can't."

Hayden searched for the words. *Lord, guide my tongue to get the point You want made.* "Are you asking me if that's okay? Because I can't give you permission to stay angry at someone."

"I'm not asking for permission." But her tone said otherwise. "I don't . . . I guess . . ." She shook her head. "I just can't make myself forgive him. No matter how much I know it's the right thing to do. No matter that I know forgiveness is for me and not him. No matter how much I want this to stop eating at me. I still can't. Not in my heart."

"I understand."

She shifted, adjusting her sling. "Do you?"

"Yeah, I do." He stared over the water, wondering where to start. "I don't know if Rafe or Remington said anything to you about me in regards to how they met." He glanced at her.

She shook her head.

"Well, long story short, because of Rafe's investigation, I had to confront my mother about my biological father. All my life, I'd assumed my father was my mother's husband, her only husband. I mean, that's a normal assumption most people would make, right?"

Riley nodded, her eyes a bit wider.

"So I asked her. Come to find out, I'd been

wrong. My father was actually Remington's godfather, Judge Daniel Tate, who had been murdered. Remington had witnessed the murder, knew the killers were FBI, so she went into hiding. She'd found my name and address in Daniel's safe, so she came to Hopewell. After she changed her name to Bella Miller, of course." He smiled at the shocked expression on Riley's face. "But that's a whole other story. Needless to say, Mom confessed that she'd had a . . . fling before she married the man I thought was my father." It still raked against him to use the word *fling*. It sounded so cheap. Meaningless.

"And she got pregnant?"

"According to her, she loved Daniel, and my father. She came back home and married my father, then found out she was pregnant." The back of his neck burned. "She knew Daniel was my father."

"Did she tell Daniel?" Riley's eyes were wider still.

"Yes. He agreed to let her husband raise me as his own, which is what happened. She never told my father, the man I thought was my father." He swallowed hard. "Or me. Until I had to ask."

"Wow." She blinked, not focusing.

"I know. I felt like someone had punched me in the gut, multiple times." Even now, several months later. "And I was angry. So angry. At Mom. At Daniel Tate. At Remington."

"Remington?"

"Yeah. She knew when she came to Hopewell who I was. She talked with my mother about it."

"Why?"

"I'm still not real sure how that all came to pass, but it's irrelevant now. Either way, all I wanted to do was hit something. Hard. Really hard. Yell at how unfair it was. How they'd hurt me. They'd lied. They'd kept secrets. They'd schemed so I wouldn't know who I really was." Hayden forced his breathing to regulate. "Even now, I still get upset."

"So you *do* understand. You haven't forgiven them entirely."

"No, I've forgiven them. But just because you forgive someone, doesn't mean the pain automatically goes away. Betrayal still hurts, even if you know the reason and semi-understand. I still have trouble trusting. Women. Close to me. Grief still hurts, even if you know the person is with God. Does that make sense?" But sitting here . . . talking with Riley . . . he felt like he'd known her forever.

And he trusted her.

Riley sat a little straighter in the patio chair. A cool breeze lifted strands of her light brown hair. "Kind of."

"One night I was reading Scripture and the Holy Spirit pressed upon me the need to pray for God to give me the grace to forgive."

She wrinkled her nose, looking absolutely adorable. It tugged at his gut. Hard. He shook off the attraction, knowing he needed to help her. "I realized that God wanted my obedience more than He wanted me to forgive. By wanting to forgive, that's Christ in me. By admitting I'm human and not able to get past my fleshy wants, that's confession. By praying for God to remove my anger and open my heart to forgiveness, that's obedience."

She sat very still, staring at him with such openness and honesty it almost hurt.

"Does that make sense?"

"In a roundabout way, yeah, it does." She smiled. "I've been trying to make myself forgive Simon Lancaster of my own strength, when I can't."

"And you were never supposed to be able to do anything alone. Everything we do is dependent on God."

"So I've been wasting all my efforts on wanting to do what's right, without being able to do so."

"Possibly." He smiled, wanting so much to pull her into his arms and kiss those lips of hers. "At least, that's what I believe."

"Interesting. I never thought about it that way. I've been trying to forgive because Scripture tells me to, but never able to get over my grief and anger."

"Have you ever prayed for God to put the ability to forgive in your heart?"

She shook her head.

"Before you do, examine yourself and make sure you truly do want to forgive, that you aren't just playing lip service because you think it's what God wants to hear."

"Because He already knows what's in my heart." She nodded. "Thanks. You really helped me. I appreciate it."

He ducked his head as heat slid up the back of his neck again. "Glad to help. I enjoy talking with you." More and more, as time went on. "So much so, why don't I take you to lunch today?" Where had *that* come from? She'd just gotten out of the hospital, for pity's sake. She didn't want to go anywhere.

But she smiled, the slow grin that made his heart respond. "I'd like that. I think getting out would be awesome." Then her face fell. "But Maddie came all this way to see me, so I can't just bail on her."

"I understand." He stood and helped her stand.

"But"—Riley looked up at him from beneath her lowered lashes—"I'm sure she'll be leaving this evening since she has to teach at Sunday school tomorrow."

"So, how about going out to supper with me?"

"I'd love to."

"Where would you like to go?"

The world tilted with the light in her eyes. "Surprise me."

Oh, surprise her he would.

Chapter Twenty-Two

"When all Israel heard the verdict the king
had given, they held the king in awe,
because they saw that he had
wisdom from God to administer justice."
1 KINGS 3:28

Hayden had slipped into the office so he didn't act like a wuss. He sure didn't want Riley see him mooning around the house, killing time until their date tonight.

He flipped through all the reports on his desk—nothing new since he'd checked late last night. Weekends were the worst: Labs and units ran on skeleton crews, and officers couldn't do a lot of the legwork. It made everyone antsy.

The sticky note he'd written to remind him to call Angola's warden sat on the edge of the desk. He'd intended to do a little research on Jasmine's dad but other things cropped up. Maybe if he could recall why Armand Wilson's name sounded familiar, he could help Riley in some way.

Accessing his computer, he logged into the proper database, then typed in Armand's full name and waited.

The computer beeped, pulling his attention to the report loaded on the monitor. Horror filled him as he read the details. Why the name sounded familiar rushed over him. Like yesterday, he recalled even the details not listed.

Private collectors who'd been acquaintances for some time each owned priceless artifacts from the Confederacy during the Civil War. Being members of a private and by-invitation-only group, they banded items of their personal collections together for special exhibits.

His buddy Lewis Pine had been a member of the group. Lewis had, over the years, told the story of his family's famous heirloom—a sword owned by General Pierre Gustave Toutant Beauregard of the Confederate Army. The sword was, Lewis claimed, passed down from father to son, genera-tion to generation, until current day. Apparently Lewis was a direct descendant of the notorious general.

Lewis had allowed the sword of Beauregard to be included in the special collection on display at the Louisiana State Museum in Baton Rouge to commemorate the anniversary of the start of the War between the States. The sword had been stolen along with other artifacts, but it had never surfaced. While the sword had been insured for over fifty thousand dollars, the sentimental and personal value to the Pine family was priceless.

Hayden stared at the screen, willing the Armand Wilson listed as one of the robbers to not be the same Armand Wilson who Riley had determined was innocent. No matter how he read the report or prayed the letters would reshuffle, the men were one and the same.

How could he help Riley now? Lewis was his friend and he'd been the victim of a crime. Surely Riley would understand his position. Especially after receiving the devastating news about Lancaster being awarded his parole.

Yet Hayden knew Riley wouldn't accept that. She'd proclaim Wilson's innocence. So to defend his friend's loss, Hayden needed to do a little investigating on his own.

He called his old friend, asked if he could come over, and received the okay from an eager Lewis.

The midday sun beat down on the hood of the cruiser. Hayden slipped on his sunglasses against the glare that contrasted against the brisk chill of the April air. A nice reprieve from the storms of late, but also a change from the usually higher temperatures for the time of year. Could that be an indication of a milder summer? He sure hoped so.

Lewis answered the door with a smile. "Hey there. It's been way too long."

"I know." Hayden gripped his hand and shook. "We need to get back to fishing more often."

"I hear ya, man." He waved Hayden inside. "Come on in. I have to admit, you've got my curiosity up." He shut the door and gestured to the comfortable leather couch in the middle of the living room.

Like Hayden, Lewis hadn't married. His living space was similar to that of most bachelors: comfortable, if ugly, furniture; table only used to set plates and glasses on; large flat screen; and kickin' surround-sound system.

Hayden sank into the soft leather. It absorbed him, wrapping around him like a comfortable blanket. "Sorry I haven't called more often. Things have been more than a little crazy." He shook his head. While true, it wasn't the reason he hadn't called in a while. Truth was, he hadn't been up to hanging out with buddies.

Where had that come from? He liked his friends. Enjoyed hunting and fishing and watching sports with them. But now that he let the thought enter his conscious, he realized it was true. While entertaining for a spell, hanging out with buddies wasn't something he really wanted anymore. If full disclosure rang true, he'd admit that after seeing Remington and Rafe's happiness together, he wanted that for himself.

Someone who he got and who got him. Someone who listened and shared. Someone to lift him when he needed it and let him do the same for her. Someone to call his own.

Someone he could trust.

The image of Riley slammed into the forefront of his mind. Somehow, someway, she'd slipped under his defenses. Under his skin. Into his heart.

"Hayden?" Lewis snapped his fingers in front of his face. "Where'd you go?"

Heat flamed up the back of his neck as he offered a sheepish smile. "Sorry. Lost in thought."

"Obviously." Lewis leaned back into the worn couch. "So, tell me what's up."

"It's about your family's sword."

"Beauregard's sabre." Lewis's eyes lit up. "Have you found it, after all these years?"

Hayden shook his head. "I'm sorry, no."

"Then what's this about?"

"I need you to tell me everything you can remember about the robbery. What the sheriff and prosecutor's office told you. I need to know."

"Why?"

Here was the booger-bear. "A friend of mine is looking into the case and she's asked me for help."

"She?"

"Yes, a lady friend."

"Ah, I see." Lewis chuckled.

"No, it's not like that." Well, he had taken her out once and was taking her out again tonight. "Not exactly."

His friend laughed even more. "Man, you're really tied up over this chick, aren't you?"

He shrugged. "Too early to tell. So, will you help me?"

"Help-you-help-her kind of thing?" He snorted. "Starting to sound like some cheesy nineties movie."

"Yeah, yeah, yeah." Hayden threw a mock punch at Lewis's arm. "Just help me out, will ya?"

Lewis stared at him. "Okay. Let me give you a little background. About ten years ago, me and some others who had Confederate artifacts kept running into each other at certain events. We exchanged contact information and kept each other in the loop about upcoming events, auctions, displays . . . stuff like that. After several months, we realized we could combine our individual holdings and create a really unique display."

"Who were they?"

"Sarah Nance, Judith Osborn, Darryl Thayer, and me." Lewis waited until Hayden finished writing before he continued. "Anyway, we called around and found that quite a few museums and galleries were interested in hosting our collection."

"Were y'all going to get paid for that?"

Lewis gave him an incredulous look. "What do you think, man? This was a quick-and-easy way to combine what we all loved with a way of making a little side money."

Made sense. "Go on."

"So, we printed up some advertising flyers and sent them out. Within a couple of months, we ended up having so many bookings that both Sarah and Judith quit their part-time jobs. Their husbands were mighty glad at that. The money was good and we enjoyed ourselves."

"Sounds like heaven."

"For us, it truly was. In six years, we had over five hundred amazing showings." Lewis pointed at the seventy-inch flat screen mounted on the wall. "Paid for all the little extras my job didn't allow for, like that baby."

"Sweet deal."

"It was. The arrangement was pretty awesome too. The four of us split the cost of our own security, which we hired in each location since our exhibit crossed several state lines and each state has its own laws regarding security personnel. We took turns traveling with the collection, so the expenses were pretty much even. We each had to carry our own insurance on our items."

"So everyone had good policies?"

"You're jumping ahead, Hayden."

"Sorry." He grinned, twirling his pencil. "Please, proceed."

"Five hundred showings and never once did we have any problems. Not even so much as the packing company we hired having an incident."

"That's amazing."

"Yep." Lewis nodded. "Until the state museum exhibit."

Hayden hunched over, gripping the pencil tighter. "Tell me about that."

"As if I wasn't? She must be some dame." Lewis grinned and propped his feet up on the battered ottoman. "We all like the museum showing because it's local so we can all attend. It'd been the first time we would all be together at an exhibit in over two years."

Hayden scribbled as fast as he could as Lewis continued.

"Because of that and the remembrance ceremony of the start of the War between the States, there was quite a bit of publicity. That, and we had decided to take a break from showings. Sarah was pregnant, so she needed to be pulled out of the travel loop. Darryl was engaged and his wife-to-be wasn't too keen on him being committed to traveling away from her so much. And me and Judith were just a little tired of the constant scheduling and such that goes into making sure everything goes off without a hitch."

"Six years is a bit long."

Lewis shrugged. "We weren't quitting, understand, just taking a break. We'd all discussed that probably Judith and I would work out some kind of schedule for us to take over all the traveling, with us getting more of the showing fees."

"So, the Louisiana State Museum exhibit would be the last, at least for a while, right?"

"Yeah. They planned a big dinner and fundraiser for the museum, using the exhibit as the main attraction. And it worked. They told me they received over two hundred thousand that night in donations." Lewis gave a wry smile. "I shoulda asked for a percentage of the donations instead of a flat fee."

Hayden nodded.

"Anyway, the big night was nice. Black tie, the elite of the elite out in sparkle and glitz, the whole deal. Great meal, funny emcee. Plenty of wine flowing. Even had one of those auctioneers auctioning off some tables and chairs that were donated, supposedly from the Confederate era."

"Sounds like a time."

"It was. Everything ended around two o'clock on Sunday morning. That was okay because the museum was closed on Sunday and that Monday. We were supposed to take down the exhibit and collect our artifacts Monday morning at eleven." He shook his head. "The museum was broken into on Sunday night."

"Was the whole collection stolen?"

"No. My sabre, of course." Lewis ran a hand over his jeans. "Judith's revolver. Darryl's money and button collection. That's all that was taken. The museum had some of its items taken too."

"I know some of the items were recovered."

"Yeah. Judith's revolver. My sabre and Darryl's collection weren't."

"Both your insurance companies paid?"

Lewis frowned. "Yeah, but don't get any ideas. We'll never get exhibit fees again. And I've lost a family heirloom." Lewis plopped his feet to the floor. "My father hasn't spoken to me since it was stolen. He'd all but demanded I not put it in the collection, but I wouldn't listen."

Hayden closed his notebook and shoved it into his pocket. "I'm sorry."

"Maybe if I wouldn't have been so greedy, I'd have listened to him. Now, we don't have that part of our history anymore." He shook his head. "My grandfather was a genealogist. It's a good thing he wasn't alive to learn the sabre was stolen. It would've killed him."

"I have to say, Riley, I agree with Emily. I've never seen Hayden so taken with a woman before." Remington batted her eyes.

Riley's cheeks burned as if they were on fire. "He's just taking me out to supper, y'all. It's just a meal." But excitement had her stomach spinning like a class-four hurricane.

"I think you should wear something sexy and knock his socks off." Emily giggled. "Sorry, that's a bad idea because I know what his feet smell like." She made retching sounds.

"Gee, thanks for that mental image." Remington laughed.

"Y'all, stop. I'll wear jeans and whatever shirt matches this oh-so-becoming sling. My problem is just that most of what I have with me is either extremely dressy or is a pullover T-shirt. Sexy's not exactly an option at the moment." Riley couldn't contain the anticipation spreading in her chest. All this talk made her feel the need to analyze her feelings toward Hayden.

And she really didn't want to get that in-depth just yet. Not when she would be leaving soon and had no idea if she'd ever see Hayden again.

The thought left her feeling lost, which scared her spitless.

"I can't believe you're going on a date just days after getting shot," Maddie murmured from her seat on the couch.

Riley opened her mouth, then shut it. She loved her sister dearly, but Maddie had always been a bit too serious. Even more so once Mom and Dad died. Maybe because she had to step in as the maternal figure, although Riley had never asked her to do that. Nor had she wanted it.

"I have an amazing blouse that will really make the blue of your eyes pop." Emily snapped her fingers. "And it's button down, so it will make the whole sling thing easy."

"Do you mind me borrowing it?"

"Of course I don't mind. I wouldn't have offered otherwise." Emily stood. "Matter of fact, I don't think I packed it up when I got my things, so it's still here in the closet. I'll be right back." She left, almost skipping down the hall.

Remington shook her head. "I have to say, I'm pleasantly surprised to see you two getting along so well. Especially after the rocky start y'all had."

Maddie's protectiveness flared. "What do you mean, *rocky start?*"

Riley needed to defuse and fast. "Let's just say Emily had a bite from the green-eyed monster regarding how Ardy and I related to one another. But she and I had a talk and everything's fine. We're good."

No one had time to respond as Emily sprinted back into the living room, carrying a hanger with a beautiful blouse. The shirt's Caribbean blue shimmered as the light caught the satiny blend.

"It's a small, so should fit with no problem." Emily held out the hanger, twisting it to show off the ruffles on the collar.

It was perfect. Absolutely perfect. "Oh, Emily, it's beautiful. Are you sure you don't mind me borrowing it? It looks brand new."

"I don't even remember why I got it, but it'll look beautiful on you."

"It will." Even Maddie had no argument.

"Where's he taking you?" Remington asked.

Riley shook her head. "I told him to surprise me."

Emily and Remington both started chuckling.

"What?" Had she done something wrong?

"Girl, you're apt to get a sandwich and chips from the local sports pub." Remington wagged her finger.

"Why would you tell a man to surprise you,

huh?" Emily crossed her arms over her chest. "That's just inviting trouble."

"Maybe you'd better eat before you leave."

Riley frowned at Remington. "Hey, that's mean. He took me to Eight Sisters last time. It was wonderful." Riley had loved that evening . . . if only it hadn't ended so early. She stared at Emily. If only she was blunt enough to ask Emily about how she'd really gotten the gash. Unfortunately, Maddie had gotten the bluntness gene.

Actually, there was a way to borrow the gene. "Emily, how's your face feeling?"

"That sounds so ominous, doesn't it?" Emily grinned, then perched on the arm of the couch. "It's fine. The doctor says there will barely be a sign after it finishes healing."

Maddie sat up straight on the couch. "What happened to your face?"

Emily cocked her head. "I had an accident and got cut with glass."

"Come on, it's just us girls here. No Hayden, no Ardy. What really happened?" Riley took advantage of her sister's opening the door.

"Seriously, it was an . . ." Emily's face fell. "Honestly, it was an accident, but not exactly the way I told Hayden."

"What happened?" Remington's tone was as soft and silky as the blue blouse.

Emily stared at the floor. "I don't want Hayden to know. Or Mom."

"What?" Riley couldn't contain her curiosity, but she wouldn't promise not to say anything either. That rule was basic journalism 101.

"I was using the glass bottoms of old Coke bottles, that much is true. I was goofing around . . . making fun of Thomas. He usually is so calm. But that night, I don't know." Emily shrugged. "He'd had a bad day at work, so he said. I was trying to cheer him up. Yeah, and maybe I was teasing a little on the mean side."

Riley could understand Emily's teasing being considered a bit mean. Been there, experienced that.

"So he got mad?" Remington prompted.

Emily nodded. "It was like he snapped or something. One minute I'm laughing and holding the glass bottoms up to my eyes like his glasses, and the next thing I know, he slapped me, hitting the glass when he did."

"Oh, Emily." Maddie moved closer to the arm of the couch and patted Emily's knee. "That's awful."

Riley blinked several times. "I can't believe it. I mean, I'm not saying you're lying, but, wow."

"It's so shocking." Remington leaned forward from her perch on the love seat and patted Emily's other knee. "Especially because Thomas comes across as . . . uh . . . well . . . um—"

"Effeminate?" Riley finished, then chewed her bottom lip. "Sorry, Em, but that's just the way he comes across, all prim and proper."

"I know. He does. And I'd just learned recently that he has a prosthesis on his lower left leg. Cancer as a teenager. So maybe that's why he took my teasing so hard. Because I was using a British accent and talking in what I call his stuffy tone, demanding my afternoon cup of hot tea." She cleared her throat. "He didn't mean to hurt me. He apologized profusely, wanted to take me to the emergency room himself."

"But why?" Riley asked. "Why didn't you let him? Then you wouldn't have had to mislead Hayden, your mom, everyone."

"Because you were embarrassed?"

Emily lifted her head, then nodded at Remington. "How'd you know?"

"I do have that psychology degree, you know." Remington sat back on the love seat. "But surely you know that just because he seemed to feel bad afterward, apologized, and swore never to do anything like that again, chances are likely that he will, right?"

"It's not like that." Emily lifted her hand to ward off the arguments everyone started to voice. "I mean, I know that. Give me some credit. I've even started seeing other people. From the very limited options here in Hopewell."

"That's a start," Remington said.

"Yes." Emily sniffed and shifted to face Riley. "Now, the big question."

Riley stiffened. Was Emily going to ask her to keep the secret from Hayden? She wouldn't volunteer the information, but if he asked, she couldn't and wouldn't lie to him. "What's that?"

"Since you can't raise one of your arms, who's going to fix your hair for tonight's hot date?"

CHAPTER TWENTY-THREE

"Arise, LORD, in your anger;
rise up against the rage of my enemies.
Awake, my God; decree justice."
PSALM 7:6

She stole his breath.

Hayden stood in the foyer of his childhood home and felt the earth move under the wood floors he'd helped his father lay.

Riley Baxter held his ability to speak hostage by her sheer beauty and grace. Hayden had never seen a woman so beautiful. The overhead light shimmered on her hair, picking up highlights of gold. Her eyes, so incredibly blue, looked even deeper with that liquid-looking shirt. But it was her smile that held him completely spellbound.

"Son, have you lost all the manners I taught you?" His mother chuckled, nudging him into the house so she could shut the front door.

"You look . . . *beamazing*."

"*Beamazing?* I'm pretty sure that's not a word." Emily grinned from the couch.

"It's a mix of *beautiful* and *amazing,* and shut up, Em."

Riley smiled wider, causing his stomach to feel as if it'd been caught in a vise. "Ignore all of them. They've had their fun at my expense all afternoon."

"Yeah, but we're bored picking on you. It's Hay's turn." Emily laughed.

"Emily, stop annoying your brother. Even though it has been a while since you've been on a date, son."

Gee, thanks, Mom. "Okay, that's it." He held out his arm to Riley. "Are you ready to escape these lunatics?"

"Yes, thank you."

"Where are y'all going?" Remington interjected.

At least Rafe wasn't here to interrogate him as well. He'd made sure Rafe had some reports to inspect at the station before he saw Maddie and Remington off in the morning. "Out to eat."

"Yeah, but where?" Emily probed.

"It's a surprise and none of your business." What was this, the Spanish Inquisition? He smiled down at Riley. "Are you ready? I don't want us to be late."

She nodded at him, then stuck her tongue out at Emily. He had to admire that flash of spunk.

291

Once he'd gotten her settled in the passenger seat and slipped behind the steering wheel, he adjusted the thermostat. A chilly evening but not cold. The weather needed to hold. "I have a confession."

She lifted a single eyebrow. "What's that?"

"We don't have reservations."

"Oh. We don't?" Her face told it all—that his sister and Remington had scared her with some outlandish tales.

Now he wondered if he'd made the right decision. Should he have taken her to some fancy-schmancy restaurant in Baton Rouge and impressed her? Second-guesses tied his gut into knots. "I had something a little more private in mind, unless you'd rather go to a restaurant."

"Whatever you want is fine with me. I trust you."

His heart pounded against his ribs. And honestly, he trusted her. Which was truly saying something. He smiled and drove toward the Hopewell Visitor Center located out off the river.

Once a bed and breakfast, the center's main building had been sold and businesses it held changed many times: restaurant, day spa, gift shop, and now a visitor's center. It'd been renovated two years ago, downplaying the building itself and changing to make it more a part of the beautiful landscape. Man-made waterfalls, lush greenery, and wooden pathways wound around the building as unobtrusively as possible.

Normally, the center's grounds were closed and the gates locked in the evenings, but the manager had appreciated Hayden's willingness to scare his rebelling teenage son on the dangers of illegal drag racing, so he'd agreed to allow Hayden in after hours.

Hayden had spent the last hour making sure everything was set up just right. He remembered his mother's stories of romantic gestures, so he did his best. He'd taken Japanese lanterns and placed them all around the base of the largest waterfall, where he'd laid out an old quilt.

On the way to pick Riley up, he'd stopped and loaded the picnic basket he'd ordered filled with items from the local deli. Fried chicken, potato salad, batter buns, and strawberry shortcake. All could be eaten cold. All delicious.

"Has Emily been a pain anymore?"

"No. Not at all. She actually loaned me this blouse."

"It's nice." Nice? What kind of lame small talk was that?

He kept his mouth shut and pulled into the center's parking lot. She raised her brows as he killed the engine but asked no questions. He had to give her points for that. He rushed around to her side of the car and opened the door for her, grabbed the picnic basket from the trunk, then led her down the private path to the area he'd set up. Nerves bunched in his every muscle.

Her eyes widened as she took in the view before her. "How? Oh my, it's beautiful."

Relief flooded him as he led her to the quilt and helped her sit. "I know how rich Mom's cooking is. I thought perhaps you'd welcome something a little less spicy."

"You shouldn't have gone to so much trouble, but this is perfect." She smiled as her gaze darted about the area. "It's just breathtaking. How did you manage all this?"

He chuckled as he handed her a bottled water. "Believe it or not, men actually can make arrangements."

"I didn't mean it like that." She smiled and took a sip. "This is lovely. Thank you."

He opened the basket and set out the food. After a quick blessing, they ate, interjecting bits and pieces of their day. He could sit on the quilt and listen to Riley talk all day long and never get tired of it. Which brought up a whole other subject he needed to tackle . . .

"Riley, I think we both can feel this . . . this . . . whatever between us." His heart felt like it would explode.

She blushed. "I know what you're talking about."

"I just want you to know, I'm serious." He cleared his throat against the lump. "About you. About us. About seeing where this goes."

She let out a long, slow breath. "I feel the same way. But, Hayden, I live in Tennessee. You live in Louisiana. It's impossible."

The main concern he'd had himself over the past couple of days. "And Rafe and Remington figured the same thing too." He leaned forward, tucking that ever-present loose lock of hair behind her ear. "I just want us to give it a chance. We'll figure out the details later."

Her cell phone chimed.

"Sorry." She glanced at the screen, then pressed a button and slipped the phone into her purse. "Text message from my editor."

The moment had passed. Hayden would let it go. For now.

He packed up the leftovers, Riley watching and smiling. "That was wonderful. Just perfect. Thank you." She stretched her legs out in front of her. "I haven't felt this relaxed in days."

"I'm glad. You probably needed it more than you realize."

"Yeah. Especially since I need to hit the ground running on my next article. I'll start calling people tomorrow."

He scooted next to Riley and stretched his legs out as well. He took her right hand. "I need to tell you something, and I don't want you to get angry with me."

Caution flashed in her eyes like hazard lights. "What?"

"I did a little digging on Armand Wilson today. I wanted to help you with the series."

"Why would I be mad about that?" She squeezed his hand. "I've asked you to help, so I invited you into my work. I'm not upset about that."

Maybe he shouldn't have had that second piece of strawberry shortcake. "The thing is, when I searched his name, I recalled the case."

She wrinkled her brow. "You didn't handle the case. I've read the file and your name isn't there. It happened in Baton Rouge."

He nodded. "The reason I recall the case is that one of the victims is a friend of mine. Lewis Pine. He owned a sword—excuse me, a sabre—owned by General Beauregard. It was a family heirloom and had been in his family since the Civil War."

She blinked, but her lips were pressed together tightly.

"They never recovered his sabre, or some artifacts of a friend of his. He'll never be able to get back something that meant so much to his family."

"But that doesn't mean Armand was involved."

"Actually . . . let me explain. The other friend of Lewis's who lost his artifact? His name is Darryl and his brother, Cam, was the pawnshop owner."

"That still doesn't mean it was Armand."

"According to both Lewis and Darryl, Cam

was 100 percent positive the guy who came in and tried to pawn Judith Osborn's revolver was Armand."

"How would he know? He saw him for maybe, what?—ten minutes?"

"He knew Armand, Riley. Cam Thayer had been at the big event at the museum that week-end. He'd bid and bought two antique chairs in the fund-raiser. He recognized Armand from his security detail."

She shook her head. "It's a mistake. I'll talk to this guy. He's wrong."

"Riley . . ."

She shoved to her feet. "I don't want to talk about this anymore. I'll prove them wrong." She popped her right fist on her hip and jutted out her chin. "I'll prove *you* wrong."

This changed nothing.

She couldn't believe Hayden had ruined a romantically perfect evening like this. Riley stomped toward the car, ignoring him as he followed.

Beautiful weather. Gorgeous setting. Apparent that he went to quite a bit of trouble to make the evening special. Great food. And then . . . then he had to go and destroy everything by all but coming out and stating Armand Wilson was guilty.

She couldn't accept that. Wouldn't.

Reaching the car, she didn't say a word, just

waited for him to unlock and open the door for her.

He knew how much she believed in Armand's innocence. If he really wanted to help, why hadn't he gone and talked with this Cam Thayer himself? Really dug for the truth? That's why Armand was in prison in the first place: Someone was too lazy to go out and actually do some poking around.

The trunk slammed, then Hayden got into the car. He started it, cracked the windows, but didn't put it in gear.

Riley still wouldn't speak, although she felt his stare burning into her. This was important to her —he was important to her—now everything was all messed up. Confusing.

"Look, I know you're mad and I'm sorry, but I won't apologize for sharing the information with you. I know these guys. They wouldn't be party to putting an innocent man in prison." He let out a heavy sigh. "This isn't easy for me. Considering my profession, I usually don't give out information."

She didn't want to hear his generosity was because of her. Riley chewed her bottom lip, not daring to look at him. She needed to say something. Anything. But she didn't trust herself not to lash out. She needed Armand to be innocent. Believed it to the core of her being. But had her need for a front-page story blinded her to the truth? Was Hayden right? Could Armand actually be guilty? Could he have been involved?

Her thoughts spun as she felt his gaze on her, never wavering, reflecting the strength of the man she'd give her heart to. Who was she kidding? He already held it.

After what seemed like an eternity, he put the car in reverse and backed out of the center's parking lot.

The drive back to Ardy's was downright cold, and Riley knew it had nothing to do with the fresh air seeping through the cracked windows. Maybe she'd judged too quickly and too harshly.

When it came to Hayden Simpson, she just didn't know anymore. Everything about him confused her. Excited her. Scared her to feel such intense emotions.

He pulled into the driveway and rushed to open her door. She remained frozen in her seat. It would be rude not to let him, and she'd already been rude enough.

Hayden seemed a bit shocked that she'd waited on him. He held out his hand to help her from the car.

Just his touch sent her reeling. The man had a killer effect on her.

He shut the car door, then put his arms on either side of her. Not touching, but close enough that she could feel the heat from his arms on hers.

Her back pressed against the cruiser. He leaned in, almost resting his forehead against hers. She could feel his breath on her skin. "There's a real fine line between wanting to help and wanting to be right, and today, I tripped over that line. Will you forgive me? Please?"

How could she resist that? Her stomach plunged.

His gaze locked on to her mouth. Hayden leaned forward, pressing his lips to hers.

Pulling her to him, Hayden wrapped his arms around her, gentle as a hummingbird's wings.

With such slowness, he deepened the kiss. It was soft and sweet, with just a hint of the emotion that lay under the surface of both of them.

When he pulled back, Riley's breathing came in bursts—ragged and haggard. His breathing was rapid as well. He'd been just as affected by the kiss. He rested his forehead against hers and stared deep into her eyes.

She couldn't move. Her body refused to obey even the simplest of commands. No man, not Garrison nor Damon, had ever literally made her knees go weak. Not by just a single kiss.

It was anything but *just* a kiss.

"Ri, please forgive me." His whisper caressed her cheek.

As if she wouldn't now? She chewed her bottom lip and nodded.

He gave her a quick kiss, a squeeze of a hug on her uninjured side, then released her. Apparently she didn't know how to stand by herself anymore because she swayed. Hayden steadied her, then left his hand under her elbow.

She let him lead her up the steps, turned to kiss him good night—the door shot open.

Rafe stood in the doorway, his face a grimace or controlled eruption, Riley couldn't tell. But that expression meant one thing only—her brother was on the warpath.

CHAPTER TWENTY-FOUR

"And I saw something else under the sun: In the place of judgment—wickedness was there, in the place of justice—wickedness was there."
ECCLESIASTES 3:16

Oswald threw the glass against the door to his office. The amber liquid slid down the stained wood to drip onto the shattered Waterford crystal.

He didn't care. All he cared about was that his world was falling apart around him, and he was powerless to do a thing to stop it.

"Arrrgggghhhh!" He cleared his desk with a forceful shove. Computer, telephone, and all crashed to the wood floor. Pens and pencils, once held in a leather-bound canister, rolled across the floor.

Heat twisted in his gut. Hot. Boiling. Angry.

He couldn't catch his breath. He fell to the

floor, hunched over, panting. Like a dog. A mangy cur.

Oswald once had a dog. A yellow lab. His father had brought him home as an early birthday present. His mother had been furious, but his dad had overruled her objections. His son, he'd said, needed a dog. Needed a best friend. He'd named the dog Brutus.

For the first time in over a dozen years, he opened the vault of his memories of his father. He rolled to his side, laying his head on the floor of his office.

He didn't remember one set thing about his father. It was more scattered images. His dad teaching him to ride a bike. His father laughing while they built the tree house in the backyard— the yard without a tree. Dad throwing him a baseball and hugging him when he couldn't catch it.

He'd followed Dad around from the time he could walk. To his shop, to auctions, to sales. Dad never told him that he was too young. He'd always taken the time to explain the process to Oswald. Answered a million questions with patience and a smile.

Attending every meet, even the ones miles from school. So proud. Bragged to everyone about his son, the track star. When he got notice of the track scholarship from LSU, Dad nearly took out an ad in the paper to let everyone know.

Then the tears running down his father's face

in the hospital when the doctors delivered the diagnosis. The prognosis. The treatment plan.

And then later, Dad just leaving.

No, he wouldn't remember those bad times. He wanted to remember the good times. Back before his father was run off by those bureaucratic spawns of the devil. Back before his life was ripped away from him.

Oswald groaned as the painful images refused to be denied.

The horrid hospital bed. The stench of disinfectant and decaying limbs. The therapy after the surgery. The pain.

He rolled onto his back, his face wet with tears. Seventeen was too young for a boy to lose . . . everything.

Senseless.

His mother . . . she'd tried, at first, but after losing her husband and the son he'd once been, she let herself descend into a dark depression. She'd drawn out the pain and misery for her own selfish purposes. Because she was afraid of being alone. Afraid of standing on her own two feet.

Ironic.

The weakling. Her depression started her downward spiral. First antidepressants. Then when those weren't enough to mask the pain of being alone, homeless, and broke, she would take anything she could get her hands on, including his pain medication. Within thirty days, she wasn't only weak, but a wasted excuse of an addict.

His mother had gone from Susie Homemaker to Debbie Doper in sixty days from the time of his father's abandonment.

Oswald endured his own drug addiction nightmare.

At least he had a legitimate reason: Ewing's sarcoma.

His mother's excuse was stupidity. And laziness. Two traits Oswald despised.

He'd learned to hate them even more in prison. The only reason he'd been caught was because he'd been stupid and lazy. But unlike his mother, he'd learned from his mistakes.

Oswald learned he had to cast off his past. He had to start over as a new man, complete with a new name. To do that, he'd had to walk on the even dirtier side of the law.

The side that reinforced what he'd learned the hard way at seventeen when his own life was ripped from him: Politicians and government bureaucrats were the worst mankind had to offer.

Spawns of Satan, not worthy to live. And it was Oswald's duty to remove them from existence.

Permanently.

"About time." Rafe's frown was apparent from the driveway.

Hayden kept his hand under Riley's elbow. Was Rafe ticked that he'd taken Riley out? Had

Rafe seen Hayden kiss her? Too bad if he did. Riley was a grown woman and could see and kiss whom she wanted. Hayden squared his shoulders. "Did I miss a call from you?"

"No. But only because Remington refused to let me call you."

He'd have to remember to thank her. "What's up?" Hayden asked.

Suddenly Rafe turned to Riley, as if he'd just now noticed her standing on the porch with them. "What?"

She shook her head. "Nothing." Riley turned to Hayden. "Thank you for a lovely evening." She stood on tiptoe, planted a quick kiss on his lips, then went inside.

"When Remington told me you'd taken Riley out, I assumed you were just being nice and getting her out of the house. Is there—?"

"What did you want to call me about?" Hayden didn't feel like going into too much detail just yet. Not with Rafe. Not until he and Riley finished their discussion about their feelings. "What's so important?"

"Your crime unit got the reports back on the truck. Two prints found. One matched the print on the infant seat. I ran them through IAFIS and got a match."

"Who?" Hayden reached for the door.

Rafe stopped him with a hand to his chest. "Ex-army. Job Wilder. Dishonorable discharge seven years ago. Has built up a reputation as quite the killer-for-hire."

Ice ran through Hayden's veins. "So it *is* an assassin."

"This guy's bad news. Has the MO to get people to stop on a deserted road, then take them out with a high-powered shot from over three hundred feet. He doesn't often miss."

Thank You, Lord, for keeping Riley from being another one of this man's victims.

"We got an address. Baton Rouge. I'm waiting on Deputy Ingram to verify and call me back. Let's go. We'll be that much closer when he calls. I'll tell you the rest on the way."

"Okay. Let me tell . . ." Who was he going to tell? Mom? Already in bed. Emily? Car not here. And no way could he explain to Riley, not with Rafe watching. "I'll drive." He spun and got back behind the wheel of the cruiser.

"Why the dishonorable discharge?" It'd already been a long day.

Rafe clicked his seat belt and slapped the dashboard. "Insubordination and anger issues. According to his military record, he was ordered to undergo several years of counseling. Report indicates he'd get better, then his temper would flare and he'd be cited. More counseling, then he'd get better. Then the whole cycle would start again."

Hayden steered back to the main road. "I don't

understand people like that. We see them way too often in our profession."

"Tell me about it. Wilder, according to his commanding officer's discharge report, is a crack shot with a rifle. He'd wanted to train Wilder in sniper school, but Wilder could never pass the psychological evals. And then his anger would flare and so forth."

"Sounds like Uncle Sam got tired of dealing with a loose cannon."

"Yeah. Too bad they trained him in combat before they cut him off." Rafe shook his head. "I'd estimate that at least 85 percent of the assassins the bureau catches are former military."

"Guess we train them well, yes?"

"Yeah. I suppose we do."

The moon shone bright on the Louisiana bayou. Sheets of Spanish moss hung like decorative drapes from the old oaks lining the road to the interstate.

Hayden sped as he entered the interstate. "What did Deputy Ingram have to say?"

"He said it'd take him less than five minutes to reach the address." Rafe glanced at the clock on the dash. "That was a good twenty minutes ago."

Pressing harder on the accelerator, Hayden wove around an eighteen-wheeler. "What's the address?"

Rafe rattled it off from memory.

"I know the area. Rough part of town." He

whipped around a small compact with more bumper stickers than should be legal.

"I want to ask you something personal, if you don't mind."

Hayden's mouth went dry. Here it came . . . "Sure."

"I think I'm going to ask Remington to marry me. What do you think?"

For a minute, his mind wouldn't comprehend what Rafe had said. Marriage. Remington. Rafe.

"I love her. And she loves me. We make each other happy, although us together makes no sense."

Remington married?

"She doesn't have any family left. You're the closest thing she has."

His ability to speak returned. "I think of her just like I think of Emily." And he did. Which was why he couldn't quite get over the whole idea of her being married.

"Do you object? To me?" Rafe sounded hurt.

"No, not at all."

"Oh."

Hayden laughed. "I'm just trying to picture her married. It's kinda hard."

"She's not exactly the stereotypical housewife, is she?" Rafe chuckled.

"Remington? Not hardly. Have you tasted her cooking?" Hayden snorted. "Man, I feel sorry for you. Mom's tried to teach her to cook a gazillion times. She's just no good at it. At all."

"So, I have your blessing to ask her?" Rafe was all serious now.

"I'm honored that you asked. I know you love her. And you'll protect her and cherish her." Hayden gripped the wheel tightly. He was losing his best friend all over again. But the image of Riley's face danced across his mind, and suddenly, the loss didn't cut so deeply. "Yes, you have my blessing. When are you going to ask her?"

"I was thinking about this summer. I haven't worked it all out yet."

Before Hayden could reply, Rafe's cell rang. He jerked it to his ear. "Baxter here."

Hayden shot down the exit, passing a pickup and minivan in the process.

"We just exited." A pause. "Yeah." Another pause. Hayden took a left.

"That's good, right?" Silence. Hayden turned left again.

"Sure." A pause. "Hang on, I'll ask." Rafe addressed Hayden. "Do you have vests?"

Stupid question for a police commissioner. He nodded as he took a right.

"Yeah, he does."

"Okay, we're turning onto Miller Avenue now." Rafe put his phone back on its clip. "They've confirmed it is Wilder's residence and he is in the house. They don't want to wait to bring him in, so they're about to take him down now."

"Here's the street. Where are they?" Hayden slowed the cruiser to a crawl.

Rafe gave him a number.

Hayden jerked the car into the driveway of a neighboring house from Wilder and killed the lights and engine. He and Rafe eased out of the car, shutting the doors silently, then crept to the trunk. Hayden popped it and grabbed two Kevlar vests. He passed one to Rafe and slipped into the other.

Deputy Ingram materialized at his side. "Nice of you to join us," he whispered.

"Wouldn't miss it." Hayden pulled his firearm from the trunk where he'd stashed it during his date. He shoved the extra clip over his waistband, then withdrew the gun.

Rafe grinned, his own firearm drawn. "Let's lock and load, rock and roll, boys."

The group crept toward the house. No porch light blazed, nor did any of the interior lights. A faint glow shone through one window, most likely from a television set.

Deputy Ingram and two others from the sheriff's office led the way. Rafe and Hayden brought up the rear as they crossed the street void of any streetlights.

A dog barked three doors down.

The men ducked behind the old Cadillac parked in Wilder's driveway. Ingram held up a closed fist.

They waited.

One minute. Two.

Three.

Ingram motioned for his two men to go around back. Rafe and Hayden moved up to cover his flanks. They approached the front door.

The dog barked again.

Rafe took one side of the door. Hayden the other. Ingram moved slightly to the right. He nodded at Hayden.

Gripping his gun with one hand, Hayden rapped hard on the front door.

"Police. Open up!" Ingram yelled.

A *pop* sounded inside. Then silence.

Ingram nodded again.

Rafe flipped around and kicked the door. Splinters flew as the door opened. The three men rushed inside, their stances firm and firearms steady.

Hayden covered behind the door and the living room while Rafe and Ingram moved deeper into the house. "Living room, clear." He moved down the hall, passing Rafe on his left.

"Dining room, clear." Rafe stepped into the hall behind Hayden.

"Bathroom, clear." Ingram stepped in the hall, just in front of Hayden.

"In the back!" one of the deputies yelled.

Rafe and Ingram ran to the kitchen and out the back door. Hayden kept his track down the hall. He checked the first bedroom. No sign of anyone.

He went to the second bedroom: nothing. He checked the master bed and bath: all clear. With a sigh, he headed toward the back door, praying they'd caught him.

Just before he entered the kitchen, he heard it: the unmistakable sound of a round being chambered in a rifle.

Hayden eased to the doorway, the barrel of his gun steady. Through the back door standing ajar, he could make out voices in the distance. He silently stepped around the corner and into the kitchen.

A man in all black, holding what looked like a .22-.250 with a scope, aiming through the open door. His back faced Hayden.

In two steps, he reached the man, the barrel of his gun on the back of the man's head. "Drop that rifle, nice and easy. I have some questions you need to answer, something you won't be able to do if I have to shoot you."

Wilder dropped the rifle. Hayden kicked it across the floor.

The men's voices got louder. "Guess we lost him. I'll get a unit out to scour the woods," Ingram said.

"Then again." Hayden leaned in toward Wilder and whispered in his ear. "That lady you shot? She's someone close to me, so maybe you should move after all."

CHAPTER TWENTY-FIVE

"See how the faithful city has become a
prostitute! She once was full of justice;
righteousness used to dwell in her—
but now murderers!"
ISAIAH 1:21

"Promise me you'll be extra careful." Maddie stood in the living room, hugging the uninjured side of Riley for the sixth time. "I feel like I shouldn't leave you."

She'd had all the mothering she could take for the time being. "Please, go. You have a job to get back to, and so do I." Riley hugged her sister back and smiled. "I'm fine. Rafe and Hayden got the guy who shot me. He's in a holding cell in Baton Rouge as we speak. I'm okay."

"Well, I *am* in the middle of this big case . . ." The hesitation was so obvious. Torn between two responsibilities.

"Go. Do your scientist thing. I want to hear all about your case when you can talk about it." Riley gave Maddie a gentle shove. "Get out of here."

Remington lifted her suitcase, still wearing the dress she'd had on for early church services. "If I didn't have to teach Sunday school this afternoon, I'd stay."

This would drag out forever. Riley gave Remington a quick hug. "Get going," she whispered.

Remington nodded. "Come on, Maddie. We'll be late if we don't get on the road now." She gave Riley a wink, then hugged Ardy and Emily.

Maddie pulled Riley in for another hug. "I love you, Ri."

"And I love you, Mads. I'll be home before you know it." Just saying the words caused a physical ache in her chest as she recalled Hayden's words. *"Give us a chance. We'll figure out the details later."*

"Let's go." Remington all but dragged Maddie out the door, down the steps, and to the car.

Ardy and Emily followed Riley onto the porch, all three of them waving as the car pulled away from the house.

When the car was no longer visible, Ardy turned back to the house. "I'm having some of my Sunday school ladies over for lunch. I hope both of you plan on joining us."

Riley opened her mouth but Emily interrupted. "Sorry, Mom. I thought Riley might be a little sad with her sister leaving and all, so I made lunch plans for us."

Ardy looked from her daughter to Riley, then back to Emily. "Well, isn't that sweet of you? That's really nice, honey. Y'all have a good time."

"We will." Emily kissed her mother's cheek,

then batted her eyes at Riley. "Are you ready?"

Riley swallowed a chuckle and nodded. She followed Emily down the steps and got in the passenger seat of Em's car. "That was slick, girl. I'm impressed."

"Years of experience in dealing with my mother." She backed out of the driveway. "Trust me, the last thing you want is to be trapped with Mom's Sunday school ladies. Ugh."

"But now you have to take me somewhere for lunch."

"I could always just take you back to my apartment and we could order pizza."

"You know, that sounds pretty good. And I'd love to see your apartment."

"Okay, but you can't tell Mom that it's not immaculate. I think she takes it personally when my space isn't as spic and span as hers."

Riley laughed. "Hey, at least she cares, right?"

"Uh, yeah. Okay." Emily made a sharp right, causing Riley to grab the bar by the handle. "So, are you going to tell me about your date with my brother last night?"

"We had a nice time."

Emily snorted. "Well, that's really filling in the details." She laughed as she made another sharp turn. "Where did he take you?"

"Um, the visitor's center."

"That's closed at night."

"I know, but he got us in."

"Interesting." Emily pulled into a parking lot to a duplex. "But there's not a place to eat there."

"Right. He brought a picnic lunch."

"Get out! *Hayden* brought a picnic lunch?" She put the car in Park and turned off the engine. "You're kidding, right?"

"Nope." Riley opened the door and followed Emily to her apartment.

Emily opened the door and let Riley enter first. "It's not much, but I like it."

"It's nice." Riley meant it.

The living room was decorated in deep browns and subtle blue. Comfortable and soothing color scheme. The furniture, while sparse with only one chair and a small love seat, was placed in a welcoming arrangement. The slate-top table held a bowl with color-coordinated glass balls.

"Sit down. I'll call in the pizza. What kind do you like?"

After they'd decided on a meat extreme and Emily called it in, she sat in the chair with the plush ottoman. "So, my brother took you on a picnic. I'm pretty impressed."

So was Riley. "At the base of this waterfall, he set out those Japanese lanterns everywhere. It was beautiful."

"Sounds like he's got it bad for you."

No worse than she had it for him. "It was just a second date."

"Let me tell you something about my brother—

he doesn't go all out. Most times, there isn't a second date. And I've never, ever, heard of him doing a picnic, period."

"Why not?"

Emily shrugged. "He says not much point in leading someone on if he didn't feel something. Whatever that means."

Warmth spread from Riley's stomach to the tips of her toes. "Well, I'd be lying if I said I didn't like him." Her face had to be redder than all get-out if the heat of her cheeks was any indication.

"I'd say the feeling is quite mutual." Emily smiled.

A knock sounded on the door.

"That was fast." Emily shot up, grabbed the cash they'd counted out and set on the slate table, and opened the door.

And froze.

Thomas Vince stood there, a glare on his face. "How dare you turn me down?" His proper accent wasn't apparent now. "Don't you realize women fawn all over me? Don't you understand how lucky you are that I bother to show any interest in you?" Despite his slight limp, he charged Emily, backing her into the apartment.

Riley stood.

He caught sight of her and took a step backward. "I'm sorry. I didn't realize you had company, Emily." He nodded at Riley, contempt fighting the scowl he wore. "It's nice to see you again, Ms. Baxter. How are you feeling?"

"Fine." What a bully! The scrawny, little, effeminate . . .

"I'm glad you're doing better." He cut his gaze to Emily. "I don't want to intrude, so I'll just speak to you later."

"No, Thomas, I told you already. I don't want to see you anymore."

His smile was as fake as his front teeth. "I'm sure we'll find a better, more private time to discuss this." He nodded to Riley again. "Nice seeing you again. Give my regards to your brother."

"Oh, I will. Certainly." And she'd tell him to kick the little jerk too.

With a puckered brow and final glare at Emily, he left. She slammed the door shut. "Sorry. Obviously, he's not taking my breaking it off with him very well."

"You need to tell Hayden about him. That man has a lot of hate in his eyes. He could be dangerous."

Emily snorted and flicked her hand. "He likes to act big and talk a good game, but that's about it. As you said, he's effeminate. And his leg is fake, remember, so he's handicapped."

Riley pointed to her face, where the gash was healing rather quickly. "But he does have a temper."

"Yeah." Emily shrugged. "I'll see. If he comes by again or calls, I'll tell Hayden."

Another knock sounded.

Emily jumped up. "About time the pizza got here."

Riley nodded, but she couldn't stop the feeling that Thomas wasn't going to just go away. Not by a long shot.

"We've been at him all night. Taken turns questioning him. He's about worn down after our in-depth interrogations." Deputy Ingram nodded at the window. "He hasn't lawyered up."

Job Wilder sat handcuffed at a table in an interview room. Ingram, Rafe, and Hayden watched him through the two-way mirror. The man didn't look nervous. Not at all. Matter-of-fact, he looked pretty relaxed.

"Let's go," Rafe said.

Ingram led the way into the room. "You remember FBI Agent Baxter, don't you, Wilder?"

Wilder glanced at Rafe, shrugged, then stared at Hayden.

"Ah, that's right, you remember Police Commissioner Simpson. He's the one who disarmed you."

Pure venom shot from Wilder's stare, but he said nothing.

"So, you want to tell us about your little business? The killer-for-hire gig?" Ingram sat on the edge of the table closest to Wilder. "We've got you for two murders, one attempted murder. Want to tell us who hired you? Maybe the judge will be interested to know you helped us."

Wilder cursed, then spit on the floor.

Rafe was on him in a flash, pressing his face against the metal table. "Let's try that again. Who hired you to kill the woman?" He relaxed his hold on him slightly, just enough to let Wilder sit upright again.

A little spot of blood where he'd bit his lip dotted Wilder's mouth. He wiped it off on his sleeve. But he didn't speak.

"There's no way you're getting off on any of these, so you might as well tell us who hired you. Why should you go to prison and he walk around free?" Ingram stood and paced the small room like a caged lion.

Rafe slammed the side of his fist against the table. "I'm going to ask you one more time . . . who hired you to kill the woman?"

Wilder lifted his gaze to him. His eyes traveled up and down Rafe's length, then he sneered.

Rafe lunged but Ingram grabbed him.

Wilder didn't even blink.

Ingram rattled off information regarding the two murders he worked. Still, Wilder sat like a stone statue.

His eyes were cold . . . dead as he moved his stare to Hayden.

Rafe and Ingram took turns asking the same questions. Wilder stared at Hayden as if in a trance.

The questions didn't stop.

Finally, Wilder spoke, his stare never faltering from Hayden. "Why didn't you go outside too?"

Hayden knew exactly what Wilder was talking about. "Gut instinct. We hadn't cleared the kitchen."

Wilder shrugged.

Hayden held his breath. The suspect had formed a connection with him. If Hayden made one false move, the connection could be broken, and they wouldn't get anything else from him. He was tired, worn down, exhausted.

Ingram headed to the door, Rafe on his heels. They said some nonsense about evidence, a witness . . . something. Hayden recognized it as a ploy so he'd be alone with Wilder.

Wilder probably knew that too. Still . . .

The door shut with a click. Hayden refused to say anything. Wilder remained silent. A minute passed. Two. Three. Four.

"Which case is yours?"

"The woman." Hayden's blood rushed, but he forced his voice and demeanor not to change.

"That's right. You told me she was somebody close to you so you considered shooting me." Wilder smiled. "Was that true? That you thought seriously about shooting me?"

"Yes."

"Interesting. Man in your position."

Hayden just raised one eyebrow. Emily hated it when he did that. She'd told him one time it looked very intimidating.

"You must be falling for her. I can understand. She's pretty hot."

Baiting him. Hayden didn't fall for it. He sat still, allowing no change in facial expression or body language. But if it weren't for his training . . . "You know, if you tell me what's what, I'll see if the prosecutor will give you a deal." He shrugged. "No guarantee, of course, but I'm a man of my word and I'll check into it."

Silence followed. A very long, very uncomfortable silence.

And then Wilder spoke. "I don't know who hired me. Order came via phone call and money got wired into an account I specified."

Hayden forced himself not to react. He paused for at least two minutes. "What was the order?"

"To take her out. Plain and simple. Kill her."

The hairs on the back of Hayden's neck stood at attention. "I need your account number to trace the wire."

Wilder tried to stare him down. It didn't work —Hayden had mastered the art by having Emily as a little sister.

"Bank of Remco, account number 2011181121."

Chapter Twenty-Six

"But you must return to your God; maintain love and justice, and wait for your God always."
HOSEA 12:6

"I just don't know if it's a good idea for you to drive alone." Ardy fretted in the living room, staring at Riley with indecision imbedded in her face. "Maybe I should drive you. Or we could call Hayden and ask him."

Just what she didn't need or want at the moment. "I'm fine. I promise. The doctor told me as soon as I wasn't taking pain medication every four hours, I could drive. I haven't taken a pill since before church yesterday."

"I'd feel better if I drove you."

"I appreciate your concern, but I have no idea how long I'll be, and you have your friends coming over to try out the new julienne recipe." Riley snagged her keys and flashed a smile brighter than she felt. "The police have the man who shot me in custody. I'll keep my cell turned on. If I need anything, anything at all, I'll call. Okay?" She didn't know if it was right for her to be so happy that the assassin was behind bars, but she was.

"I suppose." But Ardy didn't look assured.

Riley used the hesitation to her advantage. "See you later. Have fun cooking." She slipped out the front door and headed down the steps, careful not to jostle her shoulder too much. The last thing she needed was for Ardy to catch her wincing. She'd be on the phone with Hayden as fast as stink on a gar fish.

She gave a little wave to the window where Ardy's face looked whiter than the curtains and drove off. Whew, that'd been a close one. She hadn't a clue what she would've done if Ardy had held her ground.

Thank goodness for the ladies scheduled to try out recipes with Ardy.

Riley pulled off to the side of the road and plugged in the pawnshop's address into the GPS. Hayden hadn't said Cam Thayer was still the owner of the shop, but she bet he was. The GPS pinpointed her location, then calculated the route to the pawnshop. Riley pulled back on the road and followed the directions.

Riley still didn't know what to make of her date with Hayden last night. And that kiss—wowie! She still felt like swooning just remembering it.

Her knees had gone weak, and she would have fallen had Hayden's strong arms not supported her. The man did strange things to her. Made her feel things she'd never thought she'd feel. Dream of a future she never thought she'd have.

No, she couldn't think about him like that right

now. She had to concentrate on her career, her story, her series. On Armand being the innocent man his family believed him to be. That she believed him to be.

Riley couldn't be wrong about something so important.

The April day was clear and cool. Perfect weather. She let the windows down in the car, the wind whipping through her hair. She smiled. How long had it been since she enjoyed driving with the windows down, speeding along the highway? How long had it been since she relished just being alive?

Did this attitude have to do with being shot and living, or Hayden's kiss?

She shook her head. No, she'd just enjoy the wind and being free and alive.

"Exit ramp right." The female computerized voice interrupted her joy.

Riley slowed and took the exit. The drive had been way too short. Or maybe she'd just enjoyed driving alone more than she had in a long time.

Four turns and three traffic signals later, and she pulled into the parking lot of the pawnshop. Her hand shook a little. She flipped down the sun visor and opened the mirror, smoothing down her hair as best she could with one hand. It'd have to do. She wasn't here to win any style contest. She was here to get the truth.

Riley strode into the shop as if she owned the

place. Confidence was the surest way to get to speak to the person you wanted to. Journalism 201. She walked straight to the counter, smiling at the young man wiping the glass display case with a rag. "I'd like to speak to Cam, please."

He eyed her. "You a friend of his?"

"A friend of a friend of a friend, you could say."

He narrowed his eyes. "What would you say?"

She swallowed down the uneasiness twisting in her stomach. "I say you should let Cam know he has someone who'd like to speak with him." She gave him the stare of Rafe's she'd mimicked for years. "Now would be wise."

"You a cop?" But the kid didn't sound so ornery now.

She gave him a wry smile. "Do I look like a cop?" She gestured to the sling.

He pointed at the sling. "Got a wire in there or something?"

"No, I don't have a wire. I'm not a cop. I'm here to talk with Cam, and now my patience has run out." She stared him down.

He tossed the rag onto the counter. "Wait here." He disappeared behind a closed door.

Riley glanced around the pawnshop. A couple of people walked up and down the rows, talking and sometimes laughing.

The kid returned, motioning her forward. "He said you're pretty, so he'll talk to you."

Oh, so that mirror behind the counter was two-way. Interesting. She smiled at her reflection as she followed the kid. He opened the door and pointed toward a suite of small offices, then shut the door.

A hulk of a man wearing a white "wife-beater" tank top and tight jeans that had seen one too many washings stepped into the hall. "Well, now, darlin' . . . what can I do ya for?"

She swallowed down the revulsion scorching the back of her throat. "I'm a reporter working on an article on the Louisiana State Museum robbery four years ago. I understand you were the star witness. May I ask you a few questions about that?" Riley smiled and batted her eyes. It wasn't the first time she'd flirted to get someone to talk.

"Yep, I was their witness." He crossed his arms over his chest, flexing his biceps as he did. "They wouldn't have had a case without me."

She widened her eyes. "Really?"

"Oh, yeah, sweetheart. Come into the confer-ence room." He waved her into a room holding nothing but a long table with five chairs on each side. She didn't sit, just rested on the edge of the table.

"So you made their case?"

He puffed out his chest. "My eye-witness account of that security guard was the only thing that got the prosecutor to take the case to trial." He nodded. "And they needed someone to be found guilty."

"Why's that?"

"Well, for the insurance companies. That stuff they didn't get back was insured. If no one was found guilty of stealing it, the company wouldn't pay out as quickly. They'd have sent their own investigator and it could've taken years for them to get any money. My brother, for instance, he had some Confederate coins and buttons stolen. Because they caught one of the robbers and he went to prison, insurance paid him right off."

Interesting. His brother was one of the guys who had something stolen and gotten an insurance claim paid. With him being the main witness, wasn't that a conflict of interest? "I see."

"And then there was that guard who got shot." He shook his head. "The prosecutor's office needed to up their conviction rate on violent crimes."

Riley chewed her bottom lip. For a pawnshop owner, he sure knew an awful lot about insurance claims and conviction rates. "That must have put a lot of responsibility on you." She smiled as sweetly as she could muster. The man disgusted her.

"Well, yeah, but I could handle it." He leaned in, crowding her space. "Don't you worry, darlin'. I was fine. I never forget a face."

She grabbed a picture from her purse. It was of a man, about the same age and build as Armand, with the same hair color, but with very different facial features. She handed it to him. "Him?"

She pulled out the picture of Armand. "Or him?"

He glanced at the photographs, not even taking the time to really study them. "It's Armand Wilson."

Funny he remembered the name right off the top of his head.

"But which one is Armand?"

"I think you'd better leave." His tone went harsh as he shoved the pictures into her hand. "I can see you probably bothered someone else." He gestured toward her sling.

"But you didn't even look at the pictures. You said you never forget a face. So which one is Armand? You can't identify him, can you? You don't know."

His face contorted into a grimace. "You need to go."

He hadn't been mistaken on the stand. It was deliberate. "Why would you lie on the stand? Did the prosecutor bully you?"

Cam Thayer pushed her out of the conference room with a hard shove. "It's time for you to go."

"Who told you to identify Armand Wilson? Don't you care that your testimony—your lie—sent an innocent man to prison? Away from his family?"

"Go." Cam shoved her into the main area of the pawnshop, then shut the door to the hall of offices.

"But, you can't—"

"Lady, you should leave." The kid at the counter pointed at the door. "If he has to come back out here, it won't be good for you."

Riley looked around. There were no patrons in the shop anymore. Just the kid. And Cam Thayer behind the shut door.

Maybe she *should* leave.

"Thank you." She nodded at the kid and spun on her heel.

She'd done exactly what she'd told Hayden she wouldn't—she flat-out accused Cam Thayer of lying . . . of perjuring himself on the witness stand.

Riley rushed toward her car, glancing over her shoulder. She stumbled on the loose gravel in the parking lot and had to sprawl against the hood of her car. Cam Thayer could be on her heels.

Straightening, she jerked around to stare at the shop's door once more before rounding to the driver's door.

She moved around the front bumper, glancing to the shop again. No sign of either the kid or Cam. She let out a sigh. She dug in her purse for her keys, wrapped her hand around them, and then withdrew them. Riley took the four steps to the door and froze.

Her heart kinked. She dropped the keys. Her lungs refused to move air in and out.

Ice filled her veins, yet a bead of sweat popped

on her upper lip. She swallowed against a dry mouth.

And locked stares with Simon Lancaster.

"It's layered well, I'll give him that." Rafe sat in front of the computer monitor, his fingers pounding on the keyboard.

Hayden paced the West Baton Rouge Parish sheriff's office space. Deputy Ingram hovered behind Rafe, alternating between looking over Rafe's shoulder and glaring in the direction of the interview room.

The parish building manager hadn't yet ordered the air conditioner on for the day. The sweat trickled down Hayden's spine.

Rafe's cell rang, making all three men lurch. He grabbed it. "Baxter." His fingers tapped on the keys. "Yeah, but that's not working." More typing. Clicking with the mouse. "No, I don't see it. That's not the screen I'm looking at."

Ingram ran a hand over his face, then again. Rubbing.

Hayden wanted to do the same thing. Rafe was logging into the bureau's database remotely, not with much success. He'd called three people, and none had been able to assist. But he refused to give up.

"Okay, I'm there. Now what?"

Tap-tap-tap-tap.

"Yeah. Okay."

Click.

"I see it." Rafe pumped his fist in the air. "I'm in. Thanks, Darren." He set his phone on the desk. "We're in. Now, let's see if we can get past his layers."

Tap. Tap. Tap.

"Here we go." Rafe leaned close to the monitor. "Whoever did this money wiring layered well but didn't go overseas. That's odd."

"What?" Hayden couldn't keep silent any longer.

"Well, most of these types know to run their funds through Switzerland and then through the Bahamas. It messes up our tracking."

Click. Tap. Tap.

"Either he's not real smart in this part of the process, or he's smarter than we think and he's giving us a false lead."

Tap. Tap. Tap. Tap.

"You go to the trouble to hire a hit man, I'm assuming you're smarter than the average Joe." Hayden still had a hard time wrapping his thoughts around someone hiring Wilder to kill Riley.

"We're about to find out." Rafe typed, then clicked with the mouse, then typed again. Finally he leaned back in the chair. "Funds originated from an account listed to Oswald Vance."

Oswald Vance? Didn't ring any bells with Hayden, but that didn't mean anything. He pulled out his notebook and wrote down the name.

Ingram was already on another computer terminal in the room, pounding away on the keyboard.

"How do you do a split screen on y'all's system?" Rafe asked.

Another deputy hurried across the room and pressed a button for Rafe. Ah, the influence of the Federal Bureau of Investigation.

"We have nothing on him here." Ingram returned to Rafe's side.

Rafe tapped the keys, then pointed at the monitor. "Our boy did seven years in the federal country club, courtesy of a drug charge in Denham Springs." His fingers flew over the keyboard. "He was released five years ago. Had six months of paper."

"And after that?" Hayden scrawled notes with his pencil.

"That's the interesting thing. He drops off the grid after he gets off parole." Rafe shook his head. "I mean, totally off the grid. I can't find a record of a credit card, bank account, driver's license—nothing."

Ingram went back to the other computer terminal. "He couldn't have just disappeared. He has to be somewhere."

Of course he had to be somewhere. Hayden rubbed his chin. But would they find him? If someone wanted to drop off the grid . . .

"I'm not finding anything in the entire database." Rafe scratched his head. "This is just crazy. Maybe the person *is* a genius and led us to this dead end."

Maybe. But Hayden had a gut feeling.

"I found something." Ingram turned the other monitor around to face Hayden, tapping the screen.

Rafe stood and joined Hayden. "What?"

Hayden read from the screen. "Looks like Mr. Oswald Vance filed a motion with the court to have his name changed four years ago."

"A convicted felon can't legally change his name."

Hayden's blood rushed. "You can if the governor of the state grants you a full pardon."

Chapter Twenty-Seven

" 'So I will come to put you on trial.
I will be quick to testify against sorcerers,
adulterers and perjurers, against those who
defraud laborers of their wages, who oppress the
widows and the fatherless, and deprive the
foreigners among you of justice,
but do not fear me,' says the Lord Almighty."
MALACHI 3:5

"Get away from me." Riley's heartbeat echoed in her head with a heavy thud.

Simon Lancaster stepped away from the car. "I'm not here to hurt you."

"I don't care. Go away." She willed herself to bend down and pick up her keys from the parking lot. Her body went on strike and refused to budge.

"I just want to talk to you for a minute. It's important."

"I have nothing to say to you." Finally, her muscles decided to obey. Could have been the threats her brain sent out. She squatted and grabbed her keys, her stare never leaving Simon Lancaster's face.

As she stood, anger and grief pushed aside her fear. "Actually, I do have something to say to you."

He held out his arms. "Let's hear it. I know you're dying to get it off your chest."

"I think you're despicable. You took my parents from me, killed two amazing people. You're a murderer." Tears welled in her eyes, clouding her vision, but she didn't care. She'd come too far to stop now. "I loathe you. I used to stay up at night, lying in bed, imagining slow and painful ways to kill you. And the thoughts made me smile."

She sucked in air, surprised she'd said that. She'd never admitted that—not aloud, not even to herself.

"Are you done?" He took a step closer.

She backed against the car, weaving her keys between her knuckles like Rafe had taught her.

"Because I'll tell you some things I couldn't share in the parole hearings."

Riley didn't want to listen, but she couldn't make herself unlock the car and get inside.

"For years in prison, I didn't think about your parents, your brother, your sister, or you. All I thought about was how unfair the system was. And how badly I wanted a drink."

Was she supposed to feel sorry for him?

"But then I started going to church, mainly to get out of work. But it all started to make sense to me. I wanted to be clean. I wanted to be forgiven. I wanted God's love. I gave my life to Jesus and worked to get clean. Really clean. To where I wouldn't go back to drinking. Ever."

Like she could believe him? That he *wanted* to get sober? More likely, he didn't have a choice. And he became a Christian? Didn't 99.9 percent of all prisoners swear they found Jesus in jail because it looked good to parole boards? Sure worked for him.

"And when I did, I had to face what I'd done. I have to look at myself in the mirror each and every day and know I'm responsible for two people's deaths. That because of my addiction, they're dead."

"How *dreadful* for you."

"I don't blame you for not believing me. That's okay. I understand."

"Oh, thank you so much for understanding why I can't stand the sight of you. I was worried I would have to explain."

He nodded. "I deserve your hatred."

Her hand shook and her shoulder throbbed. "Don't you dare stand there and pretend you care. You don't have that right." The tears nearly blocked her vision, but she kept on. It was as if she needed to purge it all from her system.

Her anger. Her hatred. Her pain.

"You should still be in jail, rotting away."

"Would that make you happy? Help you deal with the grief I caused?"

"Yes." She snapped at him before she weighed her decision.

He shook his head. "I don't think so. I think

you've gotten in the habit of blaming me for everything. I don't think it matters where I am."

"Who cares what you think?" But she couldn't argue with him. She didn't care where he was, and she did blame him for her parents' deaths.

"You care. Because deep down inside, you know that no matter what happens to me, it doesn't change the fact that your parents are gone and I took them from you. Plain and simple, that's the fact."

Tears escaped, trailing down her face. "What do you want? Why are you here?"

"I came to warn you." He took a step closer.

She pushed the button on the key-chain remote. The doors unlocked with a click.

He froze. "No, not like that." He stepped back again. "I received a text, from a number I didn't recognize."

"And?" She just wanted him to say whatever he needed, then leave. She needed to be alone.

"Someone tried to get me to kill you."

Riley stared at him, shock stealing her voice.

"Like I said, I didn't recognize the number. I reported it to my parole officer a couple of hours ago, just like I'm supposed to, and he said he would call the proper authorities, but I wanted to tell you."

"Why? Why would you care? You did what you're obligated to do."

"Because whoever is behind this is serious. Deadly serious."

She gestured to her sling. "Obviously." And then it occurred to her. "When did the text come through?"

"Now you're getting it." He pulled out his cell phone and handed it to her.

She scrolled through his text in-box and found the text.

emimin8 riley baxter get 1 mil in cash will snd instructions whn u reply

Riley checked the date and time stamp. This morning, 9:11. She checked the number. Local area code. She didn't recognize it, but that didn't say much. "Let me write this down."

She opened the car door and tossed her purse onto the seat, then dug out a pen and scrap of paper. She copied down the text exactly and wrote down the number. With trembling hands, she passed the phone back to him, careful to avoid touching him.

"This person knew enough to think I'd accept his offer. And he tracked down my cell, which I just got Friday night."

"Why didn't you take him up on it? A million in cash is a lot of money."

Simon smiled. "It's not worth it. I've learned that the hard way." He pocketed his phone. "You take care." He turned away, then stopped and turned back to her. "For whatever it's worth, I am really sorry. From my heart. If I could go back and do things differently, I would. I can't, so all I can say is I'm sorry."

And then he was gone.

Riley slipped into the car and shut the door. Locked it. Started the car and let the engine idle. Her hands trembled. Nausea turned her stomach inside out. Bile burned the back of her throat. She felt a strong urge to retch. Coughed. Swallowed.

She couldn't get sick here.

Putting the gear in Drive, Riley sped away. Tears choked her. It was all too much. Just too much. She pressed the gas pedal harder as she got on the interstate heading back to Hopewell.

All she wanted to do was find Hayden and get to him. Let him wrap his arms around her, keeping her safe and secure.

What did that mean?

She shook her head and drove faster. Had the parole officer called Hayden? Rafe? Neither had phoned to check on her. What was up with that?

She couldn't help remembering how joyful she'd been on the drive to the pawnshop. Enjoying the weather and life in general. Now she was scared and . . . and what?

Riley exited at Hopewell. She passed the visitor's center where she and Hayden had enjoyed their picnic. Where her heart had slipped away to Hayden. The tears fell openly and freely, until she couldn't see. Once she turned down Bayonnette, she couldn't control her sobbing any longer. She pulled onto the shoulder, put the car in Park, and rested her forehead on the steering wheel.

She didn't know how long she sat there, bawling like a baby, but when spent, she lifted her head and saw the remnants of yellow crime-scene tape fluttering in the wind. This was where she'd been shot.

Perfect.

She turned off the engine and stepped from the car. She walked alongside the shoulder, keeping her footing from landing her in the ditch. The faint tape outline of where she'd fallen had faded on the road.

It wasn't fair.

"Why, God? Why?"

The birds chirped in the trees, paying her no attention.

"Come on, God. Tell me, why did You let my parents die? Why did You let Simon Lancaster out? Why did You let me get shot?" Every muscle in her body tensed as she continued to yell at the sky.

"What did I do that was so wrong? Why are You punishing me? What?"

She spun around, her head heavy and her heart thumping. And just when she thought she had no more tears left, her eyes filled again.

"I know I need to forgive Simon. I know I can't. Lord, please . . . help me." She sat on the side of the shoulder, tears streaming down her face again. "Why, God?" Her voice hitched. "I don't understand. This hurts. So much. It's so hard."

Do not mortals have hard service on earth?

Riley stopped crying, wiped her face, and whipped around. She saw no one. "Who's there?"

For hardship does not spring from the soil, nor does trouble sprout from the ground.

Now she was hearing voices? She pushed to her feet. Maybe someone was playing a trick on her. But strangely enough, the words sounded familiar.

All the days of my hard service I will wait for my renewal to come.

She steadied herself as she walked back to the car. She got behind the wheel and started the engine.

As she drove toward Ardy's, it dawned on her why the words were so familiar . . . it was Scripture. From the book of Job.

Promising that while life on earth was hard, often unbearable, renewal of spirit and eternal life was yet to come.

"We need to see the governor. Now." Rafe flashed his badge at the security desk in the capitol building. "It's urgent."

The guard lifted the receiver and spoke quietly.

Hayden's mind raced. The pardon was four years ago, right after the governor took office. Why would he pardon someone so early in his term? Most pardons, if any were granted, were executed when the governor was about to vacate office. It didn't make sense.

"Someone will be with you in just a moment." The guard spoke to Rafe, but his gaze included Hayden and Deputy Ingram.

Even with a federal badge, the capitol cops, as Hayden's team referred to those with political security detail, worked on their own time. Within five minutes a man appeared. "Agent?"

The three men turned to the suited aide. "I'm Mitchell Rogers, Governor Eason's assistant. The governor is a busy man. I'm afraid he's unable to visit with you today. If you'll just—"

Rafe pulled his badge, as did Ingram and Hayden. Rafe put his right at the end of Rogers's nose. "See this?"

The nervous aide nodded.

"This badge is issued by the Federal Bureau of Investigation. Do you know who we are?"

The man nodded.

"Then I'm positive you won't ask any more questions but will take us to see the governor, right?"

Rogers nodded. "F-follow me, please." He led them down a hallway, then another, then a turn, then . . . Hayden had no idea where they were.

Somewhere deep in the bowels of the Louisiana capitol building.

"Here." Rogers opened a door to a sitting area with plush couches and throw pillows. Two coffee tables separated the seating offerings. "The governor will be with you in a moment."

Hayden sat on the end of a couch. Rafe sat on the opposite end, leaving the adjacent couch for Deputy Ingram.

"Nice digs." Rafe smirked. "Maybe I should've gone into politics."

"Nah. You're too honest." The door opened and Rogers escorted Governor Eason into the room. Hayden, Rafe, and Ingram all stood. The governor nodded at them. "Please. Sit down." He took a seat on the couch beside Ingram. "Now, how may I help you? My assistant insisted the matter was urgent."

Rafe cleared his throat. On the ride over, they'd decided he should lead the questioning since he had the bureau's jurisdiction. "Does the name Oswald Vance ring a bell with you?"

The governor's eyes widened for a split second. "Should it?"

Hayden recognized the stiffening of Rafe's spine. It matched his own. Rafe caught the governor's slip.

"Yes, it should." Rafe leaned forward. "You granted him a full pardon."

"My staff prepares recommendations and I

review the information carefully before I make—"

"You granted him a full pardon . . . right after you took office." Rafe stood, looming over the politician. "I want to know why."

The governor's face flushed. "Well, off the top of my head, I can't say for certain. I'll have my—"

"Let me refresh your memory." Rafe sat on the coffee table directly in front of the governor. "He was a convicted drug dealer. Served seven years in prison. Had six months parole upon release, then petitioned the court to legally change his name. Of course, as a convicted felon, he couldn't. Less than six months later, you signed a full pardon." Rafe rested his hand on his holster. "Coming back to you yet?"

His face whitened. "Mitchell, why don't you leave us for a few minutes. I'll buzz you if I need you."

The aide looked perplexed. "Are you sure, sir?"

"Yes."

Mitchell stepped from the room and closed the door.

Hayden pulled out his notebook.

"No notes. I'll tell you everything, but as much as possible, I'd like to keep this quiet." For a man in his position, the governor sure seemed . . . weak.

"As much as we can." Hayden tucked the

notebook back into his pocket. This should be good.

Eason nodded at Rafe, who had stood and paced behind the couch where Hayden sat. "It was right after I'd taken office."

Rafe dropped to the arm of the couch directly across from the governor. "We already know that."

"I received a note, here, in my office. Telling me I was to grant the pardon request on Oswald Vance when it came through, which arrived that very week."

"So?" Hayden couldn't help himself from interrogating.

"There was a second sheet of paper . . ." His face turned as red as the stripes in the flag standing in the corner of the office. "Documented proof of my involvement with . . . well . . . er . . . with a woman."

"You were having an affair? And there was proof attached to the note?" Rafe shook his head.

"Yes. No. I'd had the affair prior to being elected." The governor nodded, his carefully styled hair not moving with the bounce. "You have to understand, I was newly elected. My first term. If it came out right then that I'd had an affair . . . well, you can imagine the political suicide that would be for me even in Louisiana."

"So you pardoned this drug dealer because he blackmailed you? Because you were having an affair?" Hayden couldn't believe the corruption. Well, yes, he could. But still, he always wanted to believe the best about people. And about the system.

Instances like this made it hard for him to keep doing his job.

"Had an affair. Before I took office. I ended it before my swearing in."

Did he think that made it better? More palatable? What a champ.

Rafe stood. "We'll need everything you have. The note. The proof. The pardon paperwork. And we'll need to know what he changed his name to." He pointed when the governor started to speak. "Don't lie and tell me you don't have it. I know you kept it." He glared.

The governor licked his weasel-lips. "I have the note and the document. I can get you the pardon paperwork, but I don't know what he changed his name to. I didn't know he'd even tried before. I swear." He stood, wiping his hands on his suit pants. "Can you please keep it quiet? My wife doesn't know. We have children. Our first grandson is only two months old."

Shame he didn't think about that before he started sleeping with another woman. Where were the morals? The family values he'd rode his political career on?

While Rafe continued to dig for details from the governor, Hayden couldn't keep the frustration from slithering up his spine. Without knowing what Oswald changed his name to, they were back to square one.

Only this time, they knew they were dealing with a murderer, drug dealer, and a blackmailer.

What lengths would he go to not get caught?

Hayden quietly opened his phone and dialed the station's private line. "Bob, it's Hayden. I need you to pull everything you can on an Oswald Vance. I want to know when he cut his first tooth, when he took his first step, what sports he played, and who he took to his senior prom."

"Yes, sir. I'm on it right now."

"Thanks." He shut the phone.

They might not have much to go on, but there had to be something in Vance's background that would clue them in to his future identity. Everyone carried a remnant of their childhood with them into adulthood.

Even Oswald Vance.

Chapter Twenty-Eight

"Do not pervert justice or show partiality.
Do not accept a bribe, for a bribe
blinds the eyes of the wise and
twists the words of the innocent."
DEUTERONOMY 16:19

Riley Baxter demanded his personal attention.

Oswald ran the cloth heavy with oil over the old desk. Rubbing each scratch. Buffing carefully.

She'd even managed to get his assassin arrested. But Oswald would take care of Job the minute the man was out. He hadn't refrained from killing her himself because he was too squeamish. He'd proved numerous times he wasn't a wimp or weakling. He'd simply chosen to keep his hands clean with the minor details like Riley Baxter. The joy of killing he saved for the ones who mattered—the ones who turned him into a cripple.

The revenge.

But Riley Baxter had become too much of a complication for him to leave her future to others. Even Simon Lancaster, who should want to wipe her off the face of the earth like a bug under his shoe, hadn't acted when given the chance. If Oswald cared, he'd take care of that spineless loser too. But he didn't. He had more important assignments.

If only Riley Baxter would stop interfering.

Her smugness reminded him of Governor Eason. So certain he could have his cake and eat it too. Win the governorship on his ticket of family values, his pert little blonde wife standing by his side, but as soon as night fell, he tangled the sheets with the redhead. The siren with a penchant for the arts and a smoldering look that had the governor writing checks on an account his wife knew nothing about.

Oswald had come too far, overcome too many hurdles to allow a chit like Riley Baxter to mess it up.

Smiling and flirting with the police commissioner. Endearing herself to his family. Making herself right at home in his mother's house. Gold digger.

Just like Kelly had morphed after his future died at the hands of ruthless bureaucrats.

As if she had a right.

Riley Baxter using people to further her career. Exposing that girl. Her little brother. The woman.

Oswald almost felt guilty enough to help Peggy Wilson. She'd been dealt a hand similar to his mother, but instead of giving in and giving up, Peggy had fought. Had stood up and did what she could for her children. Despite the circumstances, she hadn't turned to the first man to take care of her. She hadn't turned into a shell of a woman. She wasn't a quitter. She wasn't a loser.

In a way, he admired her. Respected her.

He didn't like what had happened to her, but that couldn't be helped. She was a bystander in the scheme of things. He had needed to change his name to start over. No way could he have a drug record following him around. He'd needed ammunition to get the pardon, and one of his cell mates had inadvertently given him what he needed when the poor sap had said his sister was having an affair with Mr. Soon-to-be-governor Eason. Pictures weren't enough—Oswald had seen them explained away when a woman was so desperate to believe the man in her life.

No, Oswald knew Mrs. Eason would need something more than a photograph. What better proof for a woman than to see her husband spending money, *lots* of money, just because another woman asked? Giving another woman the money that rightfully belonged to her?

What better vehicle than the check he signed, in his handwriting, in an account other than the one Mrs. Eason was aware of? Proof positive not just of giving himself to another woman, but giving his money to another woman. No way would Mrs. Eason allow that.

But to obtain that proof, Oswald had needed to get inside the museum. He'd been intent on not framing a soul, but then one of the partners he'd gotten for the job had requested certain heavily insured items be stolen. He'd agreed.

He hadn't expected the arrest of Armand Wilson. The conviction. The incarceration. Oswald certainly hadn't planned that part. Of course, neither had Peggy Wilson. But the situation worked for Oswald. Not so much for Peggy, but Oswald couldn't be concerned with that.

Simply put, she was expendable. Her family was expendable.

Maybe after he completed his mission to make all the devil's minions pay, he'd help her. Anonymously, of course. That would make him feel good, right, to do something nice for someone else. Isn't that what all the good folk said?

He finished oiling down the desk and set the rag back in the kit, folding it neatly. He washed his hands, then straightened his glasses before checking his planner.

If he hurried, he could make the bank before they closed. After all, he still had a business to run.

All day, Riley had waited for Rafe or Hayden to call and check in with her. Neither did. She didn't know whether she should be pleased that they weren't hovering or upset that they seemed so unconcerned. All day, she'd been split in her thoughts about Simon Lancaster. She still wasn't sure what she believed about him anymore. Or how she felt about him.

As soon as Hayden's car pulled into his mother's driveway, she rushed to the porch, barely noticing the setting sun as a beautiful backdrop. "Are either of you going to tell me about the text to Simon Lancaster?"

Both Hayden and Rafe stopped in their tracks, wearing twin expressions of confusion.

"What are you talking about?" Hayden asked.

"What about a text and Lancaster?" Rafe added.

This was most peculiar. "Didn't Simon Lancaster's parole officer call and tell you about the text he received to kill me?"

"What?" They spoke in unison.

Riley sat on the oversized rocking chair and told them about Simon's visit. "I have the number. Hang on." She went inside, grabbed the slip of paper from her purse, and handed it to Hayden. "I got it directly off his cell."

Hayden was already on his phone. "Yeah, 225 area code." He rattled off the rest of the numbers. "Call me back as soon as you have it." He shut his phone. "Why didn't you tell us earlier?"

"I can't believe Lancaster tracked you down. What were you doing at a pawnshop?" Rafe crossed his arms over his chest.

"I needed to talk to the owner. For my series." The article she'd written about Thayer's obvious deception. The one she'd already sent to Jeremy for publication in next week's magazine. "Hayden, I know you want to believe everything's on the up-and-up with your friend and all, but it's not. Cam Thayer lied on the stand. I don't know why, but he did."

She explained what had happened when she showed him the photos. "Someone told him to lie, Hayden. I know it."

He sighed. "I'll look into it, but I told you not to go around accusing people. You could have been hurt." He reached out and softly wound a strand of hair behind her ear.

The intimate gesture sent chills down her spine and raised goose bumps on her arms. She liked it.

"But I wasn't." She smiled.

He reached out and gave her a gentle hug. "Don't push it."

His cell rang and he popped it to his ear. "Hayden Simpson."

She stared up at him, admiring the defined lines of his jaw. The five o'clock shadow on his chin.

"Are you sure?"

Rafe pushed off the rail where he'd leaned.

"Yeah. Do. Thanks, Bob." Hayden put his cell phone back in its clip. "The phone number traces back to one of those throwaways."

"Hate those," Rafe muttered.

"Yeah. But Bob put in a call to Lancaster's parole officer. The man never called to report the text, which is a huge breach."

"Reeks," Rafe said. "Lancaster's up to something."

Riley shook her head. "He came to me with the news, remember? He could've just let his parole officer handle it, which we see he isn't doing anything, but Simon Lancaster didn't. He tracked me down to warn me." As far as she could tell, nothing he did was to his own benefit, which confused her all the more.

Hayden took Riley's right hand. "Do you realize he had to be following you in order to tell you this? He has an order not to come within two hundred feet of you or Maddie."

She hadn't thought of that. She'd been so concerned that the text had come while the assassin was behind bars. Still . . . she hadn't felt threatened by him. Not by anything he'd done anyway.

Hayden put his arm around her waist. "I'd prefer it if you stayed around Mom's for the next couple of days. Until we can figure some things out."

"But my article." She had to keep digging. Keep investigating. Otherwise, an innocent man would stay behind bars for a crime he didn't commit.

"I'll talk with Thayer, I promise. See what I can find out. But you need to stay around here."

She couldn't promise that. Riley knew all too well how that went. She'd seen Rafe pull the macho act more than once. She wasn't the type to sit idly by. "I have to go to my doctor's appointment tomorrow."

Rafe's sigh was exaggerated.

She turned and wagged her finger in her brother's direction. "Hello? I got shot, remember? Have to go for a follow-up appointment."

He closed the distance between them, wagging his finger back at her. "Hello? You were shot, remember? Someone's trying to take you out. You have to be smart, squirt."

"I can't very well ignore medical attention, now can I?"

"It's not like we're asking you to stay confined to a room, Ri."

"Why don't I get Emily to take you?" Hayden glanced at Rafe. "At least there's some safety in numbers and she can take you there and come straight back home."

"Like a guard?" Somehow, Riley figured she'd let it go. Emily would break any rule just for the fun of it. Especially if it would irritate her brother in the process. "Never mind. That's fine."

"Let me call her right quick and get this set." Hayden had his phone to his ear again. "What time is your appointment?"

"Ten fifteen." She smirked at Rafe.

"Hey, Em." Hayden turned away and walked to the edge of the porch.

"Maddie made it home okay, by the way." Riley had talked to her earlier.

"Yeah, Remington called." Rafe checked his phone. "Speaking of, I promised Rem I'd call and update her. I'll be back." He disappeared into the house.

Hayden returned. "Em says it's a date. She's meeting Thomas for lunch, but I assured her you'd be done by then and she'd have plenty of time to drop you off before she goes to meet him."

Riley frowned.

"What's wrong?" Hayden leaned against the porch's railing.

How much should she say? Emily hadn't wanted Hayden to know about Thomas, but when he'd come to her apartment . . . and the gash.

"Riley?"

"I don't like Thomas."

Hayden chuckled. "Who does? I can't believe Emily likes him. If it weren't for her dating him, I'd swear he was . . . well, that he didn't like ladies."

"Don't let him fool you, Hayden."

He sobered instantly. "What do you mean?"

"He's not as effeminate and harmless as you think. He's got quite a temper. Anger issues."

"What aren't you telling me?"

Sorry, Emily. "That gash on her face?"

Hayden nodded.

"He did it. Emily says the actual cut was an accident. She was holding up the Coke bottle bottoms, making fun of his glasses and prosthetic, and he reached to slap her face and the glass slid down her face."

Hayden's face twisted into horror.

"And the other day when I went to Emily's apartment with her for pizza, he showed up. Before he realized I was there, he acted very threatening. Basically told Emily how dare she try to end things with him. He changed his entire attitude when he saw me, but he was seething." Riley could only hope Emily would forgive her in time for telling Hayden. But he needed to know.

"Why didn't she tell me?"

"Because you're her brother. It's embarrassing when you let a man get away with hurting you. Even worse when your big brother is in law enforcement." She shrugged, remembering how Garrison had acted and how she hadn't wanted Rafe to know. "It's not logical, but that's the truth of it."

"I'm going to kill him." Hayden pushed off the rail.

Riley laid a hand on his arm. "Don't. And don't run over there and give her the third degree for not telling you. It won't help, and she'll only clam up. You'll alienate her and she'll feel betrayed by me, so she won't have anyone she can tell."

"So what am I supposed to do?"

"Wait and see what happens. Try to be an unobvious buffer. I'll beg her to take me to lunch or something tomorrow after my doctor's appointment so she'll break her date with him."

"The whole point of her taking you to the appointment is to break a routine in case anyone's following you and to have you go there and straight back here." He flicked a finger against the end of her nose.

"Then I'll tell her she has to come back with me so I won't go crazy in my forced exile. Don't worry, I'll think of something."

The door swung open and Rafe stood in the doorway. "Hey, supper's getting cold. Is everything settled?"

The sun had set while they'd talked. She hadn't even noticed the dusk-to-dawn lights flick on.

Riley bit her bottom lip and raised her brows at Hayden. She needed him to say it was okay because she needed to tell Emily that Hayden knew before he just blurted it out. If they were to maintain any type of friendship, Emily had to hear it from Riley.

He nodded. "Come on, let's go eat. What did Mom cook?" He placed his hand in the small of her back and they followed Rafe into the house.

"Chicken and dumplings. I'm starved." Rafe led the way.

Riley let Hayden lead her into the kitchen. She hadn't promised she would go straight to her doctor's appointment and straight back.

CHAPTER TWENTY-NINE

"Good will come to those who
are generous and lend freely,
who conduct their affairs with justice."
PSALM 112:5

"Here's what we know about Oswald Vance." Bob stood before Hayden's desk, reading from a file. Rafe sat in the chair.

"Sit down. You're making my neck hurt." Hayden motioned to the chair.

Bob sat, then continued reading. "Born in March, thirty years ago, to Fred and Karen Vance. Lived in Denham Springs, nice suburban house. Two-car garage. Nothing fancy, but quite comfortable."

Although he'd get a copy of the report, Hayden took notes. It helped him remember facts. Even the obscure ones. Fred Vance. The name rang a bell . . .

"Father owned an antique shop. Did pretty well. Again, nothing fancy but quite comfortable. Oswald was a high school track star. Got a scholarship to LSU. Was the golden boy. But late in his senior year, he was diagnosed with a type of bone cancer. Had his leg amputated. The dad couldn't deal, so he left. Scholarship was revoked. Kid got hooked on painkillers."

There was the connection. Hayden's blood rushed. "How long ago?"

"Thirteen years ago. According to the medical records, the leg could have been saved with a new surgery, but his insurance company wouldn't allow it. Said it was experimental. Guess who managed the insurance company?"

"For Your Health."

Bob nodded. "Bingo."

"We have motive." Hayden smiled at Rafe.

"There's more." Bob interrupted. "After it all, his mother became depressed. She went through the gamut of antidepressants and painkillers with the kid."

"It all fits. The insurance. The drugs." Hayden snapped his fingers as something else slipped into place.

"What?" Rafe asked.

"The money for Manchester."

Rafe's eyes widened. "Drug money."

Hayden nodded. "It all connects." He pointed at Bob. "What else?"

"There's nothing on paper after he's released from prison and is denied the name change."

That kept bothering him. "Hey, send Fontenot down to the state courthouse. Have him manually pull all the name changes for the six months following Vance's pardon. I don't think he'd wait too long. I'm sure the paperwork is buried, but there should be something there. Even if it's just the

361

judge's docket for the day. Find me something."

"Yes, sir." Bob was up and out the door in less than a minute.

Rafe stared at Hayden. "What are we missing? There has to be something."

Hayden shook his head and looked over his notes. "Motive, means, and opportunity. Everything fits. Oswald Vance is our guy."

"But who is he now?"

"That's what we have to find out."

A knock sounded, then Officer Gaston stepped inside the office. "I pulled everything I could find on Cam and Darryl Thayer, sir." He handed Hayden a file. "And the copy of the Wilson trial transcript that you requested." He passed that along as well, then slipped out of the office.

"Thayer?" Rafe asked.

"The pawnshop owner Riley went to visit yesterday and his brother." He opened the folder.

"And the Wilson trial transcript?"

"The family Riley's been writing about." He wished Rafe weren't so perceptive.

And that Gaston didn't talk so much.

"So, you're helping Riley with her investigation?"

Hayden tented his hands over the open file. "Trying to keep her from getting out there, digging into stuff on her own, and finding trouble."

"Uh-huh. And that . . . date you took her on the

other night?" Rafe leaned back in his chair, crossing his arms over his chest and scrutinizing Hayden.

So they were going to have this conversation now. "Yes, I took her out. On a date. A real date." Rafe raised his eyebrows. "I like her, okay? She's a grown woman, Rafe. I think we have a chance at something, and I plan to do everything in my power to give it a go." The hot flashes his mother complained about had nothing on the heat rushing up the back of his neck. "Okay with you?"

"It depends."

He hadn't expected that response. "On what?"

Rafe leaned forward, resting his forearms on the edge of Hayden's desk. "Your intentions. See, Riley's had a couple of really bad relationships. Sure, she picked them, but that doesn't mean she didn't get hurt. I don't want to see her get hurt again."

"I'm not playing with her, Rafe."

"I didn't think you were. But you need to proceed very carefully. Riley lives in Tennessee. You live here in Louisiana."

"Just like you lived in Arkansas and Remington lived in Louisiana when y'all met."

"True. But Rem had ties left in Arkansas she'd never severed. She knew she'd have to return one day." He grinned. "I'm just glad she decided to come back when I did."

Hayden nodded.

"But Riley has nothing here in Louisiana. You're the police commissioner, and I don't see you leaving your post. Your mom and sister are here. You're settled in Hopewell."

It was logical, but that didn't mean Hayden wanted to hear it.

"Riley's just finding her footing in her career. When she finishes this series and goes back, she'll have her choice of plum selections. Maddie's in Tennessee, the only mother figure Ri's had since Mom and Dad died."

Hayden swallowed. Again. "So, what you're telling me is to back off? For Riley's sake?"

"I'm not saying that. I'm just pointing out the obvious. There are hurdles. You need to decide if you're willing to jump them. All I'm asking you to do is make that decision before my baby sister gets hurt." Rafe ran a hand across his chin. "Does that make sense?"

"Yeah. I know." Hayden dropped his gaze to the desk, not wanting to discuss Riley's and his relationship anymore. "I hear what you're saying. Riley and I have barely discussed the obstacles." But that didn't mean he could just turn off his feelings for her. He flipped through the transcript, focusing on the testimony of Cam Thayer. "I'll think about what you said, okay?"

"That's all I can ask." But Rafe's tone didn't sound happy in the least.

His gaze landed on part of Wilson's testimony. Hayden jerked upright. "Hang on a second." He flipped the page in the report, then grabbed the copies of documents they'd received from Governor Eason.

"What?"

"You aren't going to believe this." He went back and forth through everything. It couldn't be this much of a coincidence.

"Okay. Fill me in." Rafe cocked his head.

"The check used to blackmail Eason . . ."

"Yeah?"

"Guess what the date is on it?"

"I don't know."

"The night of the museum break-in."

Rafe sat up straighter. "What's the date Eason received the note?"

Hayden held up the copy. "The next day."

"So that means, the records had to be stolen from the museum that night."

"Yep. And it's possible, just possible, that the robbery was a cover-up for what they were really after."

Rafe pointed at the paper. "A copy of that check."

"Which means, not only is Riley dead-on in her assessment that Wilson is innocent and was framed—"

"But her series is the reason Oswald put out a hit on her."

Hayden nodded. "Because she dug where he'd left a loose end. If the true theft that night was the records and not the artifacts and Riley swears Thayer's lying, Thayer just might be able to tell us who Oswald is now."

Rafe shot to his feet. "What are we waiting for?"

Hayden's blood rushed as he grabbed his keys.

He was so close to the truth, he could almost touch it. But while excited, he also knew that as soon as he solved the case, he'd have to resolve his feelings for Riley . . . and what to do about them.

"It feels strange not to have the sling." Riley gently moved her shoulder. The pain wasn't as bad as right after it happened.

"Glad you're healing. That sling did nothing for your outfits." Emily chuckled as they made their way back to her car.

"Um, Emily. I need to tell you something."

"That sounds serious." Emily unlocked the car with her key-chain remote as they approached. "What?"

"Can we get in the car first?"

They got into the car. Emily twisted in the seat to stare at her. "Okay, what's going on?"

"I told Hayden about Thomas."

Emily's face fell. "I asked you not to."

"I know, I know. And I'm sorry." She reached out to grab Emily's arm.

Emily shrugged out of her touch.

"I'm just really worried about you. I think he's dangerous."

"I can handle him. He's just a bully." Emily turned the key in the ignition. "It's my business. You had no right."

"I know. I'm so sorry." On one hand, she really was. But she knew something was off.

"I'm going to lunch with him today to tell him if he doesn't straighten up, we're finished for good." Emily's voice warbled a little.

"Oh, Emily. You should be done with him already. Look at what he's done to you."

"I told you, that was an accident."

"Come on. We both know that's not exactly true." Riley's chest ached. "I'll make a deal with you."

"Why would I agree?"

"Just humor me."

"What?"

Riley let out a long breath. "Let's go to his shop. You tell him you're going to have lunch with me instead of him. If he's gracious about you standing him up, then I'll shut up and butt out of your business."

"Sounds like a plan to me."

"But," Riley said, "if he throws a fit or loses his temper in any way, you break it off with him then and there." She eased the seat belt into place. "Deal?"

Emily sat there for a long moment. "Okay. Deal."

Riley motioned to the road. "Then let's go."

They drove most of the way in silence, until finally, Emily sighed. "I'm mad at you for telling Hay when I told you not to, don't get me wrong, but thanks for being concerned about me."

Riley grinned. "No problem. I kinda like you. Even if you are a bit of a freak."

"Ha." Emily turned into the parking lot of a large building.

The front of the store had a simple sign: Vince Antiques. Not very creative. Or original.

Riley stepped out of the car and followed Emily inside. The place was neat, smelling of furniture polish and air freshener. A bell over the door tinkled.

A young man, no more than twenty, smiled at Emily. "It's nice to see you again, Ms. Simpson."

"You too, Michael. Is Thomas here?"

"Yes, ma'am. In the back. I'll get him for you."

Riley shook her head. "Don't give him warning. He'll have time to prepare his reaction," she whispered.

Emily rolled her eyes. "No, that's okay. I want to surprise him."

Michael grinned. "Yes, ma'am."

Emily led the way into the back of the store,

then down a hall. She stopped outside a closed door. "Here we go." She opened the door.

"I don't care. I said I—" Thomas stood. "I'll have to call you back," he said into the phone before hanging it up. His expression was unreadable as his gaze darted between Emily and Riley. "This is a surprise."

"Yes. Well. Riley wanted to see the shop, so I thought I'd bring her by." Emily's voice trembled a bit.

"How nice." Thomas smiled, but it was almost as if he were baring his teeth. "Are you interested in anything specific?"

"Not really. I love antiques, and have thought about doing an article on them." She smiled, trying to gauge his reaction to their being here unexpectedly. He was hard to read. No doubt they'd surprised him.

That tone he used on the phone when they'd come in . . . it sure was harsh.

"Really? Perhaps I should show you around."

"Well, I don't know if we have time right now for me to really look hard." She raised a brow to Emily.

"Oh. Yeah." Emily turned, facing Thomas. "About lunch . . ."

Riley didn't want to appear obvious, so she turned to look at the items hanging on the wall.

"I was thinking perhaps . . ."

A pastel. Really ugly painting.

". . . we could have lunch another day. Riley . . ."

An old China plate.

". . . just left the doctor's appointment . . ."

Riley froze. "Where did you get this?" She pointed at the frame closest to Thomas's desk.

Matted inside the brassy frame were several Confederate coins and buttons. Just like the ones pictured in Armand's case file as one of the unrecovered stolen artifacts.

Chapter Thirty

"This is what the LORD says to you, house of David: 'Administer justice every morning; rescue from the hand of the oppressor the one who has been robbed, or my wrath will break out and burn like fire because of the evil you have done—burn with no one to quench it.' "
JEREMIAH 21:12

Hayden pulled into the pawnshop's parking lot amid an ambulance and several Baton Rouge police cruisers. He stepped onto the pavement, Rafe on his heels, and approached the area taped off. "What's going on here?"

A policeman stopped him. "I'm sorry, sir. You can't come any farther."

Pulling out his badge, Hayden nodded at the door to the pawnshop. "What happened?"

The cop lifted the crime-scene tape for them to duck under. "Homicide."

"Who?" Hayden asked.

"You'll have to ask the lieutenant inside. Lieutenant York's in charge."

"Thanks." Hayden and Rafe made their way into the shop.

Several police officers wearing blue latex gloves milled about. A crime unit dusted for prints.

Hayden addressed one of the uniforms. "I'm looking for a Lieutenant York."

The cop jutted his chin in the direction of the counter. "She's over there."

They approached the counter. Shattered glass littered the floor. Blood pooled under the counter, oozing from the other side.

"May I help you?" a woman in a well-worn suit asked.

Hayden introduced himself and Rafe, flashing his badge. "I'm looking for Lieutenant York."

"That's me. What are you doing here? This isn't even close to your jurisdiction."

"I know." Hayden pocketed his badge. "I was actually coming to ask the shop's owner, Cam Thayer, a couple of questions about a trial he testified at several years ago."

"Well, if the ID in the pocket is any indication, your boy is lying face down behind the counter. A .22 slug between his eyes."

"Robbery?" Hayden noticed the cash register open.

"Maybe. Too early in the investigation to answer."

Seemed really coincidental that Riley was here yesterday asking Thayer about his testimony, and this morning he was dead.

And Hayden didn't believe in coincidences.

"Anything significant?"

"Like?"

"Nothing. We'll get out of your way. Thank you." Hayden turned to head out of the pawn-shop when two chairs caught his attention. Well, not so much the chairs themselves, but the card sitting on them.

It had the description and the price, then the very bottom line read:

Appraised by Vince Antiques, Hopewell, Louisiana.

Hayden's feet took root. He nudged Rafe and pointed to the sign. "Vince. Vance." Hayden shook his head. "How could we not make the connection?" He finally found his footing and rushed out the door.

Rafe followed. "His father having an antique shop before he died. The one his father sold just before leaving them."

Hayden started the car's engine and sped toward the interstate. "Riley told me he was dangerous. Told me he'd been abusive toward

Emily." He filled Rafe in on the details as they raced along the highway. "I can't believe I didn't figure this out earlier."

"None of us did."

He reached for his cell, called into the office, and requested Bob obtain a warrant for Thomas Vince's home and business. "The man has been in my mother's home. He sat at the table with us and ate Mom's cooking."

Rafe nodded, his concentration on the road. "He fooled us all, Hayden. Not just you. I was there that night as well, and I didn't have a clue either."

Hayden glanced at the clock on the dashboard —11:20. "I'm going to call the house and quietly ask Mom to keep Emily there with Riley." He punched the speed-dial number for his mother.

"If we get Vince at his home or shop, we'll all sleep easier tonight."

Every ring felt like an eternity. Where was Mom?

"Hello?"

"Hi, Mom. What are y'all doing?"

"Hi, honey. I'm just puttering around in the kitchen. What's up?"

"Where are Riley and Emily?"

"At her doctor's appointment."

Hayden's eyes went back to the clock. "Mom, Riley's appointment was at ten fifteen."

"Oh, honey, the doctor probably ran late. Or the

girls are out shopping or getting their nails done. You know how girls are."

He didn't want to alarm his mother, but . . . "When they get back, do me a favor and have them call my cell."

"Is something wrong, son?"

"I don't think so. Mom, whatever you do, don't let Thomas near the house, okay?" He looked over at Rafe. "We have reason to believe he's the one who put the hit out on Riley, and I know he's the one who cut Emily's face."

"Oh no. She swore it was an accident."

"It's going to be okay, but I need you to have them call me as soon as they get back, okay?"

"Yes. Yes. Okay."

"Thanks, Mom. Love you." He shut the phone and told Rafe they weren't back yet, pressing the speed-dial button for Em's cell.

Rafe was on the phone but said, "I'm calling Riley's cell."

Hayden exited, heading to the police station. They needed those warrants to come through.

"Ri, it's Rafe. It's 11:27. Call me as soon as you get this message." He hung up the phone and shook his head at Hayden.

"Hi, this is Emily, sorry you missed me. You know what to do at the tone." A beep sounded.

"Em, it's Hayden. Call me *immediately*." He shut the phone as he pulled into his parking space and turned off the car. "Went straight to voice mail." He flung open the passenger door. "I don't like this."

"Me either."

"Bob! Do we have those warrants yet?"

"Oh, that's something a friend of a friend gave me." Thomas smiled.

It made Riley want to take a shower. Friend of a friend. Yeah, right. "Well, it's unique." And she'd have Hayden come by and check it out as soon as she got out of here and called him.

"I have a wonderful idea. Why don't I take you two lovely ladies out to lunch?" The charm oozed from his every pore.

He creeped Riley out. Maybe because he stared at her like he wanted to bite her head off, or maybe because she knew what he'd done to Emily and that reminded her too much of Garrison. Either way, she did *not* want to have lunch with him.

Emily, on the other hand, lit up like a new lightbulb. "Oh, that sounds like fun, doesn't it?"

Riley widened her eyes as she stared at Emily. "Did you forget? Your mom is cooking us lunch." She hoped Em took the hint.

"Don't worry. Mom's used to me not showing up. She'll be fine." She smiled at Thomas. "Where were you thinking?"

"Oh, I have a special place in mind. Shall we?"

He held out his arm, allowing them to precede him out of the office.

Something was wrong. Whether his eyes, the smarmy way he looked at her, or the heat that indicated he wouldn't accept a *no,* Riley didn't like the idea, but she didn't have a car. She fingered her purse and remembered her cell phone. At least she could call Hayden for a ride if things went south. Riley wanted to get another look at the framed box. Maybe later.

"Michael, I'm taking these beautiful ladies to lunch. Handle the shop while I'm gone." Thomas held the door open for them.

"Why don't we follow you?" Riley asked. That way, she could fake a stomachache and ask Emily to take her home as soon as she could.

"Oh, nonsense. Don't deprive me of your company. I'll drive, of course." He unlocked the doors of the four-door sedan, opening the back for Riley, seating her, then shutting the door before doing the same for Emily in the front passenger seat.

He got behind the steering wheel. "So, ladies, what have you been up to this morning?"

"Oh, I took Riley to her doctor's appointment."

"Yes. I noticed the sling was absent." He looked at Riley in his rearview mirror. "I'm assuming the doctor is pleased with your shoulder's progress?"

"Yeah. He says I'm doing great." Riley couldn't

help but wonder where they were going for lunch. Perhaps she could call Rafe or Hayden from the bathroom and have them come up with some type of emergency.

"Wonderful." He cut his gaze to Emily, then stared back at Riley in the mirror.

Little warnings tinged her stomach. The way he looked at her . . .

"Oh, rats. I've left my wallet at home. I can't believe how forgetful I've become lately." He smiled at Emily. "I think you distract me, my dear."

She laughed, but it sounded forced to Riley. Had Emily finally picked up on the creepy vibe?

"If you will indulge me, I'll run by the house and fetch it."

"No, that's okay. Actually, my shoulder's starting to hurt. Guess the doctor poked it a little too much. Why don't you just take us back to Emily's car and we'll head back home?"

"Nonsense. We're almost to my house now." He turned into a residential area. "This won't take but a moment."

"I should probably take a pain pill and lie down."

"Silly, girl. You can't take pain medication on an empty stomach." He pulled into a driveway. "Come in. Have a glass of water. You'll feel a bit better. I'll get my wallet and we'll be on our way."

Not that she wanted to be in his house, but

maybe, just maybe, she'd see something else suspicious she could tell Hayden about. "Fine."

"Excellent." He parked the car in the garage, then shut the door. "My dear?" He smiled at Emily.

Riley hung back trying to nudge Emily, but he kept his arm firmly around her friend's shoulders. Even as he unlocked the door inside the garage to the house, he kept Emily close to him. Once inside, Riley tried to pay attention to everything she saw.

"Now, where did I leave my wallet? Oh, the powder room is right down the hall. First door on your right."

She hadn't asked, but maybe she could figure something out. "Thanks." Riley winked at Emily as she headed down the hall.

After finding the bathroom, she locked the door and took a quick inventory. The man was weirder than she'd thought. Who used potpourri anymore?

She peeked behind the shower curtain. Seriously? Soap on a rope? Hadn't that gone out in like the eighties? Self-adhesive nonslip decals on the bottom of the tub?

This guy was crazy. She'd tell Emily to stay far, far away from him.

A knock sounded on the door. "Riley, are you okay? Is your shoulder hurting you? Would you like an aspirin?" His voice had risen. It came out almost nasally.

She turned on the water at the sink. "I'm okay.

I'll be out in just a second." True that. The bathroom was freaking her out.

After washing her hands and drying them on the lacy hand towel, Riley turned off the light and opened the door.

A sharp scent burnt her nose.

She drew back, then someone had her pinned.

A rag pressed against her nose and mouth. A rag with that horrid smell.

Pain shot through her shoulder.

Riley opened her mouth to yell. She inhaled the wet, smelly rag.

Room spun. Round and round and round and . . . Nothing.

CHAPTER THIRTY-ONE

"I saw heaven standing open and there
before me was a white horse,
whose rider is called Faithful and True.
With justice he judges and wages war."
REVELATION 19:11

Hayden hung up on Emily's voice mail. "Still nothing. You?"

Rafe shook his head.

"Bob, do I have my warrants yet?"

"Working on them."

"Something's wrong. I feel it."

Rafe nodded.

Hayden headed to the back door with Rafe following. "We're heading to Vince's antique shop. Bring me the warrant when it comes through."

"Yes, sir."

Gravel crunched as Hayden peeled out. "Emily never turns that stupid cell phone off. Never."

"Riley either. Said a reporter has to be ready at all times to catch a scoop."

Hayden's chest ached. Physically. Like it never had before. "I've been thinking about what you said."

Rafe shot him a glance. "About what?"

"About Riley. Me. Us. Hurdles."

"And you want to talk about this now?"

He turned down the road toward the antique shop. "Yeah, because just the idea that she could be in trouble turns me inside out."

"That's not enough."

"For now, it'll have to be."

"What are you saying?"

"I'm saying, we'll work around the hurdles. Riley and me. Together. If she's interested, that is."

Rafe remained silent as Hayden parked the car. The two of them rushed into the shop. A bell sounded as they entered.

A young man smiled at them. "Good afternoon, gentlemen. I'm Michael. How may I assist you today?"

Hayden wasn't in the mood. He flashed his badge. "Hi, Michael. I'm Police Commissioner Simpson. I need to speak to Thomas."

Michael wasn't all smiley now. "I'm sorry, sir. He's out to lunch."

"Where?"

"I don't know. Perhaps I can assist you?"

Rafe flashed his badge as well. "Was he alone when he left?"

"No, sir. He was with Ms. Simpson and another lady."

Hayden's pulse went into overdrive. "How long ago did they leave?"

Michael looked at his watch. "Maybe twenty or thirty minutes ago."

"Do you know where they were going?" Rafe pushed against the counter. "It's *really* important."

"I'm sorry, sir. No." Michael shook his head.

"Thank you, Michael. You've been a big help." Hayden nearly sprinted out the door. He reached for his cell and called the station as he unlocked the cruiser. "Do we have warrants yet?"

"Almost. The judge should be signing them right now."

"I'm going to his house. You take the shop, but have Gaston bring me the one for his house. I'm on my way now." He hung up and started to turn over the engine.

Then stopped.

381

"What? Why aren't we going?" Rafe asked.

Hayden nodded. "That's Em's car."

"They're with him."

Hayden started the car, punched the gas, and flipped on the flashing lights. "We'll have the warrant by the time we get there."

"Dear, Lord, I hope so."

But Hayden was already praying for a hedge of protection around Riley and Emily both as he sped to Thomas Vince's address.

Someone was hammering her head.

No, the banging was inside her head.

Riley moved, only to realize she couldn't. She struggled to open her eyes. To see.

She sat in a chair in the middle of a room. A very dim room. Her legs were stuck to the chair. No, not stuck. Tied. She was tied to a chair. Her hands were bound behind her.

What?

She opened her mouth to scream out. Cotton-mouthed. No, something was in her mouth. Between her teeth.

The last thing she remembered was potpourri.

No, wait. At Thomas's. The bathroom. Soap-on-a-rope. The nasty smell.

He'd drugged her. Of all the nerve. How dare he—?

Emily!

She rocked the chair, her gaze shooting around

the room. The part she could see. Not in that corner. Was that a body lying on the ground in that corner? There? Was that—?

"You are quite a hard woman to dispose of, Riley Baxter."

His voice, void of any emotion, stilled her movements. Where was he? Behind her somewhere . . . that's where his voice had come from. Behind and to the right.

"You just couldn't mind your own business, could you? You had to keep digging. Keep prying. Asking the questions you shouldn't." Thomas moved and stood directly in front of her. "I'm going to remove your gag, but I'm warning you. Don't scream."

He reached for her head, then paused. "Not because I'm afraid someone will hear you, of course, but because screaming hurts my ears." He squatted and looked her directly in the eye. "Do you understand?"

She nodded.

"Good." He straightened and removed the gag from her mouth.

Riley gulped in air. She wanted to scream. Wanted to ask where Emily was, but she needed to keep her wits. Needed to play along, pay attention, and wait for her opportunity. That's what Rafe had taught her and Maddie both.

"Water," she croaked. Get him remembering she's a human with basic needs like water. It would also give her opportunity to get some sort of feel for the layout.

"Maybe later."

Okay, scratch that.

He stared at her like she was a bug under a microscope. She'd never felt so naked, so vulnerable in all her life.

He paced in front of her. "Aren't you going to ask why?" His voice was so cold . . . so flat . . . so dull.

"You already told me."

"I did?"

No sense acting stupid. He knew she wasn't. "You said I wouldn't stop asking questions. Poking my nose where it didn't belong."

He stopped pacing and clapped his hands. "Very good, Ms. Baxter. Well done." He popped his hands on his hips. "Not that it will help you any, but it's refreshing not to have to play games."

"If I might ask a question or two . . ."

"Of course. You're a reporter. It's your nature." He spread his arms. "Please, ask away."

"Your involvement in the robbery?"

"Yes." A slow smile stretched his lips taut. "I was there. And you are correct in your assumption. That piece in my office was from the robbery. I like to display it, an inside joke that I can't be caught. However, that wasn't the reason for the robbery."

She had to keep him talking. Give Rafe and

Hayden time to realize she and Emily were missing. She made a show of looking confused. "Then why rob the museum? Those artifacts were priceless. Irreplaceable."

Just the thought of Hayden made her heart seize.

"To satisfy your final curiosity," he moved his hand as if punctuating *final,* "I'll tell you. I needed ammunition to blackmail the governor for my pardon. The robbery of the artifacts was all a cover."

A cover for a blackmail scheme put Armand Wilson in prison.

"I do enjoy owning the artifacts. It amuses me to show them to people and know that I've gotten away with such a theft. It gives me pleasure to know I pulled it all off. With the help of Cam Thayer. His brother apparently needed the insurance money for his artifacts. He'd gotten into a little bit of a financial bind and couldn't sell the artifacts outright for enough money quickly. Insurance is good about paying quickly when someone is held accountable for the crime. Did you know that?"

"Armand Wilson?"

"Oh, you were quite correct in your assumption and in your reporting. The man had nothing to do with the robbery or the shooting. He wasn't even there."

She knew it!

"Also shocking is that the guard was never

supposed to be shot. No one was supposed to be injured during the robbery." He sighed. "Unfortunately, one of the idiots involved panicked and pulled the trigger. Messy. I killed him by breaking his neck."

His bragging sent ice into her veins.

"Would you like to know how many people I've killed, Riley Baxter?"

"If you'd like to tell me." She forced her voice not to crack.

"Aren't you curious what number you'll be?"

"Not particularly."

He laughed, but it was dry and humorless. "Well, for my own amusement, then."

"As you wish."

"First there were the two doctors who failed to save my leg."

Her mouth went drier than it already was.

"Then there was the first subcommittee cochair, Mr. Vermillion. Oh, wait. I forgot the spawn of my mother and that pimp-pusher of hers. Does an infant count?"

He killed a baby? She forced her expression not to change. "So that's four."

"Very good, Ms. Riley Baxter." He rubbed his chin. "Now, let's see, next there was Curtis Goins, then Allen Boyce, then Mack Thompson. That's six."

"Seven." She knew he was testing her. Pushing to see if he scared her.

"Right. Seven. Good counting. Then Evan Coleman and Matthew Nichols. Oh, and as of this morning, Cam Thayer." He ran a finger over his lips. "How many is that all together?"

"Ten."

"Oh, this is perfect. Add that whiny brat Emily and finish with you, and that's an even dozen."

"Now, about that water?"

He laughed that callous laugh again. "You do have a one-track mind, don't you, Riley Baxter?"

She tried to shrug but nearly cried out when pain ripped through her shoulder. "Just thirsty. Whatever you used to drug me has left me . . . parched." He should like her using unique vocabulary. He was just odd enough to find that intriguing.

"I didn't realize chloroform had such a side effect. Interesting."

Maybe?

"I don't see the harm in a little sip of water." He walked behind her. His footsteps echoed in the empty room.

A basement? His basement? Surely he hadn't moved them. But where was Emily? Riley hadn't even heard so much as a whimper.

A tap came on. Spurted. Sprayed. Then ran.

The water turned off. His footsteps. One. Two. Three. Four. Five. Six. Seven.

"Here you go." He stood in front of her, put the glass to her mouth, and gave her a drink.

But now she knew there was a wall about seven feet behind her. Plumbing didn't just come straight up out of the floor.

"Thank you." It galled her to be polite, but it would be what kept her alive. He wanted her to beg for her life. To cry. To be weak. He could kill her then.

But being strong and polite, as if she were a guest—he didn't know how to handle that. It wasn't a usual response. And the unusual intrigued him.

And if she kept at it, playing him, perhaps she could keep herself and Emily alive until Rafe and Hayden found them.

Please, God, let them find us.

CHAPTER THIRTY-TWO

"But his sons did not follow his ways.
They turned aside after dishonest gain and
accepted bribes and perverted justice."
1 SAMUEL 8:3

Hayden inched the car down the road Vince lived on. He'd turned off the flashing lights before they entered the neighborhood. Now they crept along, keeping their eyes open for anything out of the ordinary.

It curdled his blood to think he'd never picked

up on anything while Em dated him. If he was right—and he'd stake his life on it—this guy was a maniacal killer. He'd always thought he'd pick up on someone that evil. Vince had been good, but hopefully not too good.

His cell rang. "Hayden Simpson."

"You got your warrants. Gaston is on his way to meet you at the residence. I'm en route to the shop."

"Thanks, Bob. Be careful. Riley and Emily are both unaccounted for and were last seen with Vince."

"You got it."

Hayden slipped the phone into silent mode and pushed it back into its clip on his belt. "Warrants came through."

Rafe nodded, his jaw so tight Hayden expected to hear the pop.

Hayden parked the car two houses down and across the street. No sign of movement from anywhere. Nobody walked their dog. No one worked in their flower beds. Nothing out of the ordinary on a Tuesday afternoon in April.

No one was aware their neighbor was a cold-blooded murderer.

A car engine sounded.

Hayden moved in position behind the car beside Rafe. Watching. Waiting.

It was a cruiser. Gaston.

Hayden waved his arms.

Officer Gaston whipped in the driveway behind Hayden's car. He gripped the warrants as he stepped to the curb.

"Get on your vest," Hayden ordered. He and Rafe had already slipped into theirs.

Once ready, Hayden led them down the street. He kept his gaze alerted for any form of movement. They reached Vince's house. Gaston was too new to send alone.

"Gaston, go with Agent Baxter and cover the back."

Rafe shot him a look.

Hayden lifted a single shoulder. He'd work with what he had. That was the best he could do.

He counted to ten, giving the other two plenty of time to get into position.

Cautiously, he rang the doorbell. He pressed against the house, weapon drawn.

No sound came from inside.

He rang the doorbell again.

Vince's car wasn't parked in the driveway, but it could be in the garage.

No response.

He rang the doorbell a third and final time. Still nothing.

Hayden banged on the door. "Police. Open up." Then he pressed himself back against the house.

Nothing.

Again, he identified himself and banged on the door.

Not even a curtain moved. No footsteps.

Rafe and Gaston eased around the edge of the house.

"Anything?" Rafe whispered.

Hayden shook his head.

"Maybe they aren't here." Rafe joined him at the front door.

It was possible, of course, but Hayden just *felt* it. They were here. In the house somewhere.

And Vince knew they were out here. For him. It was a game to him.

Hayden adjusted his hold on his gun's grip.

Let the games begin.

Riley had heard Hayden upstairs. So had Thomas. She hadn't screamed. Hadn't moved. Had just stared at Thomas.

"Your knight in armor on his white horse is here." He mocked her.

She raised one eyebrow. "Apparently."

"Should I kill him before you? Or let him watch you die?"

Her insides were liquid, but she wouldn't let him see her pain. Her terror. Her horror. "It is what it is."

"You really don't care?" His puckered brow telegraphed his confusion. "You aren't afraid to die?"

"No. Not really."

"How is that?"

"I know where I'll spend eternity, so I'm not afraid." And she'd get to see her parents again. Despite missing them, she wasn't quite ready to see them just yet.

"That whole Christian thing. Really? I thought you were more intelligent than that."

"I guess not."

Hayden banged and called out again.

Thomas stared at her. "Are you sure you don't want to make the decision? Die first or watch him die?"

She didn't know if she could watch Hayden die. Part of her would die right along with him. Riley knew that now. Sadly, it was too late.

Just when she found someone she wanted to love, wanted to try to make it work with, they were both going to die. It wasn't fair.

At least they'd be in eternity together.

"Well, if you're going to leave the choice to me . . ." He smiled, but his eyes were already dead. "I know. I'll bring up his bratty little sister. He can watch her die. Then since you've been such a particular problem for me, I'll let you watch him die before I kill you."

Again, she'd be all alone.

No, she was never really alone. Jesus was always with her. Even during the darkest hour, He was there.

"Fine." He stomped up the basement stairs, obviously irritated that she didn't respond.

She closed her eyes. *Dear Lord, if we're all going to die, please, be merciful and let it be over quickly.*

Poor Maddie . . . she'd have more grief than she could bear. Maybe Rafe wasn't with Hayden. They would have each other.

Poor Ardy. She'd lost her husband and Hayden's father. If she lost both Emily and Hayden . . . *Oh, God, be with her when she grieves. Hold her as only You can.*

"Psst."

"Emily?"

"No. I've already got her out of the house and in her brother's car."

"Who is that?"

"Simon. Simon Lancaster. I followed you after our meeting."

Oh, this was like a bad dream that kept getting worse and worse. The last person she'd get to talk to on this earth was the man who was responsible for her parents' deaths? Something was seriously wrong with this picture.

He appeared at her side. "I'm going to untie you." His hands brushed against her arms as he worked on the knots. She'd always imagined his touch would be like acid, burning away her flesh.

No flesh burning.

Her hands were free. She pulled them in front of her, rubbing where the binding had left rope burns. Her shoulder ached.

He bent over, working to untie her feet when shots erupted.

Hayden! Rafe!

Thomas flew down the stairs, holding a gun. Footsteps echoed behind him. He headed straight for Riley, a circle of blood on his left shoulder, similar to her injury.

"He'll watch you die this time." Thomas lifted the gun, pointed it straight at her head.

"No!" Hayden scrambled at the stairs, but she knew he couldn't get a clean shot. Not at that angle. He wouldn't risk hitting her.

Riley closed her eyes. She was ready. Hayden was alive. He'd survive. She was okay with that.

Pop!

Something heavy slammed into her, then slumped against her lap.

"No! No! No!" Thomas cried.

She opened her eyes to see Hayden tackling Thomas to the floor. Pressing his face into the concrete and handcuffing him.

"No, she has to die. She must die," Thomas cried.

But what was—?

Simon Lancaster lay on her, his head in her lap. He stared up at her as blood spread from the wound to his gut.

Tears welled in her eyes. She cradled his head. "Why?"

"Because. I. Had to." His eyes fluttered.

"No, you didn't. But thank you."

His breathing labored. Help. They needed to get help for him.

"Rafe! Call 911. Help!"

She brushed his bangs from his forehead and stared into his face.

"So. Sorry. Every. Thing."

In that moment, she knew. God had granted her prayer. "I forgive you, Simon. I forgive you," she whispered. "Go in peace."

The words she'd been terrified to say, to feel, weren't hard at all. She'd spent so much time angry with Simon, not considering he was capable of change . . . and now, now she knew he had.

EPILOGUE

Three Weeks Later

"I can't even begin to tell you how terrified I was, knowing you were in the house and Vince had a gun and was going to shoot you. He told me exactly what he planned." Hayden planted a kiss on the tip of Riley's nose. He'd almost lost her, and he wasn't willing to take that chance again.

Ever.

"But he didn't succeed." She smiled up at him and his heart flipped. It'd been doing that ever since she agreed to move to Hopewell. She and

Emily were going to share an apartment, and her editor had told her it didn't matter where she lived as long as she kept turning in amazing articles.

Hayden couldn't stop the smile that had taken up permanent residence on his face since she'd told him that she didn't want to leave him. Didn't want to give up on them.

Life was good. No, God was good, and He was good all the time.

"I don't know what I would've done if I'd lost you. Before we even got a chance to get started."

She pressed her finger against his lips. "Shh." She pushed up on tiptoe and planted a firm kiss on his mouth. "It didn't happen. It's over. Let it go."

But he'd never forget the fear that had burned him like fire when Thomas aimed at her. Without Simon Lancaster . . . well, he wouldn't be falling head over heels like he was.

Taking his hand, Riley lifted it to her lips and planted a soft kiss in his palm. Happiness spread over his soul.

Thank You, God. Thank You.

Riley sat beside Hayden on the hood of his car. The May sun beat down on them, but she welcomed the warmth. For far too long, she'd been out in the emotional winter, her heart buried under feet of snow. No more.

"Ms. Baxter, Ms. Baxter, look at me." Mikey Wilson stuck his fingers in his ears and waggled them at his sister, who chased him up and down the stretch of road. Thanks to Simon Lancaster's will in which he'd left his life insurance policy to the Baxters, Mikey had tubes put in his ears last week and was doing extremely well.

"Watch out . . . Jasmine will get you."

Hayden leaned over and gave Riley a real kiss. One of hope. Of promise. Of the future.

"Here he comes! Here he comes!" Peggy's voice contained myriad emotions—excitement, anticipation, love. "Oh my. Look at him. That's my Armand."

Riley slipped off the hood of the car and grabbed Jasmine and Mikey, holding them to her.

With arms wide open, Peggy ran across the street toward Angola prison. Armand dropped his mesh bag and ran to meet her.

Jasmine tried to move in that direction.

Riley held her tight. "Not yet."

Peggy leapt into Armand's arms. He spun her around. And around. And around. He dipped his head and kissed her.

"Eww!" Mikey said.

Riley laughed with tears in her eyes. She ruffled his hair. "You won't think that's eww one day."

"Double eww."

She laughed with Mikey. Hayden walked up behind them.

Jasmine looked up at Riley, her eyes filled with tears too. "Thank you, Ms. Baxter. For everything.

My daddy wouldn't be free if it weren't for you."

No words could push past the emotions clogging Riley's throat. God's justice was always just, and always right at the perfect time. She gave Jasmine a hard hug.

"I mean it. All of this." Jasmine waved her arm toward her parents. "All of it is because you believed me and wouldn't give up. I want to be just like you when I grow up." She gave Riley a quick kiss on the cheek, then grabbed Mikey's hand and ran with him toward their parents.

Armand let Peggy go long enough to lift both Jasmine and Mikey into his arms. They squealed, then showered his face with kisses.

Peggy turned and met Riley's stare. She smiled, then nodded.

Riley nodded back before turning to Hayden. "Let's go. Your mom promised to teach me how to make a roux."

Hayden wrapped his arms around her waist, lifted her off the ground, and kissed her deeply. Thoroughly. Passionately. "I'm falling in love with you, I hope you know."

Her heart fluttered. "Good, because I don't want to fall with anybody else but you."

Dear Reader,

Sharing Riley Baxter's story with you was so much fun for me. Thank you for coming along and participating in the Justice Seekers series and getting to know the Baxter siblings.

The Wilson family's struggles are very, very personal to me, as I lived through something similar. Much of Jasmine's emotions were mirrors of my own during that season in my life. I'm grateful you've allowed me to share these feelings with you.

Through the course of my research, I came across an organization whose purpose is to exonerate those wrongfully convicted, as well as reforming the justice system in order to prevent future injustices. I applaud their efforts and the strides they're making to set innocent people free. You can find out more about the organization by visiting their website at www.innocenceproject.org.

Another example of someone dedicated to the freeing of innocent people I found while researching is Dallas District Attorney Craig Watkins. I commend his and his staff's efforts. You may find out more information on him by visiting http://www.dallasda.com/Craig_Watkins.html.

I hope you've enjoyed getting to know another Baxter and seeing Hayden find love. I hope you'll read the next installment of the Justice Seekers series, experiencing Maddie's story.

Since many of my readers have commented on the yummy Southern dishes I mention in my books, I've included a few of my favorite family recipes on the pages that follow. I hope you'll enjoy them!

As an avid reader, I love to connect with other readers. Visit me on my website—

www.robincaroll.com

—and sign up for my newsletter. You can connect with me on Facebook at

www.facebook.com/robincaroll

or write to me snail mail: PO Box 242091, Little Rock, AR, 72223. I can't wait to hear from you!

Blessings,

Robin Caroll
Robin Caroll

Mama's Hot Water Corn Bread

2 cups white cornmeal mix
1 finely chopped onion
finely chopped jalapeño slices—to taste
boiling water
oil

Put about ¾ inch of oil in the skillet and heat till hot. Mix cornmeal, onion, and jalapeños. Add boiling water until mixture sticks together, about like mashed potatoes. Drop by the tablespoon into the grease, then mash with a spoon to flatten a bit. When brown, turn once.

(Contributed by Robin's mother, Joyce Shannon Bridges)

Casey's Chicken & Dumplings

1 cup chopped celery
1 cup chopped onion
whole chicken with skin, quartered
½ stick real butter
2 cloves garlic, crushed
2 tablespoons Worchestershire sauce
¼ teaspoon Tabasco
2 cans of ready-to-bake biscuits

Sauté onions, garlic, and celery in the butter until onions are translucent. Add quartered chicken and sear. Add approximately 5 cups of water and bring to a boil. Keep at boiling for 45 minutes to 1 hour. Remove chicken and debone, then remove the skin. Return chicken to water/celery/onion mixture. Add Worchestershire sauce and Tabasco. Simmer 35 minutes. Slowly and gradually drop in biscuits—each quartered. Simmer 20 minutes.

(Contributed by Casey Miller, Robin's husband)

Becca's Oooey-Gooey Butter Cake

1 box yellow cake mix
1 egg, slightly beaten
1 stick of butter, melted

Mix all together and press into 9 x 13-inch ungreased pan.

Glaze
1 package 8-ounce cream cheese
1 box powdered sugar
2 eggs

Cream together and pour over dough. Bake 30 to 40 minutes until lightly brown at 350 degrees.

(Contributed by Robin's sister, Rebecca Harden)

Dan's Pancakes

1 cup flour
1 cup milk
¼ cup oil
1 tablespoon baking powder
½ teaspoon salt
1 egg

Mix well, then cook in hot, greased skillet until bubbles form and stay open. Only turn once. Serve with liberal amounts of butter and Steen's Ribbon Cane Syrup.

(Contributed by Robin's uncle, Dan Kelly)

Lisa's Red Beans & Rice

1 16-ounce bag of dried beans (I use pinto.)
2 teaspoons or so of Tony Chachere's Original
   Creole seasoning
¼ teaspoon or a dash of garlic powder
1 pound of skinless link sausage (I use Eckrich.
   Down Home sausage is very good too.)
¼ cup chopped onions
2 cups cooked rice
Large Crock-Pot

Wash beans well and presoak them the night before (if you have time, but it's not necessary) in a ½ pot of water in the Crock-Pot. In the morning, cut the sausage into bite-sized pieces and add to water. Add all other ingredients. Cook on high for at least 6 hours, depending on your Crock-Pot.

(Contributed by Robin's sister-in-love, Lisa Burroughs)

Green Jell-O Salad

1 large package lime Jell-O
1 small package tiny marshmallows
1 8-ounce package cream cheese (mixed with sweet milk)
3½ cups of boiling water
1 large can crushed pineapple
1 carton small curd cottage cheese

Put Jell-O and marshmallows in a bowl, add hot water, and mix well. Mix cream cheese with a little sweet milk and mix well. Add to Jell-O mixture. Add pineapple and cottage cheese. Chill in square pan.

(Contributed by Robin's niece, Krystina Harden— the recipe of her greatgrandmother, Una Abi Brannon Shannon)

BB's Rouxless Crawfish Étouffée

1 medium onion, chopped
1 green pepper, chopped
2 sticks real butter
2 family-sized cans cream of mushroom soup, undiluted
3 large cans diced tomatoes
2 cans Rotel tomatoes
2 pounds crawfish tail meat (fresh or frozen)
Worcestershire & Tony Chachere's Original Creole seasoning—to taste

In a large soup pot, melt butter over low heat. Then increase heat to medium and sauté the onions and peppers until soft. Add Worcestershire and Tony's to taste. Stir in mushroom soup, tomatoes, and Rotel—mix well. Allow to simmer 15–20 minutes, stirring frequently to avoid sticking. Add crawfish tails and mix well. Lower heat slightly and simmer another 15–20 minutes, stirring frequently. Serve alone or over white rice, and garnish with grated cheese if desired. (Note: add hot water to soup/tomato mixture to thin to desired consistency.)

(Contributed by Robin's sister, Cindy Pittman)

Aunt Julie's Red Beans & Rice

(Start with Camellia Beans! It makes a difference.)

1 package dried Camellia Red Beans
2 large white onions, chopped
2 tablespoons olive oil
2 pounds smoked sausage, sliced
4 pods pressed garlic
1 teaspoon sugar
Tabasco to taste
Salt & pepper to taste
Cooked rice

Sauté chopped onions in olive oil. Add all ingredients to a large pot, cover with water plus 3 inches more. Then bring to a boil. Lower heat to medium and cook covered for about 1½ to 2 hours, checking to be sure fluid never goes dry. Taste a bean every now and then to see if it's tender.

(Contributed by Robin's aunt, Julia Kelly)

Aunt Millie's Chicken and Sausage Gumbo

3 pounds of chicken breasts and thighs (bone in &
    skin on)
4 cups Roux (see recipe below)
5 cups hot water
4 cups chicken stock
Salt & pepper
2 pounds sausage
1 can Rotel tomatoes
Cooked rice

Boil chicken breasts and thighs until tender. Place
roux (4 cups) into a 6-quart pot. Add hot water,
chicken stock, then salt and pepper to taste. Cook
for about 1 hour. Debone chicken and cut into
bite-sized pieces. Slice sausage into ½-inch
rounds. Add chicken, sausage, and can of
tomatoes to gumbo and cook about 30 more
minutes. Serve over rice.

Microwave Roux

Roux is a mixture of oil and flour that is browned
and used in many South Louisiana dishes—
especially gumbos.

⅔ cup oil
⅔ cup flour, sifted
4 cup glass measuring cup
2 cups onions, chopped
1 cup celery, chopped
½ cup green pepper, chopped
4 cloves minced garlic
½ cup parsley, chopped
½ cup green onion tops, chopped

Mix oil and flour in a 4 cup glass measuring cup. Microwave uncovered on High for 6 to 7 minutes. At 6 minutes, stir the Roux. It should be light brown at this point. Microwave another minute, more if needed, to reach a dark brown color. *Roux will be extremely hot, so be careful!*

Add the onions, celery, and green pepper to the hot roux. Stir and microwave on high for 3 minutes. Add the minced garlic, parsley, and green onion tops to the roux mixture and microwave on high for 2 minutes. If any oil has risen to the top, pour it off. Add ¼ cup hot water to the roux mixture to bring back to the 4 cup mark. Stir well.

(Contributed by Robin's aunt, Millicent Bridges)

Discussion Questions

1. Oswald wanted to start his life over, in essence, with a new identity. Have you ever felt like that? As a follower of Jesus Christ, you are given a new identity. Discuss what 2 Corinthians 5:17 means to you.

2. Riley had her own ideas of justice and had difficulty with acceptance when her ideals weren't met. What does Scripture say about our role in justice (see Leviticus 19:15 and Deuteronomy 16:20)?

3. Emily stayed with Thomas after he'd hurt her, making excuses for him and not holding him accountable for his actions. What does Scripture tell us about taking responsibility for our actions (see Romans 3:19)?

4. Hayden carried a lot of responsibility, often too much for him to handle. Does it ever feel as if your responsibilities are too heavy? Discuss how you can use Scripture to balance your life.

5. Armand's family stood in support of him during an extremely trying season in his life.

How would you react if a similar situation arose in your family? Discuss ways to be supportive of families with loved ones in prison.

6. Hayden realized how much he cared for Riley when she was shot. Has it ever taken a crisis to make you realize how much someone meant to you? Discuss how that made you feel. Consider ways to let those you love know it every day.

7. Riley's career was very important to her, almost to her detriment. Have your priorities ever gotten out of whack? Discuss ways you can strive to keep your priorities in check.

8. In the end, Simon Lancaster saved Riley and she forgave him for killing her parents. Forgiveness is often something we Christians struggle with. What does Jesus tell us about forgiveness? (Discuss Matthew 6:14–15 and Matthew 18.)

9. Simon stated he'd become a Christian in prison, which Riley had a hard time accepting. Do you believe people can change? Discuss why or why not.

10. The truth came to light that Armand had been unjustly imprisoned for a crime he didn't

commit. Do you believe innocent people are sent to prison for crimes they didn't commit? Discuss ways you can help improve our legal system.

Center Point Large Print
600 Brooks Road / PO Box 1
Thorndike ME 04986-0001 USA

(207) 568-3717

US & Canada:
1 800 929-9108
www.centerpointlargeprint.com

1/13